Exit, Pursued by a Bear

Exit, Pursued by a Bear

Jacqueline Kolosov

Hollywood Books International
an imprint of Press Americana
Hollywood | Los Angeles

Published by
Hollywood Books International
An Imprint of Press Americana
americanpopularculture.com

Cover Art: Paul Bond, "On the Transmigration of Souls"
Cover Design: Press Americana

Library of Congress Cataloging-in-Publication Data

.

Names: Kolosov, Jacqueline A., author.
Title: Exit, pursued by a bear / Jacqueline Kolosov.
Other titles: Exit, pursued by a bear (Compilation)
Description: Hollywood : Hollywood Books International, an imprint of Press
   Americana, 2023. | Summary: "In Exit, Pursued by a Bear, art -
   particularly the visual arts - is a unifying and simultaneously
   expansive theme, from "Intention's" grieving portraitist to the artists
   and female caregivers who wander the paths of "Solstice in the Jardin du
   Luxembourg." Winner of Prize Americana, these stories from Jacqueline
   Kolosov shore up against the inevitability of loss-illness, death,
   addiction, ruptures in intimacy-a testament to "the art that doth mend
   nature" from The Winter's Tale. If the bear of that late Shakespearean
   romance both upends and galvanizes the plot, then the horses, dogs, and
   ravens of this story collection act as companions, teachers, and even
   spirit guides to the human beings, each and every one bruised and
   damaged-but also shining"-- Provided by publisher.
Identifiers: LCCN 2023047516 | ISBN 9781735360195 (paperback)
Subjects: LCGFT: Short stories.
Classification: LCC PS3611.O58274 E95 2023 | DDC 813/.6--dc23/20231012
LC record available at https://lccn.loc.gov/2023047516

for Milica Trindade & Eileen Bonds

& for my daughter, Sophie,
who inspired so much of the journey chronicled on these pages

Table of Contents

The beauty of the world…has two edges,
one of laughter, one of anguish, cutting
the heart asunder.

—Virginia Woolf

There is an art that doth mend nature,
change it rather, and yet the art itself is nature.

—William Shakespeare

THE RAVEN

The capacity of an animal to cause damage
is proportional to its intelligence.
—Konrad Lorenz

When George Kokowshka first moved to the Southwest nearly twenty years ago, he relished visiting Santa Fe: its restaurants, its atmosphere, and especially its art. *These days the Wyeth Hurd Gallery is still worthwhile; and there's the Pushkin, which showcases modern and contemporary Russian art, as well as a few intriguing examples of Russian Impressionism—birch trees in winter and the like. But for the most part, Santa Fe's galleries have gone downhill, catering now to a moneyed, sunburned Americans who parade up and down Canyon Road in expensive white sneakers or those hideous mountaineering sandals that ruin even the most beautiful woman's legs.*

George is thinking precisely this as he stands before a gallery called Eco Cool, an establishment that was definitely not here the last time he came to visit his daughter. Occupying a small but coveted space on Canyon Road, the gallery seems to be exclusively devoted to brightly-painted wooden chickens wearing cowboy boots in its turquoise-bordered windows. Hundreds of them. There are blonde chickens and Japanese chickens and chickens with afros and chickens in nurses' uniforms, even a chicken done up to resemble Betty Boop in western gear.

"Do you see something you like?" a female voice asks.

George looks up at an attractive blonde in purple velveteen pants and what looks like cross-training shoes.

"No," he says. "Nothing at all." And then meeting the woman's mascara'd gaze and remembering his manners, he nods and adds, "But thank you."

Although he hasn't seen his daughter Maggie in nearly four months—a development leave having sent him out of the country in this year before his retirement—George takes his time as he makes his way down Canyon Road.

He and his ex-wife Alex may have fought virulently over their only daughter during the long years of their embattled marriage, but these days their mutual concern for Maggie is a point of connection, perhaps the only remaining one. When George

11

telephoned Alex to say that he was driving up to see Maggie, she encouraged him to try to convince Maggie to take the assistant's job at her Israeli friend Yossi's gallery in Chicago.

"Forty thousand a year, George," she said, "and Maggie could rent a refurbished studio just down the street at a great price. It would be a chance to start over, and we both know she would benefit from the stability."

Alex's words brought back Maggie's last breakdown some fourteen months ago—two weeks in a psych ward, twice-daily pharmaceutical cocktails.

"I'll see what I can do," he said.

Maggie is already waiting for George at El Farol when he arrives, the garish memory of the wooden chickens, but also his ex-wife's concerns, still whirling through his mind.

He'd hoped that tonight, their first meal together, Maggie would have left Hugo at home. He will have to deal with the creature's obstinance and demands throughout the next four days: the greeting rituals, the cajoling, the mischief, the need to be center stage.

Instead, when he catches sight of Maggie, her long dark hair twined into a messy chignon now streaked with the first hint of gray, a heavy necklace of turquoise beads making her long neck look even longer, Hugo is perched on her shoulder, his black feathers as sleek and well-kept as always.

"Daddy!" she calls before the hostess can seat him.

"Maggie." He strides towards her, and several of the outdoor diners' heads turn in their direction.

Despite her ill-fitting peasant wear, Maggie is a beautiful woman, as her mother was and is even now that Alex has come into her middle sixties. His ex-wife's beauty had always been George's undoing, the reason he put up with her demands and her criticisms for too many years, even going into far too much debt on the San Antonio house with the garden that they sold for a loss after the divorce, a circumstance that still eats at George more than fifteen years later.

Maggie has none of her mother's will, and sometimes George believes a little bit of Alex, just a sprinkling, the way a dash of cloves or cinnamon enlivens a bread recipe or a stew, would have done Maggie a world of good. At the very least, it would have made her tougher, gelled that self-preservation instinct he fears she lacks.

"Hello, magpie," George says, all too aware of the traumatic irony of this nickname, inherited on a very early trip to New Mexico when she was a child, then leans forward to kiss her, only to have his efforts thwarted by Hugo, who greets him with harsh *quorks* and flaps his wings violently, all the while retaining his tight perch on Maggie's shoulder.

"I'm amazed you can bring an animal into a restaurant," George says, "even in Santa Fe."

"We're sitting outside," Maggie says. "You're allowed to bring animals if you sit outside."

"Ah," George says, noticing a drowsy dachshund sprawled beneath a nearby table.

"Besides," Maggie adds, "they know Hugo here. He's a bit of a celebrity."

"I can only imagine," George says, relieved that he is not usually here to witness his daughter's jaunts around town with a raven, the largest bird in the crow family. *Would she become a bird lady in her old age? Was she a bird lady already? How long did ravens live anyway?* Hugo has already been around for a dozen years, and from the glossy looks of his wings and his sharp, black eye, it seems as if he has at least as many years ahead.

They look over the menu, and Hugo, still glued to Maggie's shoulder, tugs at her loose strands of hair playfully, almost as a lover would, reminding George of what he knows about ravens. Creatures of fidelity, they bond for life. As far as George can tell, Hugo views Maggie as his mate. *And Maggie?* George wonders, for the bird is far more than a pet and less a child than a companion.

A waiter passes with a platter of something smoky and red, and George is disturbingly reminded of those early days with Hugo when Maggie was still living at home in San Antonio. On the chance that she would return him to the wild, Maggie brought home roadkill, then chopped it up with a special knife and cutting board—George forbade using their own tools. It was a neighbor who spotted Maggie scouring the four-lane highway at dusk and said something to George, who had no idea of how to begin to explain. Thankfully, Maggie now feeds the raven canned dog food, chicken, and fish.

It's almost as if Hugo understands that George is thinking about him, for he hops down from Maggie's shoulder and approaches George, stopping to cock his head and look him in the eye.

"Do you think the old boy wants to be friends after all these years?" George asks suspiciously.

"Maybe," Maggie says, then chortles to Hugo.

When George laughs, his guard momentarily relaxing, Hugo draws back his beak, a sign of impending attack, and George swats at him with the menu. "Oh no, you don't."

"Daddy!"

Instantly, Hugo protests violently, his squawks turning loud and plaintive, as if George were the one attacking.

A few of the other diners turn to stare, and more than a few glare at George.

"That bird of yours is going to bite me before the meal is through," George says, after the waitress brings over a basket of bread and a bowl of olive oil.

"Don't be ridiculous," Maggie says. "He just has to get used to you again. He's very protective of me. You should be glad. He's as good, better, than any guard dog—and smarter, too."

No one would disbelieve that Hugo, who has learned to open cabinets and doors and even sticky gates with his nearly three-inch beak, is not intelligent.

Yet how much good is a bird who buries bacon in a neighbor's yard, only to return later to recover it, a bird who steals shiny objects—buttons, coins, even a turquoise ring left on some kitchen counter—hoarding them in his cage? George asks himself. *More precisely, how much protection can such a creature actually offer against an intruder who could climb through one of Maggie's shakily latched windows or jimmy the equally flimsy lock on her front door?*

George is reminded of his best friend Edgar's daughter, Hannah, a divorcee who lives in their neighborhood along with her two-year-old son and a 130-pound Great Pyrenees named Monty. When Hannah goes for a walk, her son tucked into his stroller, Monty walks at their side, alert, regal, and always on guard. A dog like Monty, this, George can understand, having grown up with German shepherds, but not this absurdly demanding bird whose nest was toppled in a summer storm just over a decade ago.

14

Hugo begins ripping off a chunk of bread, and it takes everything in George's power to hold his peace. "Miss," he says to a passing waitress. "Could we—could I—have a separate basket of bread?"

"Of course," she says, with an indulgent smile.

When Maggie first brought the injured fledgling home to San Antonio, she'd just broken up with Jacob, for the first time. The day before Maggie returned from working at a camp for underprivileged teens, Jacob actually drove across town and deposited her things in sloppily-packed boxes on George's front porch. It was during the workday when George was at school.

"The coward—if I'd seen him, I would have bent him in ways he didn't know possible," George told Alex over the telephone.

Alex, who had abandoned Texas and their marriage for her native Chicago three years before Jacob came onto the scene, just said, "Poor Mags. Well, it's good riddance to bad rubbish, but for a while it's going to be rough. Are you sure you'll be able to pick up the pieces?"

As it turned out, George didn't have to, at least not this first time. When George fetched Maggie from the airport, she held Hugo in her arms. The bird still had his pinfeathers then, and resembled a bizarre miniature gargoyle, with his hideous gray-black head and that large beak that somehow reminded George of a smiling elephant tusk.

"Who, I mean, what is this?" George asked, as she tucked the bird into a little box on her lap.

"This is Hugo," she said. "Isn't he incredible?"

"A crow?" he said.

"Hugo is a raven, Daddy. They're the largest members of the corvid family."

As if confirming his future alpha male status in Maggie's life, little Hugo squawked in agreement, nearly causing George to rear-end a Mercedes on the way out of the airport.

But in the bird's defense, when Maggie got home and saw her sweaters and books and shoes and the bits and pieces of dishware and other bric-a-brac that Jacob had thrown together, she didn't cry. No, the fledgling gargoyle's needs—his bi-hourly feedings, his daily and most rambunctious bath—pulled Maggie

15

through, a point that was difficult for George to communicate to Alex when she telephoned.

"What looks good?" Maggie asks, slicing up a sardine for Hugo, who now sits on the white linen tablecloth and makes a soft mewing sound that reminds George of a cat. Obviously, it reminds the dachshund at the next table, too, for the dog is now focused on the raven, ears cocked in bewildered attention.

"The potato saffron soup, I think, and the grilled octopus, but no," he says, "the oysters. They're not from the Gulf, are they?" he asks the waitress, who appears at their side.

"Canada," she says.

"Ah, good."

"I'll have the same thing," Maggie tells the waitress whose name is Giselle, and who, it turns out, is a massage therapist at the same studio where Maggie teaches yoga. "And a side dish of stuffed olives for Hugo."

George manages to hold his tongue, for the olives are six dollars a plate.

"Of course," Giselle says, stroking the bird's head.

"He tolerates you," George says.

"The little fellow's a lady's man," Giselle replies.

"We come here often, Daddy," Maggie says, winking at Giselle. "I told you."

A sudden breeze sends a napkin to the floor, and George twists around and down to snag it.

"You're really fit," Giselle tells George. "Do you practice yoga, too?"

Maggie splutters with laughter, momentarily looking so much like the little girl she once was, the happy little girl, that George isn't sure if he is relieved or concerned. She is, in reality, a thirty-three-year-old woman with a messy knot of hair and a purple peasant blouse that keeps slipping off her shoulder; a thirty-three-year-old woman with a history of mental instability, very little savings, and a raven that is basically another body part.

"You couldn't get my dad to practice yoga if you paid him," Maggie says now.

"No?"

Giselle, George thinks, *is looking at him almost flirtatiously*.

"My father plays tennis," Maggie says. "At least he used to

play tennis. He studied, literally studied the techniques of the professionals like John McEnroe."

"McEnroe, huh?" Giselle asks.

"I never studied McEnroe," George says. "Arthur Ashe, Björn Borg, those were my teachers. I'm self-taught, you see," and here he knows he is preening. "And for your information, I still play tennis every Saturday afternoon with Edgar."

"His best friend," Maggie tells Giselle. "A history professor."

"Ah," Giselle says, winking at George, as she turns away.

Her ass, George realizes, is shapely and full, not a skinny woman's ass. He looks away, meets Hugo's beady gaze.

"Watch out for her," Maggie says. Hugo, more relaxed now that he has had his bread and sardines and asserted his proprietary role over Maggie, squawks his agreement.

"Whatever do you mean?"

"She's checking you out. She's a maneater, Daddy," Maggie says, sopping up the olive oil with her bread, "and a very expensive one at that."

"Magpie, my dear," he says, "I have no intention of getting involved with a woman of your age."

"She's five years older than me," Maggie grins, so cunningly, that for the moment George wonders if he's misjudged her.

And if he has, *what is his daughter doing teaching yoga three evenings a week and working as a nanny for some absurdly rich people who moved here from Los Angeles? The man makes violent action films,* George recalls, *and the woman is some sort of Thai botanist from Seattle who eats a great deal of seaweed and overuses the word "like" when she speaks.*

Nevertheless, after dinner, George leaves Giselle an ample tip.

"Come back for lunch one day this week," she says, as they're leaving, "my treat."

"Maneater, Daddy," Maggie whispers, all the while smiling at Giselle and waving goodbye.

Maggie takes George's hand, and they make their way back down Canyon Road. She's already offered, twice, to let him sleep on her pull-out sofa, but they both know that would never work out. By the time George was forty, he'd reached a point in his life where a good double bed with a firm mattress and cotton

17

linens in a clean, tastefully furnished room, mattered as much to him as sex. It's been nearly a decade since he's had sex, much to his dismay, but he always sleeps in good hotels. And then there's the fact of his insomnia, which always worsens when he comes to this high altitude, thin air town.

They near Garcia Street and pause before the Selby Fleetwood Gallery, which George admits he likes, though he cannot imagine any of these pieces—a collage-like painting of a red dress, a semi-abstract composition filled with musical notes and words from philosophy, a faux primitive landscape—in his home.

"I've thought of modeling for one of the artists they represent," Maggie says, cupping her hands over the glass and standing on tiptoe to peer inside.

"Model?" George says. "And will you?"

"Maybe," Maggie says casually. "He's working on a series of reclining nudes."

"Heaven help us," George says, thinking of Modigliani's nudes and not Titian's. "How do you know this artist?"

"He takes my vinyasa class."

George trembles, fearing that the beautiful daughter for whom he once cherished such high hopes, will add nude modeling to her resume; but before he can pursue this train of thought to its dangerous conclusion, Hugo, perched on Maggie's shoulder, lifts into flight. Within seconds, Hugo is high, high above their heads, a Japanese ink drawing of a bird against a palette of purple-rose sky.

"Aren't you concerned?" George says, looking up at the brilliant creature.

"No," Maggie says, following his gaze. "If we were in the mountains, I'd be worried about eagles or owls, but he's safe here." She cocks her head in his direction, troublingly birdlike. "Don't tell me that you're worried about him?"

"No, no, of course not," George says. "How could I worry about a bird that's always ready to stab me?"

Still, watching Hugo's sky dance, as he spirals up, then barrels down, George understands, or believes he understands, for the space of those elastic moments, a space not unlike the distance between the planes of color in one of Rothko's canvases, part of the raven's allure. *Who would not want to fly like that?*

"So," George asks, as they stand there together, both of their eyes fixed on Hugo, who is flying overhead, a circus performer, a daredevil, tuned into their attention. "Have you given any thought to what your mother said?"

"About what?" Maggie says. "Mom says a lot of things."

"Chicago," George says, "the position at the gallery."

Maggie meets his eye, her blue eyes the pale blue of Modigliani's gypsy woman or the shadows beneath Monet's water lilies.

"The salary, the whole opportunity, would be excellent."

"Yossi's an Israeli," Maggie says, "and he's been divorced twice."

"So?"

Maggie laughs. "So, he's going to talk my ear off about politics, and he has a history of disastrous love affairs."

"She would never recommend a bad situation to you," George says, though he himself isn't wild about the gregarious, chain-smoking Yossi who tried to get him to buy a drawing of owls by some contemporary artist for an exorbitant price.

"How does she know what's good and bad for me?" Maggie asks.

George doesn't answer. After all, Alex did leave when Maggie was in her second year of college. Suddenly, the woman who had always been in the next room, or at least just across town, was several thousand miles away. By the time Maggie followed Jacob to Santa Fe some four years later, Alex was in Rome working on her book.

"You would at last be able to do something with your degree," he says finally.

"Oh Daddy," Maggie sighs. "I am using my degree, just not in the conventional way. Art is a daily part of my life."

George groans. How can he possibly buy this when he knows how she lives, has seen what she wears, and that ridiculous, demanding bird? She should have released the raven into the wild years ago. Instead, she spent months getting a permit. Of course, were he to bring up Hugo now, she would remind George of that pastel drawing by Picasso, the one of the Paris barmaid and her pet raven that hangs in the MOMA. The pastel had been one of George's favorite works by Picasso, whose semi-abstractions he'd found overrated, until Hugo came into their lives.

"Besides," Maggie says now, "I thought you understood how much I love it here, how hard it would be to leave."

But you don't even have health insurance, George feels like telling her, *or a lease on a decent apartment, much less a house. In six years you'll be forty, and I'll be seventy-four. The men in my family are lucky to live past seventy. Who's going to look out for you then?*

And no one, not even Maggie, could deny that she does not need looking out for. Not a week goes by, at the most ten days, when she calls wanting reassurance, advice, and all too often in tears over something as routine as a traffic ticket, an electrical storm that toppled a scrubby mesquite tree, or the yoga studio director who occasionally flips out and shouts at Maggie after her class.

George meets Maggie's eye, and the fullness he finds there is just too much, as if he can see the years of disappointment, the sadness he cannot quite grasp or understand. He wants to ask her, *Didn't we—didn't I—give you everything I had? You had the best education, endless opportunities to train as a dancer, a pianist. Surely it's not Jacob, gone from your life for three years, who's still pulling the shades down, hiding the light behind your eyes?* And yet, something about her face—the trace of violet shadow beneath her eyes, the fine frown lines rimming her mouth—tells George that it is.

Just then, Hugo comes whooshing down from the sky and alights on Maggie's shoulder. "Hi, hi, hi," he says. "Pretty bird, pretty Hugo."

Both George and Maggie laugh, and George knows they will not speak of Maggie's future again tonight. No, they will walk on together in semi-silence until they reach the St. Francis Hotel, where he will kiss her good night, then sit down in the big mauve reading chair beside the window, and read the latest biography of Kandinsky, written by a colleague at Williams College. He will read deep into the night and drink a glass of the Hennessy he bought at the liquor store two blocks from the gallery with the wooden chickens.

In the end, they do not go directly to the hotel, but stop at Maggie's place on a rather seedy dead-end street off San Francisco. The reason for this stop is to fetch the tattered volume of her friend Stanley's poetry that George will certainly not read before the Kandinsky.

"It's his first collection," Maggie says, as George takes the slim book in his hands, disturbed by the cover photo which depicts a naked woman running past a large wooden settee, her figure a soft blur. Light from some unknown source falls on her body, illuminating her lean buttocks, her legs, her slender feet. The title of the collection is *Italy*, and so George assumes that perhaps the photo was taken there, especially given the stonework in the background.

"Is Stanley a boyfriend?" he cannot help but ask, unsure if he's eager to hear 'yes' or fearful.

"Just a friend, Daddy," Maggie says. "I've been celibate for the last two years. You know that."

"I've tried not to," George says, trying not to look too hard at the low, cracked ceiling, the lack of decent furniture—only a futon in the bedroom and a makeshift table complete with four brightly-painted but un-matching chairs. The wood floors alone, scrubbed clean and bare, give the place a quality of grace; the windows are all in need of repair, and the front gate seems perpetually jammed.

"Most fathers would be glad to hear their daughters aren't sleeping around," Maggie says.

"Celibacy is a far cry from sleeping around, Mags. This celibacy," he says at last, "is it still tied up with Jacob?"

Maggie frowns, and the furrow between her eyebrows deepens.

"Well?" he asks, picturing her, a diminished figure sitting in her childhood room, a few weeks after Jacob left.

"I don't know," she says.

George leaves it at that for now, though he knows that her mother is right. Maggie should not be living in the town where Jacob's presence still lingers. So much of this place—from the Georgia O'Keeffe Gallery to the hiking trails off Bishop's Lodge Road—are filled with his memory. *How is it possible,* George ponders, *for Maggie to get over that man here?*

Realizing that the locks on several windows are not only loose but broken, George decides he will bribe Maggie to take the job in Chicago, if necessary. A new car, a week in Bali to attend that phenomenally expensive yoga retreat (though who will care for Hugo while she's gone? he can already hear her saying). After all, Alex may be selfish, but she is organized, efficient, a go-getter, as Edgar likes to say. Surely, Alex could help to get Maggie back on track.

Sitting in his hotel room two hours later, George swirls the brandy around in his glass, breathes in its scent, and fights the desire to telephone Alex, an insomniac like himself, though it's past midnight in Chicago, and she has that job now as an events coordinator for the Art Institute, the career she never had during her years in Texas.

Maggie, Margaret, Magpie, Magwitch, Mags—their bright star who exerted such a strong will from the time she was born—the nurses and then the pediatrician all said that she would be a handful, a child of real determination.

For a long time, that had been true.

For a long time, Maggie had taken both ballet lessons and ice skating, despite the fact that ice skating was a rarity in Texas; but Alex had been a skater, and she wanted her daughter to follow in this path.

And when Maggie tired of ice skating—for the practice required a forty-minute drive each way—she stayed with ballet, adding painting and piano to her repertoire.

"A cultured young woman," George's own mother said approvingly, the last time she saw Maggie, more than eighteen years ago now, in June, the summer before the old woman died. Maggie had played Tchaikovsky's "Swan Lake" for her *Babushka* on the piano, and George's mother, dignified in pearls and a violet dress, her silky white hair coiled in a braid around her head, a relic from her own time as a dancer, had sat in the armchair beside the terrace windows, her eyes closed, a smile on her fine lips, as she listened to the music she had loved since her girlhood in St. Petersburg.

And Maggie was—is—cultured. She holds degrees in English and Art History from Baylor. She can talk for hours about Jacques Louis David and especially Berthe Morisot and Mary Cassatt, for it's the female Impressionists whom she most admires. She is familiar with the works of Tchaikovsky and Schubert, and is able to improvise a piece of music with the same ease with which she once pirouetted around the tiled living room in her childhood home in San Antonio.

When was it that she first tilted towards the edge, that dark blur of blue-black, of purple-black color that seems to hold back or simply hide the

22

chaos in so much modern art? George asks himself while pouring another Hennessy. *Long before Jacob*, George admits.

There was that year when she was sixteen and wouldn't eat, winnowing down to a frightening one hundred pounds because, she told her parents, her calling was to be an angel. "I'm waiting for my wings to shine through," she said of her protruding shoulder blades.

The hospital psychiatrists wanted to diagnose anorexia nervosa, but the starving disease of high-achieving teenage girls was quickly replaced by an even more terrifying diagnosis. Maggie, the psychiatrists said, had all the signs of manic depression: grandiose visions, paranoia, a feeling of the divine. Had she shown such symptoms before? And what about long bouts of silence? Did she suffer from that, too? Crying spells? Insomnia?

There followed a year of experimenting with medications that plunged Maggie into a terrifying depression before finally balancing her out. Balancing her, yes, that was the word the psychiatrists used; but she was flatter, too, and even though she regained the weight, and more, she became less than herself, diminished.

Some nights George lies in bed and wills the God in whom he can no longer believe to grant his daughter a husband or at least a career to build a respectable, secure life. *She doesn't need a traditional family*, George reasons or tries to reason with this God, *but she does need a retirement plan, a good dentist, a reliable car.*

The constants in Maggie's life now, as far as George can tell, are Hugo and yoga and the four-year-old twins of the L.A. couple: an amber-eyed boy and girl she ferries around Santa Fe in an absurdly expensive double jogging stroller, attracting the oohs and aahs of numerous people who must wonder if the children are her own, for the mother of the twins is from Lebanon and the father, half Portuguese and half British.

It is after 2 a.m. before George finally climbs into the comfortable double bed with its sturdy mattress. The moon is full, and the gauzy curtains in his room do not shut out the light. He covers his head with a pillow and eventually slips into a dream in which he is back in those caves in Lascaux, France, with their prehistoric paintings—caves that he and Alex visited, ironically, on their honeymoon. There on the wall is an ancient drawing of a bird-headed man. The bird is believed to be a raven, and the drawing itself, a manifestation of the soul. But what sort of manifestation? Even then, ravens were associated more with the afterlife, with the dead, than the living. They may be spiritual guides for many peoples, the Native Americans particularly, but they are dangerous, too, tricksters. Rather like that God who looked on as the Germans bombed George's native city. His parents once spoke to him of people eating the bodies of the dead.

The following afternoon, George is late meeting Maggie, who is caring for the twins for the day, because he has run into Giselle at Sage Bakery on a side street off Guadalupe. He has come for the good, chewy peasant bread that reminds him of the bread his mother baked during the wintertime, and for a bowl of hot soup—tomato is today's special. He has just sat down with his meal when a female voice calls out to him.

"A good lunch for a tennis player," Giselle says, not even waiting to be invited before she joins him, carrying a bowl of the very same soup, and alongside it, a foot-long baguette and a chunk of butter.

"You have a healthy appetite," George says, watching her spread the bread thickly with butter before plunging it into the soup.

"I have a fast metabolism, and I do a lot of physical work during the day," she says.

"Ah," says George, wondering if she will elaborate. She does not.

"On your way to see Maggie?"

"I am meeting my daughter and the twins shortly," George says, curious as to just how much this Giselle knows about Maggie's life, and whether or not her knowledge might prove useful. He is aware, too, of how attractive she is, though not beautiful, for there is a meatiness to her build that he does not entirely like, being of slight frame himself, and not overly tall, unlike the Amazonian but slim Alex who towered over him physically during their marriage as she towered over him in so many other more insidious ways.

Giselle's fingernails, he notices now, have been lacquered a deep red. They were not red last night; of this, he is sure. Did she do her nails herself or go to a salon? His curiosity startles him.

Normally, he would be appalled by such garishly-painted fingernails.

"You have known my daughter for a long time?" he asks, simultaneously reminded of the lovely shape of her full ass.

"I've known her, casually, for at least five years," Giselle says, dunking more bread in her soup, for she seems to eat it this way, soaking it up, rather than taking it in spoonfuls. "We've only been friends, not close friends, mind you, but friends, for the last two," she looks down at her soup, "you know, since Jacob left."

"Then you knew Jacob?" he says, just a little worried that he is opening up a Pandora's Box.

"You could say that. We were lovers for a little while," Giselle says, holding George's eye. She has outlined her own eyes with kohl, giving her a slightly Egyptian or exotic look despite her hazel eyes and brown hair which she wears loose today and shoulder-length. "It amounted to little more than a few nights of pleasure, and it didn't happen while he and Maggie were together."

Even though Jacob and Maggie broke up too many times over the years to keep count, George is not sure he believes her. "You liked him then?" he asks.

"I'd hardly call it that. Jacob was alluring," Giselle says. "There's a tradition of gurus in yoga, and Jacob had that kind of power, or he could have had it, if he'd gotten his life together. He was a presence, and as a teacher of yoga, as a yogi, well, he was good, inspiring."

"But?" George asks.

Giselle doesn't answer.

"Do you think Maggie's over him?"

"I don't know."

"You don't know my daughter well enough?"

"I wouldn't say that. I'd say only that I don't know what makes a person get over someone. Look, I might as well be straight with you," she says, mopping up the remaining soup with more bread, "I was married before I came to Santa Fe. I thought geographic distance was what I needed to forget my ex."

"But you didn't?" George is smiling now, though there's a sick feeling in his stomach, too, as he realizes that he is sexually considering this woman.

"I still find myself dreaming about him sometimes. That royal wedding earlier this month?"

"Yes?"

"I dreamt it was my ex and me walking down the aisle to the salutes of Beefeaters and the shouts of a deluded country."

At this comment on the royal family's power, George cannot help but smile, for he has never warmed to the English despite his mastery of their literature.

"So why did you leave?" George asks.

"I wanted children," Giselle says. "He didn't."

"You have children then?"

She runs her fingers through her hair. "That's the irony or the paradox or whatever you call it. It seems I can't."

George feels himself blush all the way to the tips of his ears.

"So," Giselle says, "now you know far more about me than I know about you."

"Perhaps," George says, understanding he could say something about the tennis and in the process correct her, but he no longer feels like pursuing this. Relationships are tiring, despite the release of sex.

They talk for a while longer until George realizes that it is after 1 p.m. "I'm afraid I must go," he says, embarrassed by his apologetic tone; this woman joined him after all. "By chance, do you have a phone?"

"Sorry," Giselle says. "I left it at the studio, but I'll give you my number, in case you want to call me."

It's almost 1:45 p.m. by the time George arrives in the park. He's afraid that Maggie may have left, but no, she is there, sitting on a bench and knitting something that looks like a scarf as her charges—he sees them over by the fountain—rush the pigeons. Standing there, George feels as if his daughter is missing something. Realizing that it's Hugo's absence he's noticed, George chides himself for his mistake. *I'll be goddamned if I miss that crazy bird.*

"Daddy," Maggie says, as he approaches. "I almost gave up on you."

"I'm sorry," he says. "Something came up."

She nods, tucks the knitting into her bag, and calls to the children.

"They've grown," George says, as the twins amble over. They are dressed in overalls today, green for Clara, and a blue stripe for Ben. On their feet, they sport the same hideous mountaineering sandals that so many people wear now. All George can think is how expensive those sandals must be and of how lovely Maggie used to look in her patent leather Mary Janes.

"Where's Hugo?" Clara asks.

"What?" George asks, looking from the child to his daughter.

"I thought you'd be bringing him." The little girl pouts.

"Clara adores Hugo," Maggie says. "I suppose she got it into her head that you'd be looking after him today."

"Heaven help me," George says.

"Heaven?" Clara asks.

George shakes his head. He's forgotten how literal-minded children can be.

The children climb into the stroller, and Maggie buckles them in, gentle with them, at ease. She brushes the hair from Ben's eyes, touches Clara's cheek with her forefinger, and George feels a terrible stab of longing and loss.

Perhaps a minute later, they make their way down the street to the ice cream parlor where, Maggie tells him, the twins have vanilla or Krazy Kolors, and she always orders a double scoop of hazelnut and honey cream.

Later that evening, back at Maggie's casita, which George would rather not visit again, for in the dwindling light he sees her next-door-neighbor's collection of junked cars, crumbling furniture, and recycling. He witnesses his daughter's greeting ritual with Hugo, one she performs, he knows, at each and every reunion, no matter how little time has passed since she and the raven have been apart.

The ritual amounts to this: as soon as they step inside, Hugo hops out of his four-by-four-foot cage that dominates the living area, and onto a perch nearby. He makes a chortling noise and bows his head sideways and fluffs out his feathers, and Maggie steps forward to stroke his fuzzy head. Watching, George must admit there is something touching in this greeting, which is far more affectionate than any of his reunions with Alex ever were, even during the happiest of times.

"Hi, hi," Hugo says. "Happy Hugo, pretty bird."

"Does he understand what he's saying?" George asks,

wondering, for the first time, if the raven actually feels emotions.

"I don't know for sure," Maggie says, bowing to touch foreheads with Hugo, who chortles and gurgles, "but I'd say he does."

The greeting ceremony—for it is that, George realizes, with a formality and an order that is both scripted and oddly beautiful in the way of some choreographed yet spontaneous dance—goes on for a few more minutes.

Perhaps it is the turning of Hugo's head towards Maggie's face that is the trigger, or his daughter's caressing tone, or the way she stretches out her hand to let Hugo ropewalk up her arm. Whatever it is, it jars something loose in George's own memory: the night he and Maggie met Jacob at el Farol, and though he has forgotten it until now, it was Jacob who first introduced him to the restaurant and to the saffron and potato soup specialty that he has eaten on every visit since.

That night Maggie wore an uncharacteristically beautiful dress, a flaring sweep of crinkly red silk that brought to mind Spanish dances and heat. The dress was red, but when she moved, when the skirt billowed around her, George couldn't help but think of Hugo's wings outstretched in flight. So perhaps it was the gracefulness of her that night, the Isadora Duncan meets Pavlova allure that brings the moment back. She wore her hair swept up in a high ponytail that swung behind her as she walked, and there was a little golden bracelet of charms on one of her ankles—her left one, George remembers now. Jacob had brought the golden bracelet back from India, for he regularly visited an ashram there, where he had a guru of his own.

This golden bracelet quickly became one of Hugo's favorite playthings, and he singled it out from the other bangles and earrings and shiny things in Maggie's jewelry drawer. When was it that George last saw her wearing the bracelet? It may be that the last time was that night she wore the glowing red dress. It may have been later. The bracelet itself is not what matters.

What matters? Maggie telling him that Hugo had carried it up into the sky one afternoon not so long after Jacob left Santa Fe. "After an overnight trip," she'd said. "He refused to hop onto my shoulder, angry, I assume, because I'd left him behind."

She'd left the window open, and soon the bracelet was in Hugo's beak, and his blue-black form had vanished into the sky.

When Hugo came back from an elaborate flight display that was meant to dazzle Maggie, or so she believed—"a display meant to prove his worthiness, to re-establish his place in my heart"—the gold bracelet of charms was not with him.

How beautiful Maggie looked in that twirling whirl of red on that night at El Farol. How happy she'd been, how buoyant, as she and George walked to the restaurant, talking and laughing. That buoyancy, which was Maggie's gift, her charm, lasted after they arrived at El Farol, and waned only when 7 p.m. became 7:30 and then 7:45, and still Jacob did not arrive.

"You're late," Maggie said to Jacob when he finally showed up close to 8 p.m. She slurred her words a little by then, dizzy from the second glass of red wine she'd drunk while waiting. (Despite George's insistence, she wanted to wait for Jacob before she ordered food.)

Jacob apologized, bending down to kiss her cheek, his red hair encircling Maggie's face, the ropy muscles in his arms like the ropes of his hair.

"What kept you?" George asked, realizing he'd been gripping the plastic-covered menu with both hands for God knows how long.

"Cynthia Reynolds," he said. "She threw her back out riding."

"Again?" Maggie said, the hiss of the first syllable all George needed to know.

And George understood. His Maggie, the daughter he taught to ride a bike, to listen to a concerto, to make good Russian tea in a samovar and serve with milk and two sugar cubes, was involved with the worst kind of man. An unfaithful one and a liar. All that night, George sat there wishing he could kill him, wishing in fact that he could chop him up like the roadkill Maggie once fed to Hugo.

George relives all of this as Maggie stands in the tiny kitchen with Hugo chattering on her shoulder. Occasionally, the raven bursts into some un-harmonic song in which George recognizes bits of "Somewhere Over the Rainbow" and "Wild Thing," and Maggie joins in.

If the bird had ferried anything away into those purple-black mountains, George tells himself now, *why couldn't it have been the memory of Jacob Benedetti that he carried?* If there were any justice in the universe, Hugo would have ferried the fierce intelligence and the coiled energy that had been his daughter's lover far, far into those sacred mountains. Yes, Maggie would have been out of her mind with worry while the raven was gone. She might even have torn at her hair like the heroine of some Greek tragedy.

But what relief—what unsurpassed joy—would she have felt upon the raven's spiraling return? George closes his eyes, trying to picture it now, the brilliant blue-black bird riding an updraft across the purple mountains, the bracelet falling through the turquoise sky, lit by the annihilating sun.

BOUNDARIES, BODIES, BREATH

Now that her husband Richard is becoming Tracy, Rachel is almost grateful for Lubbock's middle-aged women with their faux tans and cleavage, and the leather-faced men who look like extras in an absurdist version of *Urban Cowboy*. Just such a couple is seated at a table by the door when Rachel steps inside Caprock Coffee on an already sweltering afternoon in late May. The woman in front of her in line has tousled, blonde hair that must take hours to style, and Rachel cannot imagine how the man sporting a cowboy hat in a place that is far more Buddy Holly than John Wayne manages to keep the thing on in today's wind.

After ordering, Rachel scans the tables and recognizes the quiet art historian from Singapore who's a regular in her yoga class. It's the first time she's seen him in street clothes. There's something sleek about him, almost feline. He might not have mastered wheel, and his eagle is still a little too much elbow and not enough knee-twined-around-ankle, but his breathing radiates calm—why Rachel likes to place her mat next to his and just listen to his deep inhale and soothing exhale, a little like the ocean of the dreamy Massachusetts summers she spent with Max all those years ago. *Could she ever become involved with the art historian whose stream-lined black and gray garb would fit her well?* Now that her husband wears pantyhose and push-up bras, it's a question that comes up.

"Will you be at Carmen's yoga class this Saturday?" he asks when Rachel approaches, holding her big white cup of cappuccino, a caffeine bomb she shouldn't be drinking this late in the afternoon, especially given her recent insomnia.

"I'm planning on it. Why?"

"It'll be her last," he says, running a well-kept hand through his thinning hair.

"I don't recall her saying anything."

"Third year of medical school: she doesn't think she can keep up."

"I'll miss her." Though she and Carmen only talk once a week after class for at most five minutes, Rachel has come to rely on her energetic attitude, her spunk.

Among the books opened on the table, she recognizes a reproduction of David's portrait of Juliette Récamier. The art historian's dark eyes are clear behind his Lennon-esque glasses.

"I'm giving a paper on portraiture after the French Revolution in two weeks," the art historian explains.

"Where's the conference?" Rachel asks.

"Montreal."

"Nice." She smiles. "I should let you get back to it."

Turning away, she thinks back to the trip she and Richard took to Paris the winter before Amy was born: the hours they spent wandering the Louvre, the way the Récamier held Richard rapt. At the time, Rachel thought he was admiring her legendary beauty; now she wonders if it wasn't the post-revolutionary heroine's femininity he was studying. And yet they'd made love almost every night of that trip, and most mornings, lingering in the white double bed in their tiny Montparnasse hotel room, the window open to the gleaming dome of Sacre Coeur beyond. Breakfast, they ate at a small café down the street where they sat at a wrought iron table, knees touching, talking and laughing, two more lovers in Paris.

It was one of their happiest times together, that trip; and now especially Rachel finds herself returning to the long walks they took along the Seine in the evenings, the lights of the city reflected off the water's surface, tiny points of bright potential, and in this way like the shared future she'd envisioned for Richard and herself. *Yes*, she tells herself, quoting Lennon, *life is what happens while you're busy making other plans, but what life should include a husband who's decided to change his sex?*

Not far from the art historian, Rachel recognizes Katie, her silvery-blonde neighbor who drives a Mercedes GT in Selenite Gray with white leather interior. Today, however, the air-brushed perfection of Katie's eyes are puffy, and she's without her trademark lipstick. Rachel is about to turn away when Katie looks up and smiles.

"Want some company?" Rachel hears herself say, sloshing cappuccino onto her jeans as she comes over.

"I would, actually." Katie's voice holds unexpected warmth, and an edge, too—an anxiety Rachel recognizes.

The last time she and Katie talked, maybe two months ago, given that Katie usually goes directly from garage to house, the family's trio of Papillons were barking in the yard at 11:30 p.m. (for God knows what reason this time). Rachel, unable to bear it any longer, had phoned to ask Katie, as politely as possible, to please bring the Papillons inside.

"Everything okay?" Rachel now says, taking note of the crimson tint along Katie's nostrils.

"Oh, I don't know. We've just begun to settle in here, and now Jonathan's taken a job in Los Angeles," Katie says, cradling her own mug of herbal tea in both hands, a gesture that makes her look small, girlish.

A hot little fist of annoyance takes hold in Rachel's belly. "Didn't you guys move here from some big city a few years ago?"

"Baltimore," Katie says. "We were in Baltimore for eight years."

Well, you drive a custom-built Mercedes that's a year old, and your three daughters all drive foreign vehicles. Your husband's salary should be able to keep you in luxury cars and pay the gas prices in L.A., so what's the problem? It's only recently that Rachel's started coming up with these contrary statements, side effects of her inability to sleep when the volcanic confusion bubbles up within her, and she wakes from some dream in which she seems to be speaking to a therapist who is not part of her past or her present.

"I grew up in Idalou," Katie says at last. "West Texas is home for me."

Rachel would have bet several mortgage payments that Katie came from somewhere back East or at least from an affluent suburb adjacent to Chicago or St. Louis. She has a hard time picturing Katie with her seashell-colored nails and neutral silk separates in tiny Idalou (named for its supposed first inhabitants) where the houses look pre-made and wear aluminum siding.

All Rachel knows about Katie's husband, Jonathan, is that he's descended from some branch of Thailand's royal family and is beautiful in the way of Michelangelo's David, his features chiseled, his ebony hair and eyes riveting. Katie's daughters, all four of whom wear their hair at waist length, are dark-haired like their father and have inherited his almond-shaped eyes and olive skin.

"When will you move?" Rachel asks.

"July," Katie says. "Leanne was accepted at Reed, so we'll go up in time to get settled before she has to leave for school."

"Sounds like a plan." What would Katie say if Rachel were

33

to tell her that during the months when Leanne was applying to colleges, Richard was investigating gender-reassignment surgeons in Dallas and Houston? Not that Katie, and the rest of the neighbors on the street, aren't all too aware of the physical changes taking place within Richard, now Tracy. Even ninety-three-year-old Dorothy Kellerman, whose eyesight and hearing are both severely diminished, can't overlook the fact that Richard's elegant, worn tweeds have given way to silk dresses and linen separates, the tapered beard he once wore now revealing skin polished by makeup.

Is it better or worse that he's talking to Dennis about the three-year-vision for the gender reassignment surgeries? Rachel asked herself when she overheard her husband discussing the process with their neighbor, a toxologist, as if he were reviewing some facet of Russian history, prior to the Revolution, to which he's devoted his professional life?

"We're going to have a garage sale next month," Katie says, "but I've already begun setting aside a few things for Amy. There's a bike in great condition and some toys and puzzles. She likes dolls, doesn't she?"

"She's wild about them," Rachel says, for her six-year-old daughter has three babies that she bundles and rocks and feeds and sings to nightly, as well as a pair of Cabbage Patch Kids that Rachel's mother sent last Christmas.

Will it be easier for Amy because she's a pre-adolescent girl, Rachel now wonders, *when Richard fully becomes Tracy, than if Amy were a boy of about the same age? What will happen to Amy's coveted status as Daddy's Girl then? Not just in the immediate future but when she's thirteen and in need of a male role model?*

Rachel can't even begin to imagine her own life as the wife of the medically transformed Richard-now-Tracy, despite the conversations they've had, the emphasis Tracy has placed on their staying together. "It's not like this neighborhood isn't full of non-traditional families," her husband says whenever Rachel tries to give voice to the faultline that's opened up within her, a faultline just a step away from that nocturnal earthquake.

Sure, their circle of university friends includes several gay couples, many of whom have biological or adopted children, not to mention the trans technology wizard and their partner. But Rachel isn't gay, and Tracy is not the man she married.

Life is what happens...

"Hey," Katie says, touching her hand. "How are you?"

"Nearly a decade of marriage, and I never came home to find my closet or lingerie drawer in disarray." Rachel attempts a smile, but her voice just trails into nervous laughter. "Now it's lipstick and higher heels than I've ever worn. I have bad balance." More nervous laughter. "It's like I've walked into *The Twilight Zone's* version of my life."

"I can only imagine," Katie says, holding Rachel's hand now. "But at least Richard—I mean Tracy's upfront about it."

"Like a butterfly that's been released from a chrysalis," Rachel says, thinking, *Like hell you understand.*

It was almost twelve years ago that Rachel arrived in Lubbock, after selling or giving away every artifact from her fifteen-year-history with Max. On the long drive out West, Rachel told herself the geographic distance from Chicago where she and Max had lived since they met in college was a godsend, despite the increasing desolation of the landscape.

Fourteen hours into the drive, she spent a sleepless night in Joplin, Missouri, where she checked into a navel orange and pink hotel room, ate vending machine Pop Tarts for dinner, and wept through a pay-per-view-showing of *Annie Hall*, which she and Max had first watched together. It remained unfathomable, really, the fact that he'd left her, and not for the usual reason—"I've met someone else. I've fallen in love with her." Nor did he say those agonizing words her friend Leah lived with—"I just don't love you anymore."

No. One afternoon in early spring, the neighborhood gardens and window boxes abloom with daffodils and hyacinths, and the cherry and crabapple trees just beginning to flower, Max came home from the Laboratory School to tell Rachel that he just couldn't "do marriage" anymore, talking about their life together as if it were a sport, like soccer or tennis, and not a sacrament, a vow.

"But I love you," Rachel had said, "and I can't believe you don't love me."

Max, beautiful, tender-hearted Max who brought every stray dog or cat home and used to sing Rachel back to sleep when she had a nightmare, took her hands within his own and said, "I do love you, Rach, but I just can't be married anymore, not to you, not to anyone."

And so began Rachel's unreal journey, the job search, the move to Texas, a state she knew only from *Dallas* re-runs, and the surreal chaos of climate-change-meet-concrete-and-ever-increasing-highways—otherwise known as Houston.

It was that night in the hotel room in Joplin that Rachel swore she'd take her time before getting involved with anyone again anytime soon.

Instead, during early October of her first semester at the university, Rachel met Richard Dunham in the rare books archive. They were the only two people there on a Friday afternoon. Rachel was officially there to look at a first edition of one of Edna St. Millay's collections, though the truth was she loved the archive's stained-glass windows, its smell of old books, and a quiet that brought back her spacious years of graduate school. (This, along with the fact that her rental house smelled of the last tenant's cats, and she had trouble getting work done beneath the fluorescent lights of her office, meant that she spent plenty of time in the archive.)

"They're cutting down a fifty-year-old live oak outside my office," Richard explained across the aged maple table, once they introduced themselves. His hair was blonde and curly, and he had a deep dimple in his left cheek that made him look boyish, young, despite his forty-six years. Since losing her virginity to a graduate teaching assistant in her first American Lit seminar, Rachel has had a thing for men in tweeds; and Richard, with his broad shoulders and agile, tennis player's build, wore his very well.

By the time five o'clock rolled around, Richard had begun packing up his notebooks.

"I'm driving out to Caprock Canyon early tomorrow morning to do some hiking," he said. "Care to join me?"

Rachel didn't own a pair of hiking boots, but she said yes immediately.

"I packed a picnic lunch," he told her the following morning as they trekked up a pink clay path, the air still tinged with the chill of morning. "I hope you like cheese and tomato?"

"I do," she said, for she'd brought along only a Cliff Bar and a Ziploc bag of raisins.

Some three hours later, in the heart of the canyon, the leaves of the trees shone orange-gold in the sunlight. "For you," he said, handing her a bottle of sparkling water. From his backpack, he produced a tartan blanket. After sitting down, Rachel loosened the laces on her new boots and watched the sandwich lunch emerge from that same pack, a lunch that included homemade oatmeal cookies and fresh fruit—there were even pomegranate seeds in the salad. Such care took her breath away. They ate, and he told her about his current research on the jeweler Fabergé's relationship to the last czar, making bejeweled eggs and unfathomable privilege as tantalizing as any good novelist. And afterwards? No, they didn't make love or even make out on a blanket she now considers culturally misaligned with his passions for all things Romanov. Instead, he listened closely as she told him of her research on Millay.

"Isn't it a little soon?" Rachel's mother said, some four months later when Rachel told her that she was engaged, leaving out the way Richard had gotten down on his knees with a diamond solitaire in that very same canyon, the hours they'd spent kissing in the drowsy late afternoon sun.

"Maybe, Mom," Rachel had said, "but I know, deep down, that this is the right decision. I love him. He's smart, grounded, and he makes me feel that way too."

"So, is there anything I can do?" Katie says, before climbing into that custom Benz that a Romanov or a Kardashian might own. They are standing in the parking lot outside the coffee shop where one of Rachel's former students calls out and waves.

"No, but thanks," Rachel replies while waving to the student.

Rachel almost wishes she could step into Katie's life. *How hard could it be to pack up a three-quarter-of-a-million-dollar home and head west with her handsome, successful husband who goes through foreign cars and vintage BMW motorcycles the way six-year-old Amy goes through shoes? Amy:* The number one concern as well as the anchor in Rachel's life. Her six-year-old daughter is smart and lovely in a way that Rachel never was, and tirelessly ebullient. Some nights when Rachel wakes on her study's day bed, the sheets sticky around her, she tells herself that she should run away to teach English abroad or drink a poisonous tea made from the oleander flowers in another neighbor's garden—until she recalls her daughter's coppery hair, her gap-toothed smile, the exultant way she calls out "Mommy!" and Rachel knows she has to keep going.

And then, though her faith in these moments is diminished or at least taxed, there are those times when she and Tracy sit together at the kitchen table where they share tea or a bottle of wine and talk about the day, the plans for transforming the screened-in porch into a greenhouse, and of course their daughter; and for that small space of time, Rachel is content—at peace—or at least as close to it as she ever was.

By the time Katie has maneuvered her Mercedes into traffic, Rachel is on her way to the elementary school where Amy is in the final weeks of kindergarten. If she walks fast, she'll be there just before the three o'clock bell, in time to see Amy in her school world.

Amy's teacher, Ms. Taylor, is a "full-figured gal" somewhere in her thirties with awful, chunky blonde highlights and a wide smile filled with teeth of such flawless whiteness they must have been cosmetically altered, unless Father Taylor is a dentist.

Entering the classroom, Rachel breathes in the comforting smells of Elmer's glue and sleepy children, and quickly spots Amy at the water table with Emily and Aiden. She looks happy, Rachel tells herself, studying her daughter's concentrated stance. These days, she is constantly on the lookout for any sign that Amy is being disturbed by the changes going on at home.

"Mommy," Amy says, rushing into her arms.

Her child crushes up against her, and Rachel's whole body turns to sun-warmed caramel. "How was school, sweetheart?" she asks, kissing Amy's forehead. which smells slightly of milk and sun.

"Good, good. I'm so glad you're here. Emily has Barbie Snacks. I told her that you would buy them for me, okay?" Amy's hazel eyes, so like Rachel's own, are absolutely in earnest.

"Maybe tomorrow," Rachel says, wishing that material girl Emily, with her shiny Tinkerbell shoes and her Tangled backpack, was in the other kindergarten classroom. Every week, it's a new battle. Before Barbie Snacks, it was a princess crown, and before that, a unicorn pillow pal for naptime.

"Why not today, Mommy?" Amy asks, wide-eyed, her left cheek dimpling as she smiles. "You told me today yesterday."

38

Ms. Taylor catches Rachel's eye, grins, so that she almost expects her to say, "Well, Mom? I heard you, too. You shouldn't make promises you don't intend to keep."

I suppose I should be grateful that Amy isn't asking me why Daddy is wearing lipstick and mascara and getting "her" nails done every week at the salon frequented by the gray-haired matriarchs and thankfully not by the co-eds who take our classes, Rachel thinks.

Ms. Taylor knows what's happening in Amy's home. Amy's already told her class—with that terrifying innocence of children—about her Daddy's new dresses and his vivid pink lipstick.

"You will be at the Parents' Dinner on Friday?" Ms. Taylor asks, as Rachel gathers up Amy's nap blanket and her threadbare Pooh.

"Oh yes," Rachel says, with affected casualness, her gaze inadvertently falling to Ms. Taylor's freckled cleavage, all too apparent in her clingy fuchsia dress.

How does she get away with it? This is an elementary school for chrissake, Rachel wonders.

"And Dr. Dunham? Will he be joining you?" Ms. Taylor's smile is so big she reveals the fuchsia lipstick staining those blinding teeth. "We'd like a head count for the meal, you see."

"I'm afraid my husband has a faculty meeting that evening," Rachel says, certain that Ms. Taylor knows she is lying. Richard stopped coming to Roscoe Wilson right after he began wearing Donna Karan separates and heels, intuiting that a kindergarten classroom was not the place to try out his emerging identity as Tracy.

"Well, at least two of the other fathers won't be here either." Ms. Taylor blinks under the bright lights, her perfectly mascara'd eyes looking momentarily garish, though her smile does not break.

Rachel stares back at the teacher, astonished by the sudden need for a fight, some release, as a sick, sinking feeling takes root in the belly.

"Ms. Taylor!" Scrawny, little Tobias rushes forwards, and then he's clamped his arms around her knees. "Ms. Taylor, Megan called me 'pie face.'"

"Let's go talk to Megan," Ms. Taylor says, laying a hand on the boy's head with a tenderness that makes Rachel want to pull her hair.

What kind of woman/mother lashes out at a kindergarten teacher? I am becoming such a bitch.

When Rachel and Richard met, he was in his second year as Chair of the university's Honors College, which meant that he taught one to two courses a year, usually in his own area of interest: Russian history, specifically Czarist Russia. After that, Richard's passion for Rasputin's murderer, the cross-dressing Prince Yusipov, began to make a little more sense.

By the time Richard was wearing skirts and twin sets to work, the Honors College had asked him to play a less visible role in their administration. "The kids might be stoners. They might be having sex in the stacks, but their parents, the donors, at least most of them, voted for Bush," Richard said philosophically.

And perhaps this is the hardest thing for Rachel to take. While her own life is falling apart, Richard—who has been Tracy professionally for the last five months—seems the epitome of calm. Is it the hormones? Or simply the release of being allowed at last to live the life Tracy believes that he was intended for all along?

"You were dishonest with me," Rachel said, once Richard told her about Dr. Markson and the surgery they had scheduled for July.

"Clarification, Rachel, I was dishonest with myself. When I met you, I really thought I could live the rest of my life as a man." Tracey stroked Rachel's shoulder, kissed her there.

How can it be that Richard now Tracy is still attracted to her? Does that make Tracy a lesbian? Given today's ever-changing gender politics, Rachel has no idea. She does know that she can't imagine making love to Tracy again. All she manages are chaste kisses and the occasional hug.

"You okay?" Tracy said just the other night when she opened the door to Rachel's study and found her lying face up on the day bed and staring at the ceiling.

Rachel turned towards this new incarnation of her husband, wishing, fiercely wishing, that this could all somehow prove to be a dream, a very bad dream. "How can you even ask that?"

"I'm still me," Tracy said as she sat down.

"You can't say that to me and expect me to really believe it." Tears pierced Rachel's eyes, and she turned away, refusing to cry with Amy playing in her room just down the hall.

Tracy tried to hug her, but Rachel tensed up, drew back. "I'm sorry. I just can't," she said, wishing she could reach out, touch the vanished beard that would never return.

"We made a commitment to each other, and we have Amy," her husband said, voice scratchy, still adapting to the hormones. Her husband's hands, Rachel thought, studying them, would always be a clue to Tracy's former life, her real life, as a man. As if "real" means anything anymore, or ever really had, deceiving Rachel as those jeweler's eggs deceived that last czar. "Amy needs both of us, especially now."

"Yes, yes, I know all that," Rachel said, recognizing the earnestness in Tracy's face. The way she leaned in felt almost like a supplication.

"But?" The question hovered in the air between them.

"You wear a bra now for god's sake." Rachel took a series of long deep breaths, squeezed her eyes shut.

"Please," Tracy said in a tone that brought back all that Rachel remembered falling in love with, the stability she once believed would ground her life in the windy land of tumbleweed.

"I'm not going to leave," Rachel said at last. "But I still don't how I'm going to manage to stay."

"We'll find a way, promise," Tracy offered. When she reached out again, Rachel tried to find shelter in her husband's embrace, the comfort of her strong shoulders, but the muscular arms that had always made Rachel feel so protected, would change with hormone therapy…

Some half an hour after leaving school, Rachel and Amy turn onto their street and soon they are at the house. "Look, Mama," Amy cries. "There's a cardinal in the bird bath."

"Yes," Rachel says, drinking in the beauty of the red bird against the backdrop of pink and purple flowers. Even now, five years after moving into this house, the garden continues to surprise her—*can this really be mine?* Standing on the lawn, Rachel surveys the foxglove and snapdragon and lobelia glowing beneath the

41

shimmering live oak, the two dozen purple irises she planted last November, and she feels almost happy.

A comfortable home, a garden, a child—yes, she wanted a daughter—and a loving, steadfast husband, old-fashioned as all that sounds despite her specialization in the life and work of Edna St. Vincent Millay, are the facts of Rachel's life that have always given her the most pleasure. This is the life she envisioned with Richard when they exchanged vows in an Episcopalian church he loved for the ritual and ceremony. ("No Russian Orthodox in Lubbock!" he once joked.) Yes, the tenure track job is rewarding, but it's also a vindication of what she's been all of her life: a reader, a thinker.

"Daddy!" Amy says, and Rachel looks up to see Tracy standing in the doorway. She is wearing a tasteful pale pink dress, definitely silk, and taupe sandals.

What I wouldn't give to see Richard standing there in that crinkly seersucker blazer he bought in Austin, Rachel thinks, as Amy rushes into Tracy's arms for a kiss.

"There's a present for our Amy," Tracy says. "One of Katie's daughters dropped it off."

"The dolls," Rachel says, stepping away when Tracy tries to hug her. "I ran into Katie at the coffee shop. She said she had some dolls for Amy."

"Oh?"

"They're moving," Rachel says, self-conscious given the details of that conversation. "L.A. I guess we'll have new neighbors."

"Yes." Tracy nods.

"No, it's a bike, Mommy," Amy says, once she steps through the doorway.

And sure enough, it's not a tangled mass of half-clothed Barbies that Rachel beholds, but the promised iridescent purple bicycle with training wheels and a wicker basket between pink-tasseled handlebars.

"Will you help me ride it, Mommy?" Amy says, already climbing onto the old-fashioned banana-shaped seat, also pink.

"Of course." Tears sting the edges of Rachel's eyes, not because her husband is wearing nail polish and taking female hormones, but because the baby who nursed at her breast for two-and-a-half years is growing up. Pretty soon, Amy will be pedaling away like that little girl in a C.K. Williams poem that Rachel read once but hasn't been able to find again. Rachel looks over at her husband, wondering if Richard—Tracy—is thinking something like this, too.

"I would have loved a bike like that growing up," Tracy says.

Rachel recalls her old blue Schwinn hand-me-down, its color a non-sequitur, and her breath seizes up in her chest. She squeezes her eyes shut and tries to imagine herself beside the quiet art historian from yoga class, tries to find his oceanic breath.

Amy pushes the pedals, but she can't turn the bike to the right. "Mommy, help me!"

"Mommy's coming," Rachel says, hurrying down the front walk, the slap of Tracy's sandals on the pavement echoing behind her own.

On Saturday morning, Rachel is the last one to arrive for Carmen's class. Through the doorway, she sees about a dozen brightly-colored yoga mats laid side by side and wonders how she'll manage to squeeze herself in. Immediately, the art historian from Singapore—*Benjamin*, Rachel remembers his name only now—scoots his mat closer to the wall to make room for her.

"Thanks," she says, rolling out her mat beside his. He nods, his pale forehead already glistening with sweat.

At the front of the room, Carmen stands on the raised platform. Her sleek black hair is up in a ponytail, and she's wearing an eggplant-colored tank top and matching leggings. She's twenty-seven at the most, newly married with a half-carat diamond on her finger, not only fluent in Spanish and Chinese, but about to start her third year of medical school—and gorgeous enough to make even the ultra-lithe and eternally lovely Christy Turlington jealous. Plus, Carmen is a certified Baptiste Power Yoga Instructor who can hold a handstand for three whole minutes without wavering.

"Let your yoga practice today be a model for how you're going to go about the rest of your day," Carmen says, striding among the sweating bodies, making an adjustment here, touching a shoulder or hand there.

Yes, those were the halcyon first weeks when she and Richard cooked, and they stayed up late watching movies from the 1930s and 40s—*Bombshell*, *The End of the Affair*, and anything starring Bette Davis—but for the most part, their life together has

43

always been a grown up's happiness, one based on career, mortgage, shared values, and plans—and at the heart of it all, the raising of Amy. Though Rachel didn't scrutinize herself until Richard told her of his medical plans, she understands now that what so drew her to Richard was his intelligence, his warmth, and, yes, his stability. This was a man who would stay, a man with whom she could build something that would last.

Beside her, the art historian is breathing evenly, deeply, and although he moves a bit stiffly, he does so with real purpose and calm. She tries to deepen her inhale, but she just can't shake what she saw a few minutes ago—the reason she's late, the reason she almost missed class.

Tracy has been growing her hair out for the last few months, so that she now wears it in a neat honey-gold bob just above her shoulders. "Why not let your curls have free reign?" Rachel asked once, for she herself had always longed for naturally curly hair and was trying to be sympathetic or at least more playful than disapproving.

But her husband, newly infatuated with the world of women's styling products, seems to enjoy the straightening iron and the salon goop that goes along with it.

This morning before Rachel left, Tracy stood at the bathroom mirror, her hair now subtly low-lighted (no chunky blonde highlights for a Romanov scholar), her face already carefully made up with the Clinique products she (like Rachel) favors. Richard's chest hair is gone, and Tracy now wears a C-cup bra. And panties. It isn't like Tracy could fool everyone, at least not yet, for her jaw remains too square, too chiseled, and her hips narrow, a male athlete's hips.

Nevertheless, with the mist from the shower fogging the glass, Rachel could almost believe the illusion, or at least the surreal dream that is becoming a reality right before her eyes. The first surgery is less than two months away. Dr. Markson will surgically remove Richard's penis and create female genitalia for Tracy.

Carmen instructs the class to move from down dog to warrior three—one of the most difficult of the balancing poses. "Imagine you're flying," she says. "Let your standing leg grow so strong, so anchored, that your arms can grow light. Reach," she cries out. "Reach."

Rachel plants her left leg and steps off, her arms extended in front of her, palms facing each other, neck and shoulders aligned. She wobbles at first, and her left hamstring cramps, but she doesn't let go. Is it the art historian's breathing that helps anchor her? Listening, she feels almost as if she is riding the wave of his breath, and pictures herself in the ocean, the water cresting up and over her body as she lies face up, a starfish, staring at the summer sky.

"Reach," Carmen calls again, and this time her hand is on Rachel's sacrum. For just a moment, Rachel feels incredibly light, but then the heat in the room becomes overwhelming, and tears stream down her cheeks.

Still, she holds the pose, holds warrior three, the most challenging incarnation, once the other people in the class, all twelve of them, assume horseman. Rachel is still listening to the art historian's breath, only now her own breath has synchronized itself with his.

During Shivasana, when they are lying side by side on their mats, their arms at rest, legs gently open, hip bones tilted towards the sky, Rachel lets her hand linger near his. Her fingertips brush his, and she tells herself that if he invites her for coffee afterwards, she will say yes. After all, Tracy has taken Amy out for brunch. They won't be home until mid-afternoon. Will the people who see Tracy and Amy together take them for mother and daughter? *Grandmother and granddaughter, more likely*, Rachel thinks, and this is what comforts her, here, now in the semi-dark.

LOCKS

Just past 7 a.m. on the last day of August, and Elizabeth finds Eva slouched against the fridge, smoothie in hand, headphones suction-cupped to her ears. Eva's blouse may be buttoned up, but her denim skirt barely covers her ass. "You can't leave for school dressed like that," Elizabeth says.

Eva glances up before turning back to the iPhone.

"I said, you can't leave for school dressed like that." Elizabeth tugs at the headphones, which catch in her daughter's hair.

"Hey, what's your problem?" Eva asks, the smudged kohl ringing her eyes making her look a little too much like a rabid racoon.

Elizabeth studies her daughter's strong, brown legs and pictures the boys—*were seventeen-year-old males surging with hormones still boys?*—staring at Eva who'd come home, more than once recently, with hickeys that she'd at least had sense enough to hide from her stepfather, Tom.

"You heard me."

Eva smirks. "And if I don't want to?"

How is it possible that this moody, often downright rude teenager with the rose tattoo on her neck and the three piercings in each ear was once the little girl who cried all the way to school for weeks when I dropped her off for kindergarten? Elizabeth wonders. "What you want makes no difference," she says, widening her stance. "Remember, I pay the bills around here."

"Oh?" Another smirk. "I thought that was Tom."

With this reminder of just how little she pulls in waitressing at the university's faculty club, Elizabeth's hand seems to take on a life of its own, and she slaps her daughter's cheek. Hard.

Shock and maybe even hatred pulse behind Eva's eyes, and shame surges through Elizabeth. "Go and put something decent

46

on, or you're grounded all week and all weekend." Elizabeth keeps her voice even and controlled, but her own strength—whatever remains of it anyway—is crumbling. Despite this pretense, she knows she's lost; what's worse, Eva knows so too.

"Mommy," Brooke calls, sailing into the kitchen in her yellow dress, her hair still wound in curlers. "Mommy, will you take them out?"

"Of course," Elizabeth says, as Eva escapes down the hall, sandals slapping against the tile.

Some seven hours later, that series of slaps—her palm against Eva's cheek, Eva's sandals on the tile—reverberates through Elizabeth who stands watching Brooke clamber over the monkey bars just outside the elementary school. Elizabeth tries not to think of what Eva is doing now, but inevitably her thoughts drift to that idiot cheerleader—Sage was it? Or Santana?—not a close friend but someone with whom Eva occasionally hangs out, a girl with a crescent of pin-prick moles above her lip who'd been caught giving blow jobs to some of the football players last spring. The football players had only gotten suspensions—after football season no less—but this Sage/Santana had been suspended for a whole month.

At least Eva's grades remain decent, Elizabeth reminds herself, as Brooke leaps from the swing in midair and, without even stumbling, lands on her feet. *Or Eva's grades were decent when she finished up junior year.*

Eva's life as a senior has just begun. She's grown so close to her friend London with her fancy little VW and the French *Vogue* she often leaves at the house, not to mention an attitude concealed beneath a pretty pixie veneer.

If Elizabeth had held her ground about enrolling Eva at that alternative school with the accelerated arts program, things may have been different. Eva did qualify for a partial scholarship, but Tom considered Broad Street Day "left wing," a dirty word in his vocabulary. Water under the bridge now.

When she'd worked with horses, Elizabeth had known how to handle a difficult situation. If a horse bullied her, she worked it on the ground, backing it up ten, twenty feet—even the length of a pasture. If the horse refused to be caught, she'd grab the long whip and slap it against ground, fence, tree, anything to keep the animal moving, until it was lathered and gave up. Rarely did the horse give her trouble after that.

At this hour, the late August sun beats down, and there's not a shade tree anywhere in sight. Brooke hurries up the stairs to the long, curving slide installed last spring. A good eight-foot drop if someone were to fall. "Careful, Brooke!" Elizabeth calls when someone jostles her.

Brooke smiles back, waves. "Okay!"

With this child, Elizabeth is determined to do things right. She's among the first parents to arrive for pickup and volunteers at the Harvest Festival and at all of the other events, even if it means taking flak from Tom. Not that she can erase all the times a much-younger Eva waited, sometimes for as long as forty-five minutes, her red backpack on her lap, and not an adult anywhere in sight. In those days, the schools weren't as vigilant, and Eva's elementary school back in Albuquerque wasn't a magnet school. Given the untethered nature of Elizabeth's life back then, she was relieved for its laxness.

"Liz," a woman's voice calls out. "Do you have a moment?"

She turns towards the tall, pale, expensively-dressed mother of the equally tall, equally pale girl in Brooke's class who might just be a model in a Hanna Andersson catalog. "It's Elizabeth."

"Oh right, Elizabeth, so sorry." The woman tucks a strand of hair behind each ear. "Gwen Alexander." She extends a manicured hand. "I've seen you around, said 'hello' at the Fall Festival and all, but since our daughters are in class together, I thought I should formally introduce myself. I'm going to be room parent along with Eli Liebowitz's mom."

"Congratulations," Elizabeth says flatly, the neutral hues of this Gwen's silk pantsuit definitely not stay-at-home-mom.

"Is Brooke your only one?" Gwen asks while Brooke, now on the swings, pumps her legs higher and higher, the chain links straining as she pushes up into the impossibly blue sky.

"My older daughter's a senior in high school." Elizabeth glances again at her watch, especially eager now to get going, "and there's a stepson."

"I so wanted another," Gwen says. "My marriage would never have survived it, much less my career. How old is he?"

"Twenty," Elizabeth replies, motioning to Brooke that it's time to go.

"So, is he here at Tech or further away?"

Eight months ago, Elizabeth could have said Kurt would be newly enrolled at the nearby community college, as he'd been on track, then, to study computer programming. He had a passion for minutiae and repetitive tasks and excelled at taking the machines apart and reassembling them, convincing Tom and even Elizabeth that he'd finally found some way to become at least partially independent.

But given the unraveling of the last few months, independence no longer seems possible. *At least not for the foreseeable future*, Dr. Judy had said. And with the vanished chance of that independence, Kurt is now an unfortunate and constant fixture in their house.

"Actually," Elizabeth says, keeping her tone neutral. "He's at home."

"Oh. I see." Gwen adds, "Well, not everyone's cut out for college."

Nearly two hours later, that conversation with Gwen still needles Elizabeth, busy now mixing the Campbell's mushroom soup, milk, peas, and tuna together. Ferreting the remaining fish out of the tin, Peaches, the overweight tabby, perches on the counter. Tom does not allow this, and Elizabeth would never allow Peaches up there if Eva or Brooke were around, but when she's alone, or with Kurt, she doesn't bother chasing the cat away. Why would she when Peaches curls into her lap and often sleeps against her back, the purring heft of him a reassurance, no matter how hard her day?

Beyond the kitchen island, at the oak table where Elizabeth ate and studied during those years with her grandmother—this one piece of furniture she brought to the marriage—sits Kurt. His hair is unkempt and too long, but he wears his habitual white t-shirt, which he always irons himself, and his usual khakis. He barely greeted Elizabeth or Brooke when they got home, not even looking up when he uttered his monotone "'What's up?'" For a while, his greeting was "'What's shaking?'"— some relic slang he must have heard on TV—but then it became "'Bonjour,'" inexplicable given that he didn't speak or read French,

49

until Elizabeth saw the skimpily-clad models in the lingerie ads stashed in his room.

After draining the noodles, Elizabeth alternates the tuna with a layer of noodles in the casserole dish while Kurt continues to cut words and phrases out of magazines and newspapers. These he turns into highly complex and not always coherent sentences which he pastes into a blue leather-bound book. Once Elizabeth made the mistake of buying the same brand of book but with a red cover, and Kurt beat his fists against the wall. She'd screamed for Tom—thank God he'd been home—who managed to wrap his arms around the boy from behind and sort of sucked the air out of him, which shocked Kurt into submission.

Kurt was eleven when Elizabeth married Tom, and although Kurt's outbursts were volatile back then, too, they were also more manageable. It's a whole different story now that Kurt stands six feet two inches tall. He may be lean, but he's strong from lifting the weights he keeps in the garage. After Kurt paid a little too much attention to Eva and London while the girls sunbathed, his hand groping around in his pants, Elizabeth started Googling group homes in West Texas and southern New Mexico. Some days she believes she can convince Tom to move Kurt into one of these places. "Remember," she tells Tom, "he's not your son; he's your brother."

"And what practical difference does that make?" is Tom's response.

Elizabeth understands that Tom and Kurt's family dysfunction is what has made nineteen-year-old Kurt the thirty-nine-year-old Tom's responsibility, but to go so far as to sacrifice his own family for this younger brother? How is it possible that Tom can't see the damage that Kurt's constant presence in their household is causing?

"Kurt," she says now, keeping one eye on the clock; it will be time to take Brooke to ballet soon. "I'm making tuna noodle casserole. We had it last week, remember?" He glances up, the scissors glinting in his left hand. He doesn't meet Elizabeth's eye. He rarely meets anyone's eye, except Tom's and occasionally Dr. Judy's. "I made it with peas. You like peas."

"Green peas, green grass, peas disappear into grass filled with snakes and a nice piece of ass," he chants and begins to laugh.

"I'll take that as a yes," Elizabeth says, trying not to register her disgust at Kurt's words.

"Mom!" Brooke calls, bursting into the kitchen and startling Peaches who immediately flees. "My white tights have a snag. Can we stop for a new pair?"

Kurt's attention flickers at the mention of white.

"*May* we," Elizabeth says. "We can try, but we'll have to leave in the next ten minutes." She sets the casserole on the counter along with a tomato from the vegetable garden that she's sliced into even rounds as Kurt's stupid, foul rhyme continues to wind through her thoughts. *Is this the sort of thing he pastes into those blue books?*

At this moment, and for God knows how long before that, he's been hunched over those damn words, each precisely cut from the pages he snips to bits before anyone has a chance to read them. And he makes these neat piles, each one equally spaced from the next, half a dozen of them on the table right now.

She's just finished wiping down the counter when Eva, with London right behind her, bangs through the screen door. Elizabeth steps into the hall just in time to see her daughter—in short shorts that are a tad more decent than this morning's skirt and high-heeled sandals—make a beeline for her room. London pauses, turns. Her white-blonde hair has been newly shorn into an even shorter crop that highlights her slate-gray eyes, also rimmed with kohl.

"Hello, Mrs. Smythy," London says.

"London." Elizabeth takes in the girl's black t-shirt, her long, lean legs in Capri pants and matching ballet flats. London smells of spices, of some expensive perfume; for a moment Elizabeth pictures her and Eva cozying up at the perfume counter at Dillard's, trying on scents, sniffing each other's wrists.

"So Brooke's in Level Two this year," London says, following Elizabeth into the kitchen where Brooke's ballet bag emblazoned with *En Pointe's* insignia rests on the counter. "My mother says Brooke's a natural."

"Is that right?" Elizabeth replies. London's mother, co-director at the studio, primarily works with the advanced and company dancers. When has she ever seen Brooke dance? Why would Brooke's ability even come up?

51

But London, her gaze having strayed to Kurt and his magazine cut-ups, doesn't answer.

And then, standing in the doorway, is Eva, no trace of the slap visible on her carefully made-up face. "Good, you're here," Elizabeth says, managing as neutral tone as possible. "I made tuna casserole for dinner, and I need you to make a salad."

"Why? Won't you be here?"

"I told you last week: your sister has ballet."

"Fine, but I'm not going to do the dishes."

"You'll help Tom, and I'll finish up." Elizabeth turns away then, aware of Eva and of London still standing there. They'll surely begin whispering about her shortly, just as they whisper about Kurt.

"Brooke," Elizabeth calls, relieved to be leaving. "We need to go."

The sound of Brooke's small feet grows stronger as she hurries down the hall, and Elizabeth hurries after her, trying to outrun the memory now pressing its way up into the light. Early autumn eleven years ago, and Eva came home from school, her words struggling to catch up to her thoughts. "Please, Mommy," Eva had said, after telling Elizabeth about the gymnasts who'd visited the school and given a demonstration. "Please. I'd do anything to be able to do what those girls do. One of them is even thinking of trying out for the Olympics."

And so, despite the fact Elizabeth would have to take off early to drive Eva to the YMCA across town where the classes were held, and come up with the tuition, for the first three months she actually managed to do it, even buying Eva a silky purple leotard with a silver starburst across the front. In between classes, Eva practiced religiously, cart-wheeling and somersaulting in the small living room, the coffee table and armchair pushed into a far corner. She practiced outside, too, swearing she'd have the splits down by Valentine's Day. And she did master the splits, Elizabeth recalls, navigating the Marsha Sharp, now crowded with rush hour traffic.

Except by Valentine's Day the lessons ceased. Money was tight, and there was the stress of Elizabeth's work schedule, the pressure from the manager to have her take on extra hours now that two of the other waitresses had quit. Really, though, what choice had she had? Elizabeth had had no one else to fall back on, unless she counted the woman downstairs who, for ten dollars, would keep Eva for the evening, plunking her down before the TV with a Hungry Man dinner.

It wasn't until the following year, once she and Eva had moved in with Tom—and Kurt—that Elizabeth had the money to send Eva back to gymnastics. For a month, maybe two, Eva had gone dressed in a fancy leotard, her dark hair pulled into a neat bun. But she no longer practiced at home unless Elizabeth got after her. And then, once Elizabeth was pregnant with Brooke and the morning sickness set in, she was relieved when Eva said she didn't care about gymnastics anymore.

So many of the people Elizabeth meets on the playground these days say they'd do anything to be thirty again. Not Elizabeth. At thirty, she was ferrying Kurt back and forth between the special school and the occupational therapist. She had Brooke in the back seat, fussing, for she was hardly the easy baby that Eva had been.

Back then, when Eva was in the backseat with Kurt and Brooke, she would focus on the landscape or sing quietly. And at home she'd curl up beside the window with a book—how she'd loved to read back then. How self-sufficient Eva had been, or so Elizabeth had managed to believe. And now? The tension between herself and her older daughter brings on a surge of grief, and Elizabeth stands silent and short of breath.

"Kurt said something troubling today," Elizabeth tells Tom that night in bed. They've just had sex, and afterwards tends to be the best time to broach difficult subjects with him.

"Oh?" Tom says, still stroking Elizabeth's shoulder.

"It was some kind of rhyme. 'A nice piece of ass,' he said."

"Did he?" Tom says, the touch of fingers against skin ceasing.

"It made me uncomfortable. You remember that incident with 'bonjour,' the lingerie ads, and then the sunbathing."

"We settled that."

Did we? Elizabeth wonders. What she says: "He's home alone with Brooke sometimes, you know."

"Kurt is no threat to Brooke." Tom's voice slices the air. "Dr. Judy doesn't think there's anything to worry about."

"Comforting himself," Dr. Judy said of Kurt's obsession with the sexy lingerie ads. At this rate, Elizabeth knows she will get

53

nowhere.

Tom turns towards her, his blue eyes—Brooke's eyes—adversarial. "I was never dishonest with you about Kurt. You know I made a promise to my mother, the one thing she asked."

"And it was too much to ask," Elizabeth blurts out, sitting up in bed, her sweaty camisole clinging to her breasts. "Who asks that of their son?"

Tom glares back, but she isn't sorry. Tom's mother has had dementia for a decade, and the house where his parents still live is a rabbit warren of dark hallways overflowing with junk. They keep the windows closed most of the time, which only intensifies the smell of mold, sweat, and stale air. Not just Elizabeth but Eva and Brooke hate going there, too—the last time Eva found a recluse spider nesting in one of the teapots. As for bringing Kurt, given his mania for order, the place is out of the question.

But Tom's mother wasn't always like this, and over the years Elizabeth has listened to Tom's stories of all the ways in which his mother made ends meet, the odd jobs sewing, doing other people's wash, selling her canned goods at the specialty shops in Albuquerque and especially the more tourist-y towns. She sent Tom to college on what she earned. Tom's father still can't sober up. Yet despite the grim stories Tom has shared about his parents—the violence and walking out—somewhere along the way they'd manage to create Kurt by the time Tom was grown.

She remembers six-year-old Eva in her purple, star-flecked leotard somersaulting across the floor of their old apartment. Eva who got lost in this arrangement. But without Tom would her time with Eva have been any better? She would have had to keep working all those waitressing hours. Horse training, or horse breaking, was not something she could have kept doing beyond her thirties, and it sure wasn't lucrative. And there sure as hell wouldn't have been any money to establish a college fund.

"We can talk to Dr. Judy," Tom says at last. "See if something can be done about his meds. But he's going to stay in this house, Elizabeth. As long as I'm alive, I'm going to take care of him."

An image of that bridge in Paris takes shape in Elizabeth's mind. Not that she's ever been there or anyplace else for that matter (other than that single trip to California); no, she saw the bridge on TV; a bridge weighed down by all of those locks—the love bridge, people call it. She shivers, the sick feeling in her belly creeping up her chest, binding her breath. She stands, walks over to the dresser, pulls off her camisole and slips into a long-sleeved shirt, then walks into the hallway. Across the darkness, Tom calls out to her, but she doesn't answer, this husband, and the only man who's ever taken care of her.

Yes, in her way, she loves him, this husband, and the only man who's ever taken care of her. Elizabeth's memories of her own father amount to a handful of old photographs, the last one taken on Elizabeth's sixth birthday. The second gallon of ice cream from the party was still in the freezer when he bought a bus ticket and took off, leaving Elizabeth's mom with a slew of bills. And after that? Not a single check or even a letter.

As for Eva's father, not long after Elizabeth found out that she was pregnant, she caught him making out with some rich, college girl in the barn. She actually walked in to find the pair of them pressed up against one of the stalls. Elizabeth had imagined his hard-on, how it must have felt against the girl's soft stomach. Minutes later, she walked out—never telling him that she was eight weeks along.

Almost five years later, Elizabeth met Tom in his sensible, lace-up shoes, his glasses case tucked into his shirt pocket. He was exactly like the geeky boys with whom Elizabeth would have had nothing to do when she was Eva's age. But by the time he sat down in her section of the steakhouse, Elizabeth looked closer to forty than her actual thirty. Besides, she liked Tom's eyes, blue as the Pacific Ocean she remembered from that single trip to visit a cousin. They'd spent the whole week at the beach. Tom's eyes were steady or steadfast eyes, she told herself. And when he left her a generous tip and asked her to dinner, she didn't hesitate.

Not long after that first date at a Chinese restaurant where they experimented with chopsticks, ate too many dumplings, and laughed over their cookie fortunes, Tom introduced her to Kurt. She first saw the boy clambering over the jungle gym. Tom had called to Kurt to come down and meet Elizabeth, but the boy had taken his own sweet time. Elizabeth didn't know then that Kurt's absorption in the jungle gym was part of his disorder. Back then, she just thought he was showing off. He'd been skinny and freckled, but what had struck her most was the fierce vitality of his rough, red hair which reminded her more of a fox's pelt or a horse's mane that had known little care and a good deal of wind.

When Tom asked Elizabeth to marry him, she pictured a house of her own in Texas where he had a job offer—"a real fresh start"—and the stability a family would mean for Eva, not to mention the break that Elizabeth so desperately needed.

In the years that followed, Elizabeth washed Kurt's clothes, fed him, and drove him to a series of special schools and therapies. For a time, he even helped her with the vegetable garden. She taught him about the necessity of not watering a tomato plant's leaves, of ensuring that the water goes directly into the roots. He even learned how to transplant iris. All these, she told Kurt, kneeling beside him on the sweet-smelling earth, were skills her own grandmother had passed down to her. "And now I'm sharing them with you."

How hard she'd tried, but when he didn't respond, no matter that Tom told her that Kurt wasn't capable of physical affection—"it's not part of his wiring"—the tenderness within her diminished, the way a plant withers when it doesn't receive enough rain and light.

"Elizabeth!" Tom calls out again. Standing in the hall just outside the bathroom, she makes no reply. She knows Eva's in there. She can hear water in the bath. She pictures the tub with fancy salts, a gift from her friend London, and on the sink the scented candles Eva's taken to buying at the mall. Elizabeth taps on the door, mutters Eva's name.

When her daughter makes no sign whatsoever, even though Eva obviously knows she's there, Elizabeth walks to the kitchen. There she grabs a towel from the rack, turns the hot tap on full blast, then washes herself at the sink, hands shaking. When she looks up, catches her reflection in the window above, she's amazed at the lines carved into her forehead, the haggard look in her eyes. The image of London's mother, Carin, svelte in her black leotard, her golden hair in a dancer's knot, as she hurried off to class, flickers through Elizabeth's mind. *Damn her and her daughter*, she thinks, painfully aware that curses and anger will get her nowhere.

The clock on the stove reads 12:13 a.m. Elizabeth will have to be up at 6:30 a.m. to help get Brooke ready for school, and in this state sleep will not come soon, if at all. In the cupboard, Elizabeth reaches deep into the cabinet for the bottle of women's multivitamins into which she's stashed a few sleeping pills from the prescription the doctor filled once the chance of Kurt going to college turned to shards. She puts one on her tongue, welcomes its bitter taste.

Three weeks later is the last Thursday of September. It's a brilliant, turquoise day with temperatures in the mid-eighties, and Tom comes home jubilant as a schoolboy who's just won a big prize. "Lizzy," he calls, bringing forth a long-neglected nickname. "Lizzy."

"What is it?" she says, stepping in from the backyard, newly-picked tomatoes in her hands.

"Good news," Tom says, pressing a bouquet of red roses into her arms.

While Elizabeth trims the stems and then puts the roses in water, he tells her that the firm is going to promote him. "That's wonderful," she says, startled. "When did this happen?"

"It hasn't happened yet, but Charles Tobin talked me up at the meeting today, then said one of us engineers is going to be given more responsibility and a substantial raise, and you know what?"

Almost breathless with his excitement, she pricks her finger on one of the thorns. "Oh my God, you got it."

"Not yet," Tom grins, "but his eye kept coming back to me. Afterwards, he praised the work I did on the Guitierrez job. If that's not a sign, then I don't know what is."

"That's fantastic," Elizabeth says, trying not to let her mind race ahead and imagine all that they could do with the extra money.

He plucks one of the roses, tucks it behind her ear. "Let's go out to dinner tonight."

She laughs, steps back, slightly off balance. "Shouldn't we wait until it's official?"

"Come on," Tom says with uncharacteristic lightness. "I mean, when was the last time we did anything like go out to eat, just the two of us?"

"God knows, but who's going to watch Brooke? Eva has cheerleading practice. She won't be back before 8."

"It's all arranged," Tom says, then goes on to say that the secretary's teenage daughter—"a very responsible girl" and implicitly unlike Eva—will stay with Brooke. "I'll order pizza for them, and you and I can go out to that Italian place you're always talking about."

Elizabeth feels a surge of tenderness towards her husband. She'd mentioned the Italian restaurant maybe once and is surprised Tom even remembers. "And Lisa Miller's daughter knows about Kurt? She'll be comfortable with him?"

"Yes. Don't worry so much. It'll be fine."

Elizabeth feels her body relax. "Remember, with the pizza, only cheese for Kurt, okay?"

Tom's smile gets even bigger. "That's my girl."

Not just Tom's certainty but his remarkable enthusiasm is contagious, and as Elizabeth dresses for the evening, she actually puts on lipstick and her silver teardrop earrings. Not since their anniversary did they go out to dinner—the Olive Garden near the mall, but this Italian place isn't part of a chain. No, *Bella Italia* is run by two brothers from Brooklyn. The tiramisu is supposed to be heavenly, and the shrimp scampi as good as any of the restaurant reviewers had ever eaten. She slips on her good shoes and pictures the two of them sitting by candlelight, sharing a bottle of Chianti, and talking about the future.

And for the first time, Elizabeth discovers, stepping into the restaurant with Tom's hand on the small of her back and the air fragrant with garlic and oregano, the real thing proves to be as good, if not better than, she imagines.

Over the next few days, Elizabeth lets herself dream, just a little. The promotion may not be official yet, but Tom's told her it's only a matter of days. So, on Tuesday, before picking up Brooke, Elizabeth passes Ashley Furniture, turns around and pulls into the parking lot.

"Anything I can help you with?" asks the saleswoman, aglow with bronzer and too much mascara.

"Just browsing," Elizabeth says, relieved when the woman backs off, freeing her to wander. A velvet-y chocolate sofa catches her eye. Oh, the hours she and Brooke could spend reading there and watching movies. Maybe Eva would even join them, and it would be like the days, three or four years ago, when they sat eating microwave popcorn and watching *The Lion King* or *The Princess Bride,* none of them getting up to pee, nothing breaking the spell of togetherness. Sometimes Brooke would fall asleep in Elizabeth's lap, her legs stretched across Eva; soon Eva, too, would nod off, and Elizabeth would just sit there and gaze at her two daughters.

Inevitably the saleswoman returns. "Beautiful, isn't it?" She strokes the fabric with her well-manicured hand. "And we have a payment plan."

"Good to know," Elizabeth says, glancing at the price tag: $1200. Even with a promotion, that would be a lot to spend.

"Here," the woman says, attuned to Elizabeth's new wariness. "Take my card."

Elizabeth nods, begins making her way out the door and into the parking lot. It's a fifteen-minute drive across town, and she doesn't want to be late. "$1200," she repeats, turning the key in the ignition. Well, no matter: it feels so good to dream, something she hasn't done, not really, not since she was pregnant with Brooke.

Later that week, Elizabeth is running late, which means no time for Brooke on the playground, just a hurried stop at the store for dinner makings before they leave for ballet.

"I'm sorry, rabbit," Elizabeth says, once the little girl barrels out of school, hand in hand with Aria.

"But my friends are staying after today. I want to play with them. *Please*," Brooke pleads.

"You have ballet later. Tomorrow we can stay until 4:30, okay?"

"Fine." Brooke stomps her feet in the dust. "But I don't see why it's you who always has to make dinner."

Elizabeth stops, stares at Brooke. "Making dinner is my responsibility. That's all there is to it."

When she thinks about it later, it's probably this guilt—ridiculous, really—over denying Brooke an hour out of doors after the long school day that makes her susceptible to Brooke's plea that they stop at the Tastee Freeze on the way home from ballet, a decision Elizabeth comes to regret almost as soon as she parks. Just a few yards away she spots Eva, and by then it's too late to get Brooke back in the car—she bounds out as soon as Elizabeth cuts the engine. Unbelievably, or perhaps all too expectedly, Eva is sitting on a boy's lap, straddling him is more like it, and his hand is inside her t-shirt. Watching and licking her cone, London is there, too, sitting opposite Eva and the boy. "Mommy," Brooke says, not seeing her sister yet. "Come on!"

Elizabeth's palms are sweaty, and so are her underarms, and her mind flashes back to the way she'd let Eva's father fuck her in the back of his red Camaro (as if that car wasn't a cliché in and of itself). How stupid she'd been, and how blinded by love—or lust, more like it, though she hadn't known the difference back then—and she's dead sure Eva doesn't either.

"Eva," she shouts, stepping in front of Brooke to block her view.

Eva turns, her lipstick blurred, but she doesn't get off the boy's lap.

"Brooke," Elizabeth says, "I want you to wait for me in the car."

Brooke stamps her foot, pouts. "But Eva's here, and you said we could have ice cream."

"Eva's going to get in the car, too. I need you to wait for me, okay?"

"But—."

"Hey Ma!" Eva says, freezing Brooke where she stands.

"Don't 'hey ma' me," Elizabeth says, glancing back towards Brooke who thankfully keeps moving towards the car.

Eva just laughs, and so does the boy. "Get off this boy now, and get in the car, or I swear, you will not be allowed out all semester, and," she stares down that white-blonde-pixie London with her huge slate-gray eyes, "you will not be allowed to talk to your friend here on the phone. In fact, I will confiscate your phone."

"For what?" Eva's eyes look dreamy, or more likely stoned.

With London focused on them both, Elizabeth leans in close to Eva, breathes in the pungency of sweat and that spicy scent London wears, too, and whispers, "For practically fucking this idiot in public, that's for what." The boy nearly falls backwards, and Elizabeth breathes in the smell of pot.

She yanks Eva to her feet then, already bracing for the pushback, but this time Eva actually lets her lead her to the car where Brooke is waiting, not yet ready to give up on ice cream. "But Mommy, I was counting on the chocolate dip with sprinkles."

"I'm sorry, Brooke, not today," Elizabeth says, trying, and not too successfully, to lose the harsh tone.

Thankfully, once they're on the road, Brooke stops pleading for ice cream and begins counting off how many grand jetés she did and in what order while Elizabeth steals glances at Eva through the rearview mirror, wondering what in the hell she should do. Tell Tom that some boy's hands were up her daughter's shirt at the Tastee Freez? Tom's reaction to finding Eva with Josh in July still burns, how he'd brought Eva's father's "Mexican" blood into it. *As if that had a goddamn thing to do with anything,* Elizabeth had thought but not said, her husband's latent racism, which surfaced early on in their marriage, one of the things she's tried to think or rationalize away.

Just when Elizabeth believes they've hit rock bottom, the following afternoon Tom comes home early, cursing his Turkish colleague, Erol Adman. "It's bad enough we have all these foreigners in our neighborhoods and schools," he says, pouring himself a 7 Up. "It's the university's business if they want to hire a Muslim over one of their own, but Jamison Design is a Christian firm."

It takes a while for Elizabeth to understand that it's Adman and not Tom who's been promoted, and really, shouldn't she have known better than to get all excited when nothing had been settled?

More alarmed by his jerky movements, by the perspiration prickling his brow and seeping through his shirt, than appalled by the resurgence of prejudice, Elizabeth says, "Maybe we shouldn't have been so certain."

"What are you talking about? All the signs were there." Tom's jaw tightens. "The partners have been praising my work all month, and Charles looked directly at me at the meeting when they announced the promotion, and afterwards I told you what he said."

"Yes," Elizabeth replies, futilely carried back to her ballooning hopes.

"And the promotion would have been mine if it weren't for Jamison's son. That spoiled brat comes in as late as 10:30 some days, tosses work on my desk, barely explains a thing, so that I have to go and talk to his father."

Elizabeth has witnessed Jamison's son's rudeness to Tom. This son is twenty-nine at most. At the company picnic, his eyes flitted over them as if they weren't even there. Even so, Tom's thinking is so crooked. But to bring up these contradictions, Elizabeth long ago realized, rarely gets them anywhere but into a huge fight.

"I've given that firm nine years," Tom continues, digging around in the cupboard now, certainly in search of the gin. "How many days have I been there before 8 a.m. while Adman is never there before 8:30, and I don't think I've seen him there after 6 p.m. Ever. But Adman has a degree from Baylor just like Jamison and his son, so that puts him in the club."

"Try to calm down," Elizabeth says, focused now on the amount of gin Tom's pouring. "You could be wrong, you know."

"Who are you kidding?" he asks. "Adman has that fancy degree, and his grandfather worked in some ambassador's office. He's always talking about it, the years he spent in England visiting the crown jewels. You'd think the guy had tea with the queen, but it impresses the hell out of Jamison."

Elizabeth closes her eyes, the headache already sinking its claws into her skull. If only she could lie down and take one of those pills that will help her forget, for a few hours anyway. She still has four left. Would four be enough to disappear for the next twenty-four hours? As if such a thing were possible—ever.

On and on, Tom's words like the beat of a hammer against wood. "Bad enough these people are spouting on about rights, taking over American jobs while their own people blow their country to hell. They kill children and bomb the so-called sacred sites."

Elizabeth's eyes snap open. "My god, Tom!"

Tom steps closer, his eyes menacing despite his shaking hands. "I'm not making any of this up. It's all over the papers. You know it as well as I do. Besides, I thought I could talk openly to my wife at least."

"Erol Adman has nothing to do with any of that," Elizabeth shouts, scalded by all the things that Tom has said over the years about foreigners but especially about Mexicans while Elizabeth has increasingly stopped calling Tom out, tired as she is, and determined to just get through the day. Any wonder, then, that Eva now dismisses, even treats her with disgust?

62

Tom's red face grows even redder. "I work my ass off every day for this family. And here you are taking Adman's side."

"For God's sake, Tom, I am not," she says, exhaustion making the words themselves too heavy to carry. All she wants is to curl up into a ball, or just bury herself beneath a pile of blankets.

"Then what would you call it?" he asks.

Elizabeth's head continues to throb.

"Well?" he presses.

Elizabeth rubs her fingers into her temples. "I'm not the enemy here."

Tom waits, the pupils of his blue eyes wide as two tiny black holes.

"Erol Adman isn't Muslim," Elizabeth says at last. "He's Greek Orthodox."

Tom splutters with laughter. "Where did you come up with that?"

"I didn't come up with anything," Elizabeth says, relieved only that Brooke and Eva are still at school; as for Kurt, not for the first time she's glad that he's in the garage lifting those damn weights.

"Then what in the hell are you talking about?" Tom asks. "He's not from Greece."

"His wife told me all about their son's baptism in July at the company picnic," Elizabeth says, wanting to tell Tom that you don't have to be Greek to be Greek Orthodox. She never went to college, but she at least knows that.

"That's ridiculous."

"No, it's not," Elizabeth says. More pulsing behind her eyes; the headache fully owns her now. "She told me the Orthodox baptize their children with oil, not water. The Admans drive up to a church in Amarillo most Sundays." She waits for what will come next, her heart a trapped sparrow, Tom staring at her as if she has lost her mind—*and maybe*, she thinks now, *she has*. But living like this, how will she ever manage to find it again?

"You disappoint me, Elizabeth," Tom says finally.

They stare at each other for a moment, regarding each other with what just might be hate, before Tom turns and leaves the room. Two, maybe three minutes later, she hears him turn the keys in the ignition of his old Cherokee and drive off.

By the time she's washed her face, swallowed too many Aleve, and changed out of the sweaty t-shirt, Elizabeth must rush to pick up Brooke. She manages to cut the time on the playground short, as her daughter chatters on about the 100 she got on the spelling test, spelling out every word she got right.

"S-T-U-P-E-N-D-O-U-S, P-E-R-I-W-I-N-K-L-E, Q-U-E-U-E. Isn't that great, Mommy? Can, I mean, may we at least stop for ice cream?"

"Not today, sweetheart."

"But Mommy!" Brooke's small feet kick the driver's seat.

"Not today, Brooke!" Elizabeth says, the headache now moving into her jaw.

"Fine," Brooke pouts. "But I thought you'd care."

"I do care. I just need some quiet." Elizabeth's hands are clenched around the steering wheel, and she remembers how she used to ride with a loose rein, aware that some horses would buck or rear if there was too much contact. With a loose rein, the horse had to find its own limits beneath her hand.

"But I'm the only one who got a 100. Miss McCormick put a gold star on my test."

"And I'm very proud of you," Elizabeth says, trying to squint through the relentless glare when she inadvertently swerves into the next lane, and the driver of the silver Tundra lays on the horn and gives her the finger.

"I don't see why we can't just stop."

"Please," Elizabeth says. "Stop! Stop right now! I need you to be quiet."

After an astonished stare, blue eyes wide with hurt, Brooke does quiet. Why is it just then that Elizabeth's thoughts turn to the horse she just let go of on the mesa one hot afternoon, the horse that threw her, fractured her collarbone. She'd let that horse run off, not caring as she lay there in the dirt, if it got hit by a lone semi or even if she got fired. No, too stunned by pain to think or even care, she'd just lain there, blood in her mouth as she stared up at the sun.

That night and on the four nights that follow, Elizabeth takes a pill-and-a-half so she can really knock herself out, going so far as to refill the prescription the day after the fight with Tom. The first two nights she climbs into bed beside the already-sleeping

Brooke, waking well before 6 a.m., and leaving no sign that she was there. Yes, the pills leave her feeling groggy, but there's no way she can get through a day without some bit of rest. Meanwhile, Tom glowers, his mood intensified by his belief that not only doesn't Elizabeth support him, but she's failed him as well.

Her only break, astonishingly, comes from Eva. Sure, she seems smug about the reason for Tom's explosion—impossible for her not to piece it together, the fact that he didn't get the promotion. His moody rudeness to her mother is all Eva needs to conclude that there's been a big fight.

But at least she doesn't say anything outright, and by no small miracle Eva does her requisite chores without Elizabeth having to ask.

The day of Brooke's ballet lesson comes around again, and Elizabeth drives to the high school to pick up Eva who's no longer allowed to hitch a ride with London after the Tastee Freeze incident. This means that after backtracking to fetch Brooke, Elizabeth has to take another fifteen minutes to drive further downtown. Fortunately, Eva is waiting for them, her white skirt, a little too see-through, but at least it touches her knees, billowing around her legs in the wind. London is there, too, and she waves to Elizabeth, who ignores this gesture. When Eva climbs into the car, her headphones are around her neck instead of over her ears. But her nails are the same outrageous shade of blue as her friend's, and Elizabeth pictures the two girls whispering about Eva's pathetic family as they polish their nails far enough in the schoolyard to share a cigarette during lunch.

"Hi Brooke," Eva says, after nodding to her mother. "How was school?"

"We're reading the *Ramona* books, but you know I already read the first two," Brooke says, before rushing on to tell Eva about the paper maché dog she's making in art; and to her credit, Eva seems to listen. She even asks a few questions that keep Brooke talking.

The light at the end of the tunnel turns out to be the light of an oncoming train is how Elizabeth comes to think of what happens later. Maybe half an hour before leaving for ballet, she's in the kitchen finishing the lasagna when Kurt emerges from his room holding out a pink t-shirt, his hands shaking. "She ruined it," he repeats God knows how many times. "My shirts are white, W-H-I-T-E. I don't wear pink. Real men don't wear pink."

Little by little, it dawns on Elizabeth, what has caused this tantrum in Kurt. It's Eva's hot pink t-shirt, and somehow it got mixed in with his wash. He continues to rant, and Elizabeth wants to hurl the spatula at him. No, it's the lasagna she wants to hurl, one long noodle at a time.

"Now, Kurt, it's an accident, you know that," she says instead. "We can bleach the t-shirt, or we can simply buy a new one."

"This one was my favorite," he says, still holding it out, waving it like some sort of demented proof. "My favorite," he repeats.

Each one of these t-shirts is exactly the same, Elizabeth wants to say as Kurt stands looking dejectedly at the shirt just as Eva emerges from her room. (*Why does it have to be just at that moment?* Elizabeth will ask herself later.) Eva's headphones cover her ears so that she probably hears next-to-nothing of what Kurt is saying.

"You! You! You!" Kurt rushes at Eva who puts out her arms in order to fend him off.

"What the fuck?" Eva says, stumbling backwards.

"We don't swear," Kurt shouts, sounding so much like Tom at that moment that Elizabeth is launched back to that awful afternoon of the failed promotion.

"Oh yeah?" Eva says, making her way towards the table where his precious magazine cutouts, all in neat piles, are arranged.

It's with wonder and a perverse sort of exhilaration that Elizabeth watches as, with one long sweep of her hand, Eva wipes the table clean, scattering Kurt's carefully-made piles to the floor.

Kurt is shaking with fury, but at least he's standing still, or he is for a few flashes of the imaginary camera.

Until Brooke is there, too, standing in the doorway, beginning to cry. "Get to your room," Elizabeth tells her, watching Eva pick up Kurt's metal scissors. "Get to your room, Brooke, and lock the door."

Brooke does as she's told.

"I hate you, you know that, you fucking loser," Eva shouts, brandishing the scissors at Kurt. "I hate you and your stupid white shirts, and if you come any closer, I'll stab you with these. In fact, I might just stab you for the hell of it!"

"Eva," Elizabeth says, stepping towards her daughter, so dizzy with this mad escalation even her eye sockets have begun to hurt. "Put the scissors down."

Eva's own face is full of loathing when Eva turns to her mother. This rage, with no doubt, this rage isn't just directed at Kurt.

"Give me my scissors," Kurt demands, his voice less chaotic, though his face is splotched fuchsia.

Eva looks as if she just might plunge the scissors into or through his hands.

And what then? Elizabeth's eyes are riveted on the scissors when the front door opens.

Tom's voice cuts through, more knife than scissors. "What in god's name is going on? I heard the shouting from the driveway."

"Here, take your fucking scissors," Eva says, hurling them at the ground at Kurt's feet before pushing past Elizabeth and Tom to rush out the door and into the heat of early evening, braless and beautiful in a sheer white t-shirt.

"Mommy," Brooke calls from her bedroom doorway. "I'm going to be late for ballet."

By the time Tom reaches Kurt, the boy—with the strength of all his nineteen years—is banging his fists against the wall, hitting the plaster so hard that it's just a matter of seconds before he puts a hole through it.

Almost instantly Tom's briefcase is on the floor, and Tom is at Kurt's side, where he puts him into a kind of stronghold to keep his younger brother from hurting himself. And the house.

Elizabeth knows that she should stay and help Tom, but there is her tearful younger daughter in pale pink leotard and filmy white skirt, hugging her ballet bag to her chest. What Brooke just witnessed, what she heard from behind the closed door, makes Elizabeth want to press her face to the floor and weep. How is she ever going to give Brooke the life she wants for her given the way they live? Look at how Eva's life is unraveling. How can it be possible that when Tom proposed, talked up their new life in Texas, Elizabeth believed that she was doing right by her older daughter? Or by anyone, including herself?

"Mommy," Brooke calls again. "I'll be late."

"No, you won't," she says, forcing herself to move. "We'll leave now and get there in time."

As he continues to hold Kurt, Tom stares at Elizabeth, his brow pinched, mouth open, eyes frighteningly wide.

She almost hesitates, then remembers how many times he refused to hear her out about the group living. Time and time again, her husband refused to hear. *This is his mess, isn't it? Well then,* Elizabeth tells herself, *so be it.*

On the driveway, Elizabeth finds Brooke in her pink ballet slippers. The fact that she's already put them on tears at Elizabeth, this attempt in her daughter at some sense of normalcy. At last, they are in the car, and Elizabeth turns on the ignition and pulls out. "It'll be okay, baby," she says.

Through the rearview mirror, Brooke's face is a mixture of fear, trust, something indefinable, and otherworldly, the kind of look that catapults Elizabeth back to the morning the nurse first laid Brooke in her arms. How she'd gazed into that tiny, wrinkled face, the eyes that unreal deep blue-gray of the unborn womb-world. Looking at Brooke, holding her, Elizabeth had felt buoyed, weightless, and a little bit afraid; not unlike the way she'd felt while swimming in the Pacific, her arms and legs propelling her ever further into that soundless, unknown world in which she understood she must conserve her breath.

Elizabeth turns onto Indiana, and minutes later the car climbs the ramp onto the freeway. Brooke's face is pressed against the window now, and Elizabeth imagines the heat of her daughter's breath fogging the glass. Why is it now that this other memory surfaces? This one of Eva the autumn after she started kindergarten? For weeks afterwards, Eva had climbed into Elizabeth's bed at night, pressing her small body against her back, her breath on Elizabeth's skin warm and damp. "Mommy," she'd whisper, "Mommy." And Elizabeth, when she'd answered, had said only what? Had she reassured Eva? Told her that it would be okay? She clicks into the left lane and accelerates, but nothing comes back to her. No words. There is only Eva's body against hers and the tug of "Mommy."

Not that she ever admitted it, but Elizabeth never relished the physical closeness of Eva's nighttime visits, the girl's sharp knees an antagonist to Elizabeth's aching need for sleep—oh, the endless sorrow of that time with each day bringing its own mish-mash of fresh worries.

Amazing, really, when Elizabeth thinks about it, that up until the end of her pregnancy with Eva she continued to ride the horses at a new barn on the other side of Albuquerque. Deep into the eighth month she rode, not even thinking about the risk, not when she was so in love with the feel of wind on her back, tangling her hair, the sweaty, salt-smell of a horse's body beneath her, the two of them moving almost as one.

She considers the spooky Arabian that bolted at paper bags, napkins, the rare bee. The Appaloosa with legs like a giraffe's that tested her on almost every ride. Despite the danger, she'd loved or at least been enthralled by the challenge, and how others had admired her for the focused way she'd always handled the unexpected. Yes, she'd had an excellent seat. Still, with horses there were no guarantees. What if the Appaloosa or the Arabian or any one of the others had thrown her? Even the safest horse could be unpredictable given an unknown variable—a squeaking bicycle chain, sudden rain, a grackle cartwheeling through the air...

"Mommy," Brooke calls. "You aren't even listening."

Elizabeth glances in the rearview mirror, sighs. "I'm sorry. What is it, baby?"

"*Eva*. I've been asking you about Eva."

Elizabeth scowls, afraid of some turbulent question she won't have any idea of how to answer.

But the question, when it comes, is relatively simple, on the surface anyway. Why then does something open inside of Elizabeth who thinks first, not of Eva, but of Kurt sitting at the oak table with his cut-outs and his piles of magazines and newspapers? Yes, Kurt is the one who comes to mind; Kurt, who has claimed so much of the energy in increasingly shorter supply.

"Well?" Brooke says, her voice quiet.

While Elizabeth searches for what to say, a series of honks and cusses sends her swerving, and she manages to right the car just in time. *Concentrate*, she tells herself, fixing her gaze on the dotted yellow lines even as her mind defies her once again, or perhaps makes the inevitable connection to the incident with Eva late last week, once Elizabeth discovered Eva's middling grade on the first literature essay. Writing had always come naturally to Eva, so why the low B? Elizabeth asked. And when Eva didn't reply, Elizabeth asked her daughter, "Did you even read *The Great Gatsby*?"

"What the hell? You weren't spying on me, were you?" Eva replied, her startled fury revealing all that Elizabeth needed to know.

"I want you to realize your potential," Elizabeth said.

Eva rolled her eyes, summoned a lopsided grin. "What does that even mean?"

"It means you could go to Tech, even get a scholarship. If you apply yourself."

Elizabeth held back from bringing up the stupid antics with the even stupider boys, and she didn't go near the pot—or London.

Eva only laughed. "No need to worry, Mother. I'm going to go to college; but you can't possibly think I'm going to stay here and go to Tech."

Now it was Elizabeth who felt as if she'd been slapped. "What do you mean? Tech's a good school."

"Maybe so, but I want to go to New York, study fashion or graphic design. You're out of your mind if you think I'm going to stay here."

Into her consciousness surfaces an image of Eva flashing her scissors, wrecking Kurt's piles. *I must be out of my mind*, Elizabeth thinks.

"Mommy," Brooke calls out, "answer me."

"Eva," Elizabeth says, summoning what remains of her calm, "of course she'll come back. She just needs a few hours." *After all, right now, what other choice does her older daughter have?*

"Okay," Brooke says, but she doesn't look convinced. Instead, she turns to look out the window where, Elizabeth's grandmother used to say, the unlived life is. Not that Elizabeth ever understood what her grandmother meant by that. And now, whatever life Elizabeth has yet to live, is quickly taking the hard shape of that weighted bridge in Paris. As if such a thing could have anything to do with love—has she been wrong about all that too?

She pictures coming back to the house to find Kurt wearing yet another snowy white t-shirt with his perfectly creased pants which he lines up on the padded hangers in his closet. Yes,

Kurt will be there, she realizes, a strange giggling taking hold. With Tom's help, Kurt may have already realigned his piles.

There's no way for Elizabeth to explain any of this to Brooke; no way to tell her that Eva will be out the door as fast as she can escape. As for Brooke? A whole decade lies ahead still, but what does that amount to when the years keep speeding up? Brooke will grow up and away from Elizabeth; she may even come to despise her and Eva does. And how will Elizabeth bear that?

From nearby comes a series of furious honks, and Brooke cries out.

But Elizabeth is drifting. No longer thinking about the unlived life, no longer thinking about anything at all, she relinquishes her hold on the dotted yellow lines.

INTENTION

Seventeen years, and it's like we never left, Emily thinks, slouched in a booth at the Red Dragon, Caitlin and Anton just opposite. Take away the owner's graying sideburns and the addition of brown rice to the menu, and nothing seems to have changed. Over sweet potato dumplings, sesame noodles, and spicy eggplant, they talk about the coming art show, their voices melding with those of the other diners. But eventually, as Emily expected, Caitlin brings up their old mentor, Cora.

"Em?" Caitlin says. "You okay?"

An image of Cora sitting in the rose armchair by the window in a pale blue room in the nursing home blooms in Emily's mind. "I was thinking about Saturday," she says, idling with her chopsticks. "Cora confused me with an aunt—"

"I'm sorry." Caitlin covers Emily's hand with her own.

"At least she remembered that her aunt had been a nurse. She died in a bombing somewhere in Normandy during World War Two," Emily says.

"When I think about her wonderful classes," Caitlin begins.

"But she can still paint, some days anyway, her best days." Emily forces a hint of brightness into her voice. "At least one of the nurses is very supportive. Cora's given her several sketches. I've no idea if she realizes how valuable they are."

"The art's become muscle memory," Anton says.

Emily nods, struck by the phrase's rightness, especially coming from Anton who's never been forthcoming with praise of Cora. The two of them clashed from the start. Or, as Emily sees it, Anton wasn't exactly receptive to criticism, and the fact that Cora was a woman certainly didn't help.

Emily considers saying something, but Caitlin leans back, face pale, perspiration prickling her forehead. Her dark hair has come loose from her long ponytail, and she looks more like a teenager than a woman who'll turn forty-two in July.

"The baby's kicking."

"Breathe, Cait," Anton says, rubbing her back.

"I don't think she likes the red chile," Caitlin says. "We'd better go."

"Let's." Emily signals the waiter for the check.

Twenty minutes later, they pull into the gravel drive of Emily's property. In the six years she's lived here, she has primarily worked on the garden, so abundant now that it wraps around the front of the house. At twilight, the delphinium is the blue of Renaissance paintings, and the silver-green lamb's ear has taken on the sheen of the moon breaking free of the clouds.

Inside, the hallway opens onto a living room warmed by shades of umber and dark yellow. There's the red couch and glass-topped table that she bought after Nick left, four wooden chairs from a local thrift shop, and here and there her mother's quilts.

"I'm a little uncomfortable with you giving up your bed," Caitlin says as Emily's two Pyrenees stop just a few inches short of jumping on her.

"Nonsense, I told you already: the bed has an incredible mattress." Emily strokes the silky head of one of the dogs. "It will make a world of difference for you to sleep on it tonight."

Caitlin turns to Anton, rests her head on his shoulder. "We should check on the boys. Can you call Melody? I'm wiped out."

"Sure." He kisses her, and she turns to go.

"I'll come with you, Cait," Emily says.

"I appreciate this, all you've done," Caitlin says, as she sits down on the bed.

"I've been dying to get you back out here, you know that," Emily replies.

Caitlin smiles and stretches her long legs; her ankles are swollen, and exhaustion shadows her eyes.

Emily lays a hand on her friend's shoulder. "You have enough support? And what about rest?"

"Rest doesn't exactly come with the territory," Caitlin says, and laughs.

Emily frowns, reminded of the half dozen shows that Anton's had these last years while Caitlin's been busy with the children.

"Come on, Em, they'll be in high school before I'm fifty-five," Caitlin says, before grimacing, her hands finding her belly.

"Kicking again?"

Perspiration freckles Caitlin's upper lip. "She generally does around this time."

Emily says, "I'd better say good night then. I hope she lets up so you can sleep."

"Tomorrow's the show," Caitlin says, "so she'd better."

It's close to noon by the time Emily, Caitlin, and Anton step into the Khoury Gallery, which occupies a renovated warehouse on Buddy Holly Avenue in the Depot District. Tonight's opening will showcase the two women's artwork, an event that's been a good six months in the making.

Samuel Khoury comes towards them, arms outstretched. "Caitlin," he says, gathering her to him. "You look beautiful."

"I'm enormous," she says, "with ankles like an elephant."

"But elephants are so intelligent, and such good mothers." Samuel's arms linger around Caitlin who laughs and kisses his cheek. Emily just stands there staring. Sure, Caitlin traveled to Lubbock from Brooklyn the day before; but it's not like she's new to Samuel, much less the kind of artist who needs to be feted.

In all the years that Emily's known and worked with Samuel—seven at least, he's never hugged her like that. A slight man more beautiful than handsome, Samuel moves like a dancer, or like Emily's favorite horse, Tobias, a light-footed Arabian whose canter is velvet. Samuel's mother Fatima is Lebanese, a beauty even now that she's nearing eighty, and one who still lives with her son. Even Samuel's admitted that any woman who came into his life would have to reckon with his very formidable mother.

While he goes into the small kitchen to make tea and fetch sandwiches, Emily studies the Cora Houck self-portrait that she finished some nine months ago, just before going into the care facility. Samuel refuses to sell the painting, loving Cora's work nearly as much as Emily does, an affinity that has solidified the bond between them.

Here in the portrait's colors and textures, Emily can still find Cora as she once was. Always in motion, Cora had been a woman who could quote from Martin Buber, Groucho Marx, and Elizabeth Bishop all in the space of a working afternoon. When Emily considers how quickly Cora's remaining faculties deteriorated once she entered Garden Oaks (not that there hadn't been signs—piles of dirty dishes, confused appointments, mismatched clothes and shoes), it seems even more of a miracle— yes, nothing less than that—the way Cora managed to stay focused long enough to create this gorgeous work with its bold, loose brushstrokes.

Up close, one would never recognize the outlines of Cora's wide face: the strong, high-bridged nose, full mouth. In order to see Cora—to see that this is a portrait—one has to stand far enough away. Only then do the brushstrokes align into a human form. *Yes*, Emily thinks, *the painting is a triumph.* If this is to be Cora Houck's last word, then it not only shouts but reverberates, a testament to a long, productive career.

From the other side of the gallery, Anton approaches, gestures to a wall dedicated to Emily's portraits. "That your work?"

"Everything I've done in the last year."

"Well then, I should take a look."

"Alright, thanks," Emily says, surprised. *When has he ever shown an interest in her work? Could this be a peace offering? Or at least a truce?* She recalls some of the things he's said over the years about portraiture. And last night, at dinner, it was the logistics of the show he focused on.

Meanwhile Caitlin wanders over to one of her own sculptures, a massive female nude. Despite the figure's size—the fullness of her breasts, hips, thighs—there's a vulnerability to her that Emily noticed as soon as the piece arrived. The woman's shoulders curve forwards.

"Tell me," Emily asks now, "were you thinking of Rodin?"

"I was!" Caitlin grins. "All those sculptures in the gardens outside his house, remember?"

"I do," Emily says, the two having gone to Paris their last year of school when Caitlin's parents surprised them with tickets. A whole week spent in museums or out on the rain-lit streets or tucked into the eaves at the Luxembourg Gardens where they sketched the tenacious children at play in their raingear.

At the Rodin Museum, the roses in the garden were skeletal, and the horse chestnut trees had lost their leaves, the yellow-brown petals littering the ground. Melancholy it may have been, from a certain point of view, yet it was the perfect setting for Rodin's sculptures, and the two of them had been in such a good mood.

Beside her, Caitlin begins to cry.

"What is it? What's wrong?" Emily asks.

"Oh, let's just say that I'm excited, nervous, and raging with hormones," Caitlin says, pink splotching her cheeks and neck. "My first show since Vic was born, and so much of this has to do with you."

Emily gives Caitlin's shoulder a squeeze, and her scent of talcum powder and hint of bread dough bring a hundred other moments rushing back. "I wouldn't give me too much of the credit," Emily says.

"Why not?" Caitlin wipes her eyes, grins. "I've worked harder—and with more focus—getting ready for this show than I have in years. Now if this one will just be an easy baby, I can build some momentum."

"You will." Emily says, even though Caitlin's told her that she still does most of the shopping, fixes dinner, puts the boys to bed each night. Family life, even once it's become pastel light and flickering brushstrokes in the work of Berthe Morisot or Mary Cassatt, continues to come at great cost for a woman artist.

Samuel returns with tea and sandwiches, takes in Caitlin's wet cheeks and obvious discomfort. "Everything okay?" he asks.

"Sure," Caitlin says, "just pre-show jitters."

"If you say so," Samuel says, not looking entirely convinced as he sets down the lacquered tray.

Over sandwiches, cucumber, and mint along with finely-sliced tomato with feta and basil, all beautifully arranged, they talk about the night ahead. On the other side of the gallery, Anton is talking to the well-established and utterly commercial Lucille Croft, heiress to a ranching fortune. It's hard to tell Lucille's age, given the work she's had done to her face and boobs, never mind the more recent reshaping of her butt. Lucille is attractive, sure, if artificial and moneyed are one's thing, with platinum blonde hair down to her shoulders and chunky gold and turquoise jewelry that sets off her perpetual tan. For three months each year, Lucille travels to Paris and to some of Italy's quaint hill towns to paint scenes reminiscent of the Merchant-Ivory films that Emily remains a sucker for. One of the more expensive restaurants that caters to the affluent students' parents showcases Lucille's paintings, along with the Caprock chardonnay. The paintings sell for a good one thousand and up, and the restaurant unloads at least two each month, more at Parents' Weekend and football games.

Anton has always been a magnet for certain women, an attraction he knows how to work to his advantage. Today, though, Emily's appalled to see the two of them standing so close. The very fact that Samuel is the commercial or "trite" Lucille's gallerist also aggravates Emily, and the current flirtation becomes just more salt in the wound.

Unlike Emily, Caitlin doesn't seem bothered by Anton and Lucille. Once the sandwiches are finished and Samuel picks up the tray, she says, "Alright then, Em, your turn. Show me what you've got."

There are five canvases. Three are studies of a teenage girl named Tilly who rides at the barn. One of these Emily created from a series of sketches and photographs, having observed Tilly closely for a month while she rode. The studies of Tilly have been done in watercolor, gouache, and pastel. They are full of movement, light, and life, the kind of energy that Emily associates with the sunny sixteen-year-old—all Tilly thinks about are horses. There's no doubt in either Samuel's mind or Emily's that the "Tilly Series" will sell. The other two are done in oil: the first is a portrait of Cora's roommate, an eighty-five-year-old widow named Sylvia, whose eyes are the blue of the Texas sky at noon on a cloudless day.

For a time, Emily thought about painting Cora, but was in no way ready to open herself up to the emotions and memories that would be released if she tried. Emily alone remained. These days there are moments, too many of them, when Emily wonders if the vacancy she feels without Cora is here to stay. Other than her work and the students who pass in and out of her life, what does she have? Her house with its garden, her dogs, a few friends, and many more acquaintances. But at the end of the day, no one needs to know where she is. No one needs her.

Sylvia, despite being confined to a wheelchair, was so remarkably full of life that Emily came to believe she had found the girl and then the vital woman that Sylvia had once been. While Emily worked, Sylvia narrated stories of Lubbock in the 1940s when Nineteenth Street, now a six-lane thoroughfare, was unpaved; when families kept horses in their backyards; when the increasingly gentrified neighborhood where Emily lives consisted of a patchwork of houses including the one that lost all of its north-facing windows in last month's hail storm.

Caitlin admires the composition of Sylvia and especially the colors; but as Emily expected, it's the largest in the group that holds her rapt. She noticed Anton studying it as well. Also done in oil, with several layers of gesso underneath in order to build up the textures, the canvas spans thirty-six by forty-two inches. The composition is unusual for Emily but not because of the size. She revels in the physical movements the large canvases require, something she learned from Cora. What's unusual is the restraint with which she's used color here, allowing herself a palette composed primarily of browns with just the slightest hint of green and a pink like the primroses in her garden.

"Who is she?" Caitlin asks, taking in the gold-flecked, hazel eyes, doe-large and maybe a bit too startled, the feeling of affectation intensified by the half-parted lips set in a face with high cheekbones, a peaked chin. The woman's hair, strawberry blonde in reality, is redder in the portrait, pulled away from her face by a pink elastic that picks up the highlights in her hair.

"One of the art students." Emily chooses her words carefully. Though she and Caitlin talk every few weeks, and email more often, Emily has said nothing about her volatile and very brief relationship with Rebecca, and not just because she'd been Rebecca's teacher. Emily had never been attracted to a woman before, and she's never felt that way since. No, the relationship with Rebecca came on the devastating heels of her parting from Nick, the man with whom Emily lived for two years, the man she believed she would marry, with whom she might even have had a child.

A month into her time at the care facility, while Cora slipped further and further away, Nick sat Emily down and told her that he was leaving. "I'm sorry," he said in that same quiet way with which he spoke to animals. "I just don't believe in us enough. Not for the long haul."

Emily no longer remembers how she said goodbye to Nick who left within the week, having already lined something up (so that she understood he'd been thinking about this for a while). The last she heard he was training horses in Tucson, working with a woman close to Cora in age who claimed to have some ancestral connection to them. Upon learning this, Emily found herself seized by the perverse desire to go out there and paint her. Instead, she drove out to the barn on the north end of town and signed up for riding lessons. There Emily met the steadfast Arabian gelding that she continues to ride and realized that Nick had given her, or at least enabled, an unforeseen gift.

Some five months later, Rebecca erupted into her life; a force to be reckoned with, though some days she was more like a small child who has some claim on you. Or perhaps, Emily realized in the months since that last night, the need lay within Emily herself.

"Will she be at the opening?" Caitlin asks.

"I don't think so." Since that last night—Rebecca's hands on her throat—she has thankfully stayed away, though Emily's keenly aware of herself looking out for Rebecca at the market, the university, along the footpath where they sometimes ran.

"Still so self-composed," Caitlin says, and though she's teasing, Emily hears something else, something more jagged beneath her words.

"What?" Emily says. "I don't understand."

"Your self-control," Caitlin says. "It never fails you."

"What are you talking about? I thought we were talking about a painting here."

"If you say so," Caitlin says.

Emily wants to say more, but Anton chooses this precise moment to join them.

"Ah, now, this is the painting I wanted to talk to you about." He holds Emily's gaze just a moment too long, but she dismisses the possibility that Anton, of all people, can read how she's feeling.

He and Caitlin may have paired off during the first weeks of their MFA program, but Emily has always disliked Anton, who struck her from the start as self-absorbed, egotistical. Later, when Anton hooked up with another art student from Birmingham while Caitlin was at an out-of-state workshop during their second semester, Emily's dislike turned more hostile. Pretty soon she noticed the other times when Anton had coffee with pretty undergraduates, likely students from the Intro to Painting classes they all taught during that second year. If he'd been unfaithful to Caitlin back then, what was he doing now with his wife grown occupied with their two boys? And pregnant again.

Not that Emily would claim to have any insight into how to make a relationship work. The two years she spent with Nick were her longest run with any man, her parents having divorced before she was three. Her mother has a Ph.D. in endocrinology, and sometime during elementary school Emily consciously understood that her research was and likely always had been mother's one true love.

Her father remarried about two years afterward, not a younger woman, but a woman fifteen years older with two daughters of her own. By the time Emily was in fifth grade, the youngest of these daughters was in her last year of high school, and the other in college. The people Emily considers to be her father's real family have always been welcoming, inviting her for holidays and personal milestones, which she sometimes attends, but not too often. Having been raised by a woman who rarely socializes, Emily has always lingered on the margins, studying faces, gestures. She's a portraitist after all.

Back at home later that afternoon, Emily slips outside, needing a reprieve, time to clear her head, before she's back on duty at the gallery for the show. Beyond the hollyhocks and iris that return with increasing vigor each year is the raised vegetable garden she built with salvaged railroad ties. There she harvests the first of her lettuces, a buttery bib and the spicy arugula the rabbits won't touch.

Afterwards she makes her way to the side door, pauses on the threshold to the kitchen, struck by the sounds emanating from the bedroom: low and guttural. And although she fights it, pretty soon it's Nick she's thinking of, Nick lying beside her after love-making, the lines of his fifty-three-year-old face a comfort and a map she once believed she knew how to read. Nausea rises. As the sounds from her bedroom continue, all Emily feels is a growing need to escape.

She places the vegetables on the counter and hurries through the kitchen; then she's out the door again and stands breathing deeply, the kind of breathing she uses to relax and connect with her horse at the start of a ride. Her two Great Pyrenees, huge white clouds of fur with long, feathery tails and soulful eyes, look up at her.

When is it that she remembers that Anton has borrowed her car to drive out to Ransom Canyon? Anton is intensely passionate about few things, and one of them is bird watching; why he set off on his own just after they returned from the gallery, his binoculars slung around his neck. Does that mean she's read it all wrong? Maybe what she heard wasn't sex. Caitlin may have gone into premature labor, or is in some sort of serious distress. Emily's about to go back inside when the side door opens and Samuel steps out, disheveled only in his dark hair. The white shirt he favors is still crisp, as are his gray trousers.

"Oh my god. You've got to be kidding me," Emily says, only now noticing his white Saab parked across the street.

Samuel looks past her, the hint of crimson in his cheeks the only sign. "We changed the sheets."

"How considerate. Thank you very much," Emily says, backtracking to that embrace at the gallery, the way Samuel and Caitlin held onto each other for too long. "Tell me: how long has this been going on?"

"We've written back and forth, spoken on the phone," Samuel says, but too quickly to convince Emily. "I'm sorry about your bed. Really. But please, Em," he touches her shoulder, "don't make too much of this."

"Me? Are you out of your mind? She's nearly seven months pregnant, or haven't you noticed?"

Samuel just shakes his head, his dark eyes impenetrable beneath his luxuriant fringe of lashes.

The air seems to leave Emily's lungs, and she swallows hard. "You weren't even going to tell me about any of this, were you?"

Samuel, sheepish, red-faced, only shrugs.

"I can't believe this. You and I worked together on this show for months, Samuel," she says. "Caitlin's probably my oldest friend. And you," she pictures Cora's self-portrait, "I thought there was some real trust between us, some understanding."

"There is," Samuel says. "This is not about you and me, Emily."

"This is my house, and you were in my bed."

"I know. I don't feel good about that part at all. I just wish you wouldn't take the rest personally."

She tries, once more, to say something not full of emotion, but already Samuel is saying goodbye, moving away, reminding her of how much he has to do before tonight. He brushes past, kisses her cheek, flees.

Anton comes back less than an hour later. "It's so quiet," he says when he finds Emily in the kitchen trying to focus on the eggplant dish she'll take to the gallery. "Cait sleeping?"

"It would seem so," Emily says, though really she has no idea. Caitlin simply hasn't come out. Emily heard the shower running, but other than that, nothing.

"Good. She's been working so hard."

Anton goes to the refrigerator for the orange juice. His forehead and neck are red from the sun, and he looks almost foolish, this big man with his bunch of wilting flowers. Does he have any idea what his wife is up to? And how would he react were Emily to tell him what's been going on while he's been out scouting birds? Instead, after he gulps down the juice, she hands him a vase which he carries over to the sink, fills with water.

"Anything exciting out there? The birds, I mean," she says, almost glad to have some secret over him.

"Kestrels mostly; there was an owl."

"Really? An owl?" All these years in Lubbock, and Emily has still never seen one, except for the permanently injured owls at the wildlife center.

"A great-horned owl just sitting in a live oak. He opened only one eye to look at me, decided I wasn't worth the interest."

Emily feigns a laugh, pours herself a glass of juice. Only later does she remember Samuel telling her that for the Lebanese, an owl sighting on the eve of a big event is anything but auspicious.

That evening the gallery's high-ceilinged rooms are perfectly lit, and a good thirty people are milling about. Sure, some are taking advantage of the free food and wine (a very good Sauvignon Blanc and an even better merlot). But there are serious collectors here too, including a hotshot from the university administration. A few unfamiliar faces stand before individual pieces for a long time, moving closer, stepping back, again and again.

Dressed in her uniform of white linen pants and black silk blouse, Emily takes it in; but deep down she remains preoccupied with Caitlin who, some two hours after Anton's return, appeared in the kitchen wearing an empire-style dress, her hair in a loose bun, teardrop pearls in her ears. She looked beautiful, as Emily expected, but she also seemed remarkably calm. If Emily hadn't seen Samuel leaving the house earlier, if she hadn't heard them, she would never have suspected that Caitlin was doing anything other than sleeping.

Anton is wearing expensive-looking jeans and a camel sweater, and his hair is slicked back to expose a forehead not burnished but burned by sun. Always, he has worked with mural-sized work, and tonight more than ever he radiates a scintillating energy. The show may be for Caitlin and Emily, but he's the one most at ease in this environment of celebration and yes, adulation. Some five minutes after they arrive, he's already wending through the pockets of conversation, drawing admiring glances from many women as well as several men.

Beside her, Caitlin tugs at a pearl earring, her shoulders tense, even though she's smiling. The timing's terrible, yes, but Emily just can't resist. "So, about this afternoon: did you simply plan to not say anything?"

A rush of pink, almost like a rash, suffuses Caitlin's cheeks. "Good grief, Emily," Caitlin says. "I wish you could just let this go. Especially now. Look where we are."

"That's right: let's do that. I work my ass off setting up this show with Samuel, a relationship I've built over years, *years,* and then you show up, and the two of you have sex in my bed. And all you have to say is 'good grief'? 'Let it go'? Do you have any idea how totally inappropriate all of this is? What a slap in my face?"

"I'm sorry for that. Really, I am. It was stupid, unthinking. But you're taking this all a little far, don't you think?"

"No," Emily says. "No, I don't."

"God, Em, it's so hard to be around you sometimes."

"Hard? What's that supposed to mean?"

"You're really good at making a person feel like shit is what I'm talking about. You're so superior. So beyond reproach."

"Superior? I'm sorry, but that makes no sense at all."

"Doesn't it?" Caitlin stares down at her feet before looking back at Emily.

"What about all those needling little questions about my life with Anton? The small digs. I know you don't like him. Yeah, sure, you're careful not to overstep, but you seem to know just how far to go before pulling back. Even now, you act as if you don't understand."

"That's because I don't." Emily steps away from Caitlin, disbelieving this is the friend she thought she knew so well, and simultaneously wondering how her shock at Caitlin screwing Samuel in her bed has become a critique of Emily herself. How has Caitlin managed that? To make it worse, Caitlin looks as if she's about to cry.

"I'm sorry about Samuel," Caitlin says. "About today: just know that we didn't plan it."

All at once Emily feels both hot and cold, dots of perspiration prickling her forehead. She stands before Caitlin, the roof of her mouth and her tongue suddenly dry, as she remembers something Nick said not too long before he left. Some Saturday or Sunday when all he wanted to do was lie on the couch in front of CNN, and Emily got agitated. He'd told her to relax, to not feel compelled to accomplish something all the time, to not make him feel compelled to either.

The two women stare at each other until Samuel's intern, a courtly graduate student from Beirut, steps between them to ferry Emily and not Caitlin away. All she feels is relief as he guides her over to one of the Tillys.

A middle-aged man with a linebacker's shoulders stands before the gouache, Tilly and her mare suspended in pirouette. It's the most colorful and dramatic of the group. And the most expensive. The buyer's teeth are so straight and white they must be implants, given the weathered features of his face.

"Ah, Emily, good, good, here's someone who's eager to meet you," Samuel says. "This is Brandt Scanlon. He's so interested in your work."

In truth, Brandt Scanlon's purposes are far more decorative. The painting's destination is his daughter's bedroom.

"She's eleven and all she cares about is horses, spends all her free time at the barn. That keeps her away from the boys." He laughs.

Emily nods, trying to look pleased, though the exchange with Caitlin has left her raw.

An hour passes, then two. People do stop to study the portrait of Sylvia. Not that Emily believes it will sell. There's a gravity to it that very few people could live with, Emily having painted the old woman's deeply-veined hands, the age spots

84

marring her skin, the wrinkles fanning out from her eyes and mouth. Sylvia's blue eyes, though, are brilliantly alive, their color echoed in the sky seen through the window behind her, but also in the silver-blue sheen of the wheelchair, the arm of which Emily has captured in the lower right corner. Were someone to get all symbolic, they might even compare that blue to the blue of the Madonna's robes or to the sky in the religious paintings of the High Renaissance. Emily wasn't thinking of that. It just felt pleasing: right. But now, given what Caitlin's said—a high bar, isn't that what an artist strives for?—this rightness from which she's always derived strength, taken refuge, has been called into question: no, judged.

If Cora were still lucid, Emily could talk to her about all of this, and particularly about this vacancy rooted within herself; a windy, hollow feeling she has more and more trouble banishing; its physical counterpart the dust storms that blow in from nowhere on these high plains.

"Who are you?" Cora says some days when Emily comes to the nursing home, staring at her with a blankness that is anything but childlike. Other days, the bright, jewel-toned days of alizarin crimson or canary yellow, Cora will remember. "Emily," she says then, seizing Emily's hands, her features coming alive, "hello." And for a dazzling, dizzying few moments, Emily almost lets herself believe that they will talk again as they used to. They will talk, and Cora will understand.

But that recognition never lasts.

Pretty soon Samuel approaches Caitlin, once more cupping his hand around her elbow, then steering her away from the locals and over to Herbert Watkins, the classics scholar the university managed to woo away from Rice. Herbert Watkins, Emily now registers, is standing before one of Caitlin's women. If he were to buy the sculpture, Caitlin would get some terrific exposure. And just then, instead of pleasure for her friend, it's something not pretty, not quite jealousy but certainly not good will, that Emily feels.

When is it that Emily finds that single husky voice within the crowd? When the muscles along her rib cage constrict, and her breath shortens, as it did when Rebecca pinned her arms that last terrible night? Emily wills herself to just ignore that presence—as if Rebecca might vanish, as if such a thing was possible.

But it's inevitable that she must turn, and when she does, Rebecca is kneeling on the floor beside Samuel's mother, Fatima, who is smiling. The fact of Rebecca here, her portrait just beyond, on top of the stand-off with Caitlin, propels Emily out onto the street where the air has thankfully cooled enough to create a real breeze. *How could she have dared to come?*

Footsteps. The door jingles closed. She turns. It's Anton, his slicked-back hair glinting in the lights coming from inside. "You okay? You're not looking so hot."

"I needed a break, some air, a bit of quiet." Emily speaks too fast. Has he been watching her? She turns back towards the gallery, aware of Rebecca still sitting with Fatima. Not that she'll look at Rebecca. No, Emily focuses instead on Caitlin who stands with Herbert Watkins and Samuel; his hand continues to cup her elbow, a lover's gesture if ever there was one.

Anton taps the cigarette against his palm before lighting up. "The woman in there," he says, "the one from the painting—there was something between you, right?"

And though he doesn't say it, Emily's sure she hears the words he's thinking, and the feeling along her spine is that zero to the bone that Dickinson describes.

"Something, I suppose so. Let's leave it at that." More than anything, Emily's ashamed that it's Anton, of all people, who's seen through her.

Although Samuel is standing very close to Caitlin inside, Anton himself seems impassive, his eyelids half closed as he exhales smoke. "It might help you to know that Cait and I understand each other," he says after a while.

The composition—the arrangement of Anton's words—she tries to find a shape for them in her mind. *Is it possible that he's known all along about Samuel? Or, if he didn't know earlier, he does now, and it doesn't seem to matter.* And for years she's censored and, yes, condemned his unfaithfulness to Caitlin. The reality, the absurdity of it, could almost be funny. Except it isn't.

"Not that you would understand," Anton continues. "And did I say how sorry I was to hear about Nick?" He smiles, smoke escaping through his lips. "Of course, you've always modeled yourself on Cora. Your ideal. She gave everything she had to her art, her students, and she lived a very full life."

"Don't bring Cora into this," Emily says, his smoke filling the air around her.

"Always so sensitive." He shakes his head. "That's your problem, always has been. Try to relax a little, Em. Take things in stride. You'll find life's a lot easier that way."

"If I want your advice, I'll ask for it," Emily says, once more reminded of that snake at the barn, the visceral fear she experienced when she went to fork hay and found the creature coiled around the steel tines. A harmless snake, but that wasn't the point. As if Anton knows anything about her life, yet it's Anton who registered Rebecca, and now all of this. A man like Anton is hardly harmless, and how stupid, how utterly naïve, to invite him to stay in her house. Though it was Caitlin she invited. Not Anton, though it was inevitable he'd come. The smoke, the heat of the night, the alcohol—she feels dizzy, unsettled. "Excuse me," she says, stepping around him. "I have to get back to my show."

"Well, of course. Don't let me stop you," he says, and bows theatrically.

Back inside, a muscular woman—a toxologist to whom Emily has only occasionally spoken to at the barn—stands before Rebecca's portrait. The toxologist has an eye for quality and status, from her custom saddle and German riding clothes to the costly sheen of her skin and hair. *Yes*, Emily thinks, *this woman who keeps two Swedish warmbloods at the stable will pay the asking price.*

The real Rebecca, Emily sees out of the corner of her eye, is continuing her conversation with Fatima. The old woman is gesturing with bejeweled fingers, her wrists equally adorned. Rebecca tilts her head back, laughs, and Emily is slammed back to their last night together, the way Rebecca pinned Emily's arms above her head with one hand, and with the other applied pressure to Emily's neck. The terror that must have registered in her own face, a terror in which she believes Rebecca found pleasure, is somehow there in the portrait.

But it is only now that Emily understands this.

That last night, after Rebecca left, Emily stayed up all night packing her things into a series of plastic containers, dumping her own out in the process. Looking at the portrait now, with the toxologist beside her, talking about how "startling" the work is, "how powerful," Emily wonders if the portrait, completed some three weeks before that terrible night, might have been an omen.

"It's an incredible piece," the toxologist is saying. "Normally I would never even think of buying a portrait of a stranger and hanging it in my home."

Emily turns, tries to ground herself. "It's not the individual person I'm interested in as much as a particular emotion, an impression."

"Of course, and what an impression." The toxologist—Judith her name is—competes in Eventing. She's an aggressive, determined rider. Emily, as her trainer has said, is too passive, doesn't quite trust herself. In Emily's mind, this is why the old Arabian is so good for her. Still, it's becoming time for her to move on to a more athletic horse, or so the trainer says. The talented Carmen has been suggested, and also a black Friesian sport horse. But Emily doesn't want to leave her Arabian. The rhythms of his body are familiar, beloved, and when she presses her cheek to the whiskered warmth of his muzzle, and breathes in earth, shit, air, and sweat, a peace suffuses her, something she rarely finds anymore.

"'Intention' is a very apt name, very provocative," the toxologist says.

"You think so?" Emily stands, puzzled. *What goal, what intention, had there ever been with Rebecca? With Nick, yes; with Nick, she had made plans, though they'd come unraveled. But when Rebecca came along?* Emily was intensely lonely and more than a little bit broken. *Intention? Surely not the violence, or the threat of violence, with which the relationship ended.*

Afterwards, Emily burned the sheets.

"Hey." Rebecca's voice.

Emily keeps her eyes on the toxologist, who smiles at Rebecca. "I'll be looking at your face for a long time," Judith says.

"I'm flattered," Rebecca says, "but the credit goes to Emily, my former teacher."

Emily shifts to glance at Rebecca's face then and is stunned to see what appears to be affection. It's now that Anton comes over, smelling of cigarettes and something more pungent. He introduces himself to the toxologist, though his eyes are on Rebecca.

"I know your work," Rebecca says to him.

Anton grins. "I'm flattered."

"I took a bus to New York a while back," she continues. "I can't remember the name of the gallery, but I'll never forget the canvases—a series all in blue named for sacred sites in—"

"Laos," Anton says. "I spent six weeks in Laos, visiting the remaining temples, learning a little too much about the fallout from Vietnam."

"My uncle was in Vietnam," Rebecca says, another thing that Emily didn't know.

Not that there had ever been much talk between them. They communicated through the work during class—Emily standing at Rebecca's side, studying, gesturing. And later, even before the sex, it was all about movement and touch. They went for long walks, hikes in the canyon.

Some evenings they worked in Emily's garden and then went inside and made soup or a slow-cooking stew. With Rebecca, at least in the beginning, it had been like those exhilarating days when Emily found her rhythm in painting. Or the days she rode across the few remaining fields out here, and in the process rode out of her thoughts, fears, and regrets, the strength and heat of the horse becoming a part of her.

Or perhaps the two of them became a part of something larger. Exhilarating until that night, Rebecca's hand on her throat, her knees pinning Emily's wrists. Despite the air-conditioning, she feels overheated, dizzy. The clutch of people surrounding her are too close, and again she longs to go outside, collect herself, clear her head.

Emily tries to think of a way to break away, if only the toxologist would move out of her way. But Judith has planted herself beside Emily, as Rebecca and Anton talk about the escalating violence in Syria, in parts of the Deep South where Rebecca is from.

Once, she told Emily that she'd grown up down the road from an old plantation where there had once been slaves. Their ghosts wandered the property, Rebecca said, that county having seen more lynching than any other in the state of Louisiana. Had she been telling the truth, or lying?

The toxologist continues to stand there. Emily is trapped, the spinning sensation in her head only intensifying. The woman is talking about horses now, telling Emily that she's welcome to try out one of her own warm bloods.

"Andante is too risky. I'm going to put her in full training, but Valentina would be perfect for you. She's still young, only seven, but she wants to please her rider, and she's such a steady mount."

Emily's eyes burn, the back of her throat strangely scratchy, raw.

"You have more strength than you realize," the toxologist continues. "It's there in that portrait. I'm absolutely serious. Go ahead, ride Valentina."

A purple-blue haze fills Emily's line of vision, and soon her knees are buckling, and she's falling, the toxologist's arms reaching out to catch her.

It feels like an instant, the gap of time before Caitlin is there at her side; *there* being the trundle bed in the small room at the back of the gallery. Caitlin is there, and so is Samuel. And now Caitlin is bending over her, Caitlin's belly flush against Emily's chest. Caitlin holds a cool cloth to Emily's forehead.

"How are you, Em?" Caitlin asks, what seems like real concern in her eyes. Why then can't Emily trust it?

"It was so hot in there, the air got close. Your husband's smoke," Emily says.

"You fainted," Caitlin says, "but that woman, the doctor, caught you."

Emily feels her body tense, afraid that the toxologist is nearby.

"Another one of the Tillys just sold—this one to a pediatrician newly recruited by UMC," Samuel tells her. "She and several other people want to talk to you. In a few minutes, you think you can manage to get up and go back in, yes?"

"Samuel," Caitlin scolds, "give her a bit of time."

Emily sits up, drinks the water that Caitlin holds out to her. What Emily wants is to stay right where she is. *No, it's all been far too much. This day.* What she really wants is to go home and sleep for a long time.

Caitlin touches her shoulder. "Em, even if you're not up to going back to the gallery, there is someone who really wants to see you, someone you should see."

Again, the confident, rather mannish features of the toxologist come to mind. "I can't—"

"Yes, you can. Listen." Caitlin's voice softens. "She's wearing a beautiful red dress and matching shoes. She says she knows you from the nursing home."

For one irrational moment, Emily imagines it's Cora who's come; she came to all of the openings featuring Emily's work, as long as they were within a day's drive. Thing is, Cora never favored red.

"The woman in the portrait out there," Samuel says. "Cora's friend."

"Sylvia?" Emily pictures the old woman's bright eyes, the zest she continues to find in life despite her diminished body, her diminishing opportunities. "But how did she get here?"

"Her daughter brought her," Samuel says. "They're having a wonderful time. This Sylvia's planted her wheelchair beside the portrait and has gathered quite a circle around her. My mother's probably seething with envy."

In spite of everything, Emily begins to laugh. She thinks back to her talks with Sylvia at the nursing home, the comfort between them like late afternoon sunlight. With Sylvia, she experienced a joy and peacefulness like those best moments in riding, or when she disappears into her painting, becoming a part of the process and the energy and the spirit behind it. The ego, the edge of personality, it vanishes then.

"So what do you think?" Caitlin says.

"Be realistic," Samuel says. "There are people waiting, Emily. This is your night."

"It's Caitlin's night, too," she says, without resentment, thankfully.

Caitlin flushes, and she turns to Samuel for—what is it she's looking for there? Help?

"Of course," Samuel says. "The show belongs to both of you. Another reason to—"

But Emily isn't listening. "I'm a painter, for God's sakes," she says. "The astonishing this is that it's taken me so long to see."

Samuel sits down beside her, places a hand on her back. "Try not to get more upset."

Emily closes her eyes, tries to recapture the feel of the brush against the canvas as she painted Sylvia's portrait. The eyes are a wonder, but it was the attention she gave to Sylvia's hands that provided the most satisfaction. Sylvia's fingers remain long and slender, despite the way age has gnarled her legs, crumpled the toes of her feet. Sylvia had been fond of dancing, she'd told Emily, had even won some dancing competitions with her husband.

Another sound interrupts the quiet, the slick glide of wheels on the wood floor. Emily looks up. Sylvia is there, ensconced in her wheelchair. Just as Caitlin said, she's wearing a high-necked scarlet dress and matching shoes, and her white hair has been pinned carefully into place. A corsage—a white gardenia—adorns her left wrist. Billy Holiday's flower. And hovering at her side is her daughter, a handsome woman with Sylvia's snowy hair.

"There you are, Emily," Sylvia says. "High time you got up, wouldn't you say? There's a room full of people out there, and all of them have come to see you."

"I'm so glad you're here, Sylvia, and your daughter, too," Emily says, the knots inside her loosening. "And yes, you're right, it is, time to get back, though you've outdone me with your red."

"Glad you're seeing sense," Sylvia says kindly, but she is also tapping the patent of her shoe against the wheelchair, so that Emily can picture her talking effusively while a nurse or most likely her daughter—*Margaret*, Emily remembers—helped her get ready for tonight.

Emily smoothes back her hair, gets to her feet. Her wristwatch reads a quarter to ten. In an hour, an hour and a half at most, the opening will be over. She has no doubt that Sylvia and Margaret will stay until the very end.

As for tomorrow, Emily will leave Anton and Caitlin to themselves while she goes to see Cora at the nursing home. Maybe she'll even get Samuel to drive them to the airport. That way, she and Sylvia can tell Cora all about the evening. Even if Cora doesn't take most of it in. The important thing will be for Emily to let Sylvia do most of the talking. Emily herself will listen, eager to see the night's events through someone else's eyes. Yes, Sylvia's eyes. Tonight, it is this older woman's perspective, and not least of all her resilience, that Emily needs.

SEEING RED

Four thirty in the afternoon on July 12th, and the high's 103. The armpits of my silk dress are sweat-stained, my feet swollen. I may have spent the last six months alternating yoga with interval training, but right now I feel about as supple as an elephant with a pedicure. Ever since I pulled into Lubbock, a big sky-ruin of a town I swore I'd never set foot in again (and were it not for Sebastian I would have stayed on the highway until I reached Fort Worth), I've been all hard edges and negative thoughts.

Until I step into the Mariposa Café, and the only man I know over forty who can get away with leaving the top two, even three buttons of his Egyptian cotton shirts undone without looking desperate or ridiculous stands, kisses me on the cheek. "Renata," he says, taking my hands in his own. "I've never seen you looking better."

"You're kidding, right?" Not that I want to be thirty-five or even forty again, but what I wouldn't do to have a glow that wasn't induced by Clinique and a standing appointment at Microderm.

"Hardly." The wrinkles at the corners of his eyes fan out like tiny waves. "You're a vision, Renata, an absolute vision."

"And so are you," I reply, and Sebastian tilts his head back and laughs.

The server, a co-ed with an azure bob and kohl-rimmed eyes, seats us in a booth by the window. The café features over-the-top chandeliers and eggplant walls adorned by bad art in gold-leaf. It's a café that Thomas likes to frequent, except that Thomas, I learned via email, is in Calcutta. ("You've got to be joking?" I wrote back, not bothering to bring up what Sebastian and I both know—Thomas is neurotic when it comes to rare viruses, contaminated food and water, as well as crowds.)

"It's so good to see you," I say after I down my ice water.

"Of course it is," Sebastian says. "Still you hesitated about stopping off here?"

"My biggest humiliations to date have both happened in this town."

He rerolls a shirt sleeve, the thread-count so high the fabric shimmers. "Everyone says the Spanish are bad, but you Russians surpass us hands down when it comes to exaggeration."

"Dramatic, Sebastian, there's a difference," I say as I take my first sip of the very good Chenin Blanc he's ordered and praise his choice.

We drink a toast to reunions, and Sebastian settles back in the uncomfortable chair. "Now tell me all about your year in the sunshine state," he says. "How many undergraduates did you have again: fifty? fifty-five?"

"Two preps and four sections bring the numbers to sixty-three," I say, having gone over the size of the classes and the amount they underpaid me more times than I'd like to admit. "Photography went as planned, but life drawing in this age of social media and iPhones is taxing." I sigh, take another sip of wine.

"The iPhone's become another appendage," he says. "Now that students can buy ebooks, it's impossible to know if they're surfing the net or looking at texts during class." And more philosophically: "At least you artists don't have to parse student grammar. All this technology, and they've forgotten how to write a sentence. 'U' for 'you'—what next?" He pours us each a bit more wine. "Imagine when they're running the country."

"It could be worse," I say. "Let's face it. It has been."

Sebastian raises a bushy eyebrow. "Has it?"

"Sure. Trump certainly flipped through Strunk & White."

"Let's not go there. I want to hear about your new work. From all that I've seen on your website, it looks like you've taken a very bold approach." He raises his glass. "Cheers."

This time, when I reach for my glass, I catch something sweet underlying the tartness: a hint of green apple, possibly pear. The fact that he's interested in my series of re-imaginings of Elizabeth Siddal, Pre-Raphaelite muse and an artist in her own right (though far too belatedly acknowledged), warms me far more than the wine. Even though the topic will inevitably lead us back to Thomas whose monograph focuses on Dante Gabriel Rossetti, who both idealized and eroticized Siddal's beauty and her deteriorating health in drawings and paintings made over fifteen years.

Not that I don't expect to get to Thomas eventually, being far too curious about the reason he's actually in Calcutta, which I find nearly impossible to imagine. And his daughter, Alicia, I'm dying to ask: is she there too? Alicia would be sixteen now. Alicia, unlike her germaphobe father, would thrive in Calcutta. Hell, Alicia would thrive anywhere.

"The resemblance between you and Lizzie Siddal is stronger than I realized," Sebastian says, studying one of the images on a sleek laptop. It's my recreation of Lizzie in profile, red-gold hair flowing loose, eyes upturned so that they catch the light, investing Me-as-Lizzie with a look that is both dreamy and purposeful.

"It's mainly about the skin and the hair. Remember, the camera—or its filters—can be most forgiving. Lizzie Siddal died at thirty-two. I've got twenty years on her."

"And the advantages of advanced skincare and modern medicine."

"Touché," I say, and reach for the wine. It's my turn to top off our glasses.

He clicks open another image, a photographic recreation of myself as Lizzie dressed in a close copy of one of her gowns and stretched out on a divan that I created by repurposing an old piano bench and a low-slung armchair.

"This one is particularly stunning. The directness of your gaze is electric and more than a little unsettling," he says.

"Precisely my intention," I say, pleased. "Can you believe Rossetti sketched and painted her more than thirty times. And in all of them her eyes are closed."

"A side effect of the laudanum?"

"To some extent, though I wouldn't overplay the addiction. No, he kept her eyes closed to ensure that he controlled how she'd be seen."

"Which makes your own vision long overdue," Sebastian says. "Why then don't I find the dying Ophelia among any of the images on your website? Not that I'm not relieved, a little bit anyway."

"Are you?" I set down the wine, suddenly light-headed. "Why?"

"You may be dramatic, but macabre doesn't suit you."

"Lovely of you to say so, but I have done several recreations of Millais's Ophelia. I had a silver dress just like the one she wore custom made. I'm just not satisfied with what I've created yet." I laugh a little grimly, reminded of my own hours posing in the bath—at least I had the benefits of indoor heating and heat lamps.

"Millais's a tough act to follow," Sebastian says.

"Talk about an understatement. Have you any idea how many thousand people stand in front of that painting at the Tate Britain each year?"

"I do, yes. I've stood there among them, at least half a dozen times over the years."

What Sebastian doesn't know is that Lizzie Siddal posed for Millais's painting for five long hours by lying in a bath filled with dirty Thames water. It was winter time, and the candles beneath the tub warming the water went out. Millais failed to notice. And Lizzie didn't say a word. Not when the sum that Millais was paying her amounted to almost six months of wages in the milliner's shop where another Pre-Raphaelite painter spotted her just a few months before. Lizzie contracted pneumonia immediately afterwards, and a doctor prescribed laudanum for the pain. It was as easy to buy as Tylenol in those days, and it didn't take very long for Lizzie to become addicted.

Not that Lizzie posed for the Pre-Raphaelites for money alone. She wanted to learn from these men, both her sex and her lower-class background barring her from any formal training. If she hadn't caught pneumonia and started the laudanum (the Victorian doctor's drug of choice for men but especially for women), what might she have accomplished? That question, and the mixture of furious anguish accompanying it, kept me up on far too many nights.

As a career academic, Sebastian knows that a feminist slant on Siddal and the Pre-Raphaelite Brotherhood is a good twenty years too late. Not that feminism is my angle, not exactly, such neat binaries having always been too prescriptive for the questions that run through my own work, and especially for my search for signs of the strong personality that occasionally emerges in the scattering of letters and references to Siddal by other artists and writers; and most of all, in the perseverance with which she practiced her art.

"Renata?" Sebastian lays a hand on my own. "I asked you about your recreation of the Millais. What is it that's not working in your version?"

"Her vacuous expression, especially in the eyes," I say, almost feeling Ophelia's sodden gown against my skin once more.

"Her face isn't the focal point, but it's a millstone dragging me down, down, down. I can't look away from her eyes and slack jaw. I can't, or I won't accept it," I say, reminded of the immersion sessions in my own bath, the heat lamps bringing perspiration bubbles to my flushed skin.

"Renata?" Sebastian is watching me from beneath his heavy eyebrows.

"Sorry," I say, and smile. "Now tell me, what's in Calcutta?"

The laugh lines fanning Sebastian's eyes vanish. "Thomas is on his honeymoon."

The words land like a punch, though the hurt, at this point anyway, is less about Thomas and more about his daughter. Alicia was eleven when we met, a chubby kid with sun-bleached hair and eyes the color of crocuses. By the time he and I split up, she'd sprouted half a foot and could have modeled in *Vogue*, though fortunately she has no interest in high fashion, or boys. Or at least she didn't then, spending most of her time with the ragged dogs and broken-winged birds she was always nursing back to health. God knows what's changed in the twenty-two months since I left.

"So," I say, trying not to gulp the wine. "Who's Thomas's lucky girl?"

"A biologist from India."

By the time he tells me that Thomas's biologist studies salamanders, he's laughing his rich baritone laugh, one that almost puts me at ease, and people around us are staring. Ordinarily, I wouldn't mind except that across the way I recognize the Valkyrie from the art department who blocked my hire. The Valkyrie once wore her long flaxen hair loose like some kind of Nordic Selkie, though she now has it cropped into a spiky and most unflattering pixie, which pleases me to no end. Dressed in a Peter Pan-collar blouse and plaid skirt, the sort of thing someone wears to Catholic school, I can almost believe she bought the get-up in the children's department at Dillard's.

The waiter brings us another bottle of wine, and the gravlax arrives, laid out on a glass tray with horseradish, capers, and fine slices of toast.

Sebastian raises his glass. "I'd say a toast is in order."

I spoon a few briny capers onto my plate. "Thomas's

marriage?"

"God forbid I'd be as tasteless as that, though I've always said you were too good for him. I, on the other hand, well we both know I'm a catch."

Sebastian may be playful by nature, but something in his voice, and in the set of his jaw, which has kept its strong line despite the fact he'll be sixty-three come February, tells me that he still hasn't given up on the possibility of "us" even though I no longer live in this town.

He knows all about my poor choices when it comes to men. How could he not since he was the one I fled to, swollen-eyed and incoherent, after Thomas dumped me the same day I returned from a job interview in Fort Collins because, Thomas said, a distance of eleven hundred miles just wouldn't work. "A coward," Sebastian pronounced him before pouring me a glass of brandy and tucking me into bed in his daughter's old room with lavender walls and a row of stuffed animals on the dresser.

I look down at my hands, at the taupe nail polish I slicked on in the hotel room, the silver ring with the turquoise stone that Thomas and Alicia chose for me in Taos when I actually believed we were becoming a family.

"To your job in Minnesota," Sebastian says at last, once more raising his glass.

I offer my best smile. "Remember, it's just a year-long gig."

"Always so hard on yourself," he says. "You've broken new ground with the Siddal portraits, and they're running a search. You told me so yourself."

"I also told you that I've been to this rodeo before."

"Even so, I have a good feeling about you and Minnesota."

I stare back at Sebastian, his gaze as sincere as it is playful.

"All that snow in the winter will be good for your Russian soul, Renata."

"You're ridiculous," I say, certain the Valkyrie is watching me—she's looked over at least once, though I'm determined not to meet her horn-rimmed pixie (or is it evil fairy) gaze.

The sweat stains have spread to my breasts, and I've no doubt there's a discernable V around my cleavage. Sebastian must see it, too; what was I thinking wearing clingy silk on a day like today; so what that the rest of my clothes are dirty?

I lay my palm on the table with such force I nearly knock over my glass. "You're so sure when you know nothing about the school, the department, what they're offering."

"Call it intuition," Sebastian says. "I've told you about my grandmother's fortune-telling skills."

I lean back in my chair and laugh. "Please don't tell me that we're relying on crystal balls now when it comes to my future?"

"I'm talking about faith," he says, placing a warm hand on top of my own, "and the ability to stay-the-course."

"Woody Allen's 'just keep showing up'?" I ask, both wanting and not wanting to retract my hand.

"It comes down to a lot more than that, but sure, why not, if that phrase suits? You certainly do."

"As good as all of this sounds, and trust me, dear Seb, I appreciate every word, bear in mind that I'm going to be fifty-five in October—fifty-five."

"A good Sangiovese needs about that long to reach its peak of flavor."

"I'm not a bottle of wine," I say. "Besides, you know this isn't my point."

His eyes, beneath their heavy brows, are unwavering. "What is your point then?"

"My point? I should have at least one hundred thousand in retirement, and a house, or at least a down payment on a two-bedroom condo. Maybe even a dog."

"There's no reason you cannot have a dog," he says, the familiar playfulness returning. "A small dog would be very easy to manage. Not a Chihuahua—a dog like that would give you a constant headache. Perhaps a spaniel, or no, one of those spunky little terriers?" He places his elbows on the table, leans closer, smiles. "You know, dear Renata, you do remind me of a terrier."

"I don't chew slippers, and I don't want a dog," I say, nudging my feet out of those killing sandals.

"Well then," he leans close. "What is it that you want?"

The breath seems to leave my lungs. Didn't my father ask me pretty much the same question that last night of my visit while we sat on his deck and watched the sunset, the sky briefly transformed into a pool of orange-raspberry sherbet? *It's a little late for you to take a real interest in my life now,* I felt like saying, though I couldn't say anything of the kind, not then and certainly not now that he's careening towards ninety and taking a medicinal cocktail to ward off another stroke, which is inevitable given his own father's fate.

Growing up, days tumbled past when my father barely spoke to me beyond the perfunctory questions about school. How, then, to explain the July night he and I took flashlights and searched the grounds behind the tennis courts for a stray kitten? Forty-five years ago. Yet I remember the comfort of holding her all the way home, the tiny creature's gravelly purr vibrating through my fingers, my father and I humming along to the radio. The kitten, Tabitha after the charmed daughter in "Bewitched," grew into a cat the color of a loaf of bread. A cat has nine lives, they say, but a person only has one.

"Well?" Sebastian says again, very tenderly this time.

"I want to be married," I hear myself say. "I want to have a child. I'm too old to have a baby, but why not a stepchild. Someone exactly like Alicia would be nice."

"Darling Renata," Sebastian says, loosening my fingers from the wine glass and enclosing my left hand in both of his own. "You were very good for her."

I lean in and say, "It worked both ways."

"I know." Sebastian drops his gaze, as if studying something on the plate of gravlax. "It's been five years, and there are days I come home and still expect to find my Maria. We used to go for long walks around the neighborhood, and even after she turned twelve she continued to sling her arm through mine." He shakes his head slightly, adjusts his glasses, and I wonder if he might actually be fighting tears.

"I've never admitted this to anyone," I say, "maybe not even to myself, but I would have stayed with Thomas just to hold onto Alicia. I was a part of her life. We went camping. We did laundry. Hell, I was the one to tell her about Tampax."

"Thomas must have been relieved at that. And yes," Sebastian says more earnestly, "children do ground us. Never mind the unpublished articles, the work that goes unrecognized; they're there at the end of the day, for a while anyway."

"You know, I sent her a book on her birthday, and she sent me a Hallmark card that said 'xo Alicia.' That's it. XO as in tic-tac-toe, I've crossed you out, or my dad has."

"Ah Renata, you must remember that she's a teenager and so easily distracted. The frontal lobe won't fully develop until they're in their twenties."

"Frontal lobe? Sebastian, what are you talking about?"

"The frontal lobe, the seat of judgment."

"Come on, Sebastian, I really don't think Alicia's frontal lobe has much to do with it." The furrows between his eyes deepen, and all at once I understand, and a sickish feeling begins taking over. "That biologist: she's pregnant, isn't she?"

Sebastian nods, and the silver overtaking his dark hair stands out like a big fat streak of lightning. A baby was the one thing I could not have given Thomas, though God knows we tried, all the while I worried myself sick that I'd become pregnant and then go in for the amniocentesis, only to find out that the fetus had severe abnormalities. "How old is this salamander-studying biologist?"

"Forty-one, forty-two," Sebastian says. "It's difficult to tell a woman's age, especially someone whose eyeglasses are as big as moons."

"Really?"

"Her vision is terrible," he says, and presents me with a smile. "She's pretty, sure, but she doesn't have your energy, your j'ai ne sais quois, and definitely not your charm."

"But she's fertile." *Her eggs, unlike mine, are still viable, though at forty, they're nearing their expiration date.*

"So it seems," Sebastian says.

"Where did this fertile salamander expert come from anyway?" I say, picturing a sleek amphibian with eyeglasses. "Not Calcutta, though I imagine there are plenty of salamanders there."

"She's Greek or possibly Armenian. Before coming here, she was teaching in the Midwest, some small college on the Great Lakes. A very good place for salamanders. But Tech promised her tenure."

Thankfully, the server arrives just in time to stop an onset of tears that will run my mascara. He brings another basket of bread and two bowls of their very cold, very spicy gazpacho with

101

creamy dollops of sour cream. I plunge my spoon into the whiteness, scoop up jalapeño, feel it sear my tongue.

"Now tell me, how is your father?" Sebastian asks. "You came straight from Albuquerque?"

"Except for a stop for gas and the requisite Dairy Queen cone in Muleshoe."

"Ah yes, Muleshoe, with its sweet smell of feed lots. I still can't believe PETA hasn't gotten around to them yet." Sebastian gave up red meat ages ago, this Spaniard who comes from a region famous for its bullfights and its beef. His beautiful hands rest on the table. With their long fingers, his hands are a pianist's, though Sebastian's instrument is the cello. I've heard him play several times, Bach and an unusual piece by Camille Saint-Saëns. He played beautifully and with what I can only call compassion. Not that I could see past the haze of Thomas back then, or the haze of Thomas and Alicia.

I look up, sure the mascara's running now. *Why in the hell don't I wear waterproof? Because you normally don't hold your life up to the light*, that voice inside me replies. *Normally you're really good at keeping it buttoned up, zipped.* "My father is old," I say. "At eighty-nine he's finally old."

"There's no escaping age for any of us," Sebastian says, "though I'd hardly call either of us elderly. And you, darling Renata, are giving the years a particularly good run for the money."

"Thanks for that," I say, reminded of the quiet pleasure I found in recreating Elizabeth Siddal's one self-portrait, the care I took with the lighting, determined to play up the planes of my face, turning the laugh lines and crow's feet into their own geography, the age spots too.

After the server clears away the soup bowls, we sit for a while, quiet amid the buzzing talk and brisk movement of the café, and I remember Sebastian telling me that his own parents are still alive and living in that village not far from Pamplona. If Sebastian's going on sixty-three, they've got to be close to my father's age, though it's possible they're more like eighty. I imagine them like the other Europeans I saw in the Pyrenees, the ones who could still walk up and down a mountain well past their eighth decade. Thinking about that now brings a kind of solace. If I keep up the yoga and the intervals, that could be me.

"Given all that you've said about Alicia, I should be equally honest, if not more so," Sebastian says, and spoons a few of the last capers onto his plate.

"You're always honest, Sebastian," I say.

"Yes, well," he sighs heavily, "there are days I think I should have gone back to Spain. My little Maria is in college now in Madrid. Did I tell you that?"

"No," I say, realizing I've never really given much thought to Sebastian's daughter or her age. She was already out of the country by the time I arrived in Lubbock.

"Maria just completed her second year. She's studying mathematics. Such an analytical mind." He looks down at his spoon nudging the capers. "I was foolish to let Catalina take her back. Along with a check, I sent my daughter a Steif pony for her last birthday, to add to her collection, the one she took with her. 'I'm too old for toy horses, Papa,' she told me over the phone. She left just before starting high school, and now I only see her for a month in the summer and at winter and spring holidays."

"I'm sorry," I say, Sebastian's own sorrow pulling me out of my own.

"So, tell me," he says, "when do you go to Minnesota?"

"Mid-August."

"And in the interim?"

"I'll visit an old friend from grad school and her family in Louisville. I've been out of touch with her, with lots of people, this past year."

"One piece of advice, if I may?" Sebastian says, as the server arrives with two tiny cups of espresso. I usually douse my coffee with cream, but today I savor the bitter taste and the smoky aroma of freshly-ground beans.

"You're asking my permission?"

He shakes his head, and I'm reminded of a Bronzino in the Uffizi, the portrait of a courtier who looks less like a lesser Machiavelli and more like a knight. I'm reminded, too, that those shocks of silver in Sebastian's hair have taken hold in just the right places.

"Go ahead," I say, sloshing espresso onto the silk.

"Don't shut out the people who care about you. Thomas is a coward, and this university made a real mistake in not hiring you, but there are better things ahead. Much better, Renata."

I'm tempted to make a joke, if only to keep myself from hoping and especially from counting on those better things, but all that comes is my father sitting in the church pew, his bushy eyebrows and his hair unkempt despite the crisp whiteness of his shirt. In the thirty-seven years since my mother's death, he's continued to send his shirts out to be ironed.

My father was eight years younger than I am now when she died. Yet as far as I know, he never had another woman after her, never even dated. To this day, he plants yellow dahlias on her grave in May just before her birthday, and a well-dusted photograph of my mother in her nurse's uniform still graces the mantle; several others look out from other corners of the house.

In their honeymoon pictures from Jamaica, my mother wears a floral-print bikini and a big straw hat and sunglasses. She's smiling—they both are—but it's the eyes that, as the poet-mystics say, are the windows to the soul. Sebastian's eyes are sienna with flecks of green. They're the kind of eyes that you can rest in, buoyed. He's looking at me, and there's gentleness in his expression but resilience also. Or am I wrong about that? I've been wrong too many times to count, especially when it comes to men.

"What do you want, Renata?" Sebastian asks at last.

His eyes are bright and attentive behind his glasses, and there's so much I want to say about the want—the need—to come home, except that I no longer know where home is anymore. I've never said anything about the row of oak trees my father planted when my sister left for college. They're two stories tall now. When I left, he bought me a plane ticket to London. I close my eyes, imagine myself swimming through the Adriatic, the salt taste of the water, the way it buoyed me, and soon I'm saying it, what I believe Sebastian has waited so long to hear.

Three hours later I'm in his bed, and he's snoring gently, a muscular arm—all those years of playing the cello and tennis—resting on my pillow. The evening light is coming in through the curtains of the open window, and it casts everything in an amber glow. I'd forgotten how gorgeous the light at this time of day can be here.

Sebastian mutters something in his sleep, and beyond the window the fountain on the patio is muttering also. It was beside that fountain, some sort of faux pink marble, that I first met Thomas nearly four years ago. He was a newly-minted full professor after twelve long years. I'd been in Lubbock for just over a month, having stepped in at the last minute to fill a vacancy in art, the woman who held the job before me having decided not to come back. That's what the hiring committee actually told me. I later learned that she was doing very well for herself painting frescoes on rich people's walls in Santa Fe; but when I interviewed for the job, I thought her decision was an omen.

"Don't think of it like that," Thomas said after I was stupid enough to tell him—a man I'd just met—I had a weird feeling about the position.

"Then how should I think about it?"

"As your opportunity," Thomas said. "You had a show in New Orleans, right?"

"Nashville."

"Even better."

"You think so?" I swished my fingertips through the water of the fountain and wondered if this blue-eyed art historian, who specialized in the Pre-Raphaelites and casually mentioned my resemblance to Elizabeth Siddal, might know something that I needed to hear.

"Absolutely. The art department will be doing a search, and you've just come off a high," Thomas said, with a lopsided smile I found endearing. Then. "Besides, Milton Samuels is talking you up to the dean."

I actually blushed; I was that eager to gulp down Thomas's optimism. In fact, optimism may have been the sexiest thing about Thomas, blonde, hairless men having never been my type. And Thomas, a non-practicing Episcopalian from Pittsburgh who smelled like the Johnson's Baby Powder he probably still uses so generously (something he'll have in common with his newborn), favored movies starring George Clooney and Julia Roberts. And most nights he read thrillers. Not that he didn't know his field. He wrote a pretty good book about Dante Gabriel Rossetti, the member of the Pre-Raphaelite Brotherhood who finally married Elizabeth Siddal. Fool that I was, I took that as a sign when I should have tuned into the fact that Rossetti put the marriage off for more than eight years, and had many, many lovers in between.

Thomas kept saying he was sure I'd get the tenure-line job until one day, abruptly, he stopped. He knew the department had offered the position to a young MFA out of RISD, but he let the Valkyrie's junior colleague tell me the news. The Valkyrie, who favored a violet-black lipstick that year, didn't meet my eye again until the semester ended, and I cleared out my office. By then, I'd had fifteen years of packing and unpacking my boxes and arranging my few pieces of furniture in rent houses in Fresno, Nashville, and even Lowell, Massachusetts—not to mention a forgettable series of college towns in the Midwest.

What if I'd chosen Sebastian the night of that party instead of Thomas? *Dead-in-the-water, Renata.* I reconsider Sebastian's sienna eyes—how those green flecks glinted like emeralds while we made love. Would I be a fool to trust him now? Too many men, especially those fluent in the romance languages, have charmed me out of my underwear, only to find some reason to exit, stage left, just as I've begun to believe in a future.

There was the Venezuelan in London who told me that I was his white Russian, his saint, as if that wasn't sign enough that I should run. I may not have known a thing about Lizzie Siddal back then and her sittings for countless Madonnas and temptress virgins, but I knew plenty about the practice of putting a woman on a pedestal, so as to not see her at all; a woman who came to exist only as a figment of the man's own imagination and need. And sure enough, the Venezuelan, Mariano of the voluptuous lips, soon transferred the position of "sainthood" to one of my friends. A gamine who lived on scones and tea, worked for Ralph Lauren, and was distantly related to the Rothchilds. Their alliance certainly didn't hurt Mariano's career—an edgy gallery picked him up, and soon he was featured in *ARTNews*.

And after Mariano came two Italians, though the significant one, the one who reconfigured the kaleidoscope, was Giovanni. More than fifteen years ago, I rode around on the back of Giovanni's Vespa, my arms wrapped around his trim hips, all during those months in Florence. Giovanni bought me a gauzy white dress and insisted that I wear it out with him with nothing underneath And I did. Within three weeks of our first meeting, at the Uffizi no less where we stood talking beneath a Botticelli with an intimacy that, to me, felt like destiny—*yes, Renata, you were beyond gullible*—I moved into his dank apartment, a bona fide garret on the sixth floor of a seventeenth century building. Nights I could hear the rats in the walls. Giovanni said they were mice not rats, but I saw the size of those droppings. They littered our floodlit workspace when we woke in the mornings.

I slip out of Sebastian's bed, walk over to the window. The fountain's running, and the smell of sage lingers in the air. I never told anyone, not even Diana, my closest friend at the time, about the pregnancy. I couldn't bear to let anyone else experience Giovanni's reaction. I sure as hell didn't want to re-experience it. But what if I'd had the baby on my own?

It's a question I've asked myself before. Not that I've forgotten what Sebastian said earlier about the futility of regret. But isn't there a sort of comfort in knowing that I could have had a child, that my body could have made a human being? Or is it really just torment, and in this way not so different from, dare I admit it, yes, from Lizzie Siddal's grief over her own stillborn daughter? It was that loss, far more than the unfaithfulness of Rossetti, that I believe pushed her over the edge.

"Renata."

Even with my eyes closed, I can picture Sebastian there behind me, his hair disheveled, and his face without the glasses almost boyish in this forgiving light. And I know that if I don't say something right now, if I don't find some reason to tell him that this just isn't going to work, that tonight was a mistake, a beautiful mistake and something that shouldn't get in the way of our friendship, I will stay here, not just tonight but for many nights. And wouldn't that just fuck everything up, the uncomplicated life I'd begun to envision for myself in Minnesota?

The air the afternoon I left the clinic in Florence was pristine, and I tried to tell myself that the blue sky, the moldering but still beautiful buildings, and the smells of espresso and gasoline meant that I was going to be all right. Truth is, I wasn't all right for three or four years at least. There was the warm feel of the blood in the cotton wadding my underpants, and the salt taste of my tears. I was nearing thirty-five, my biological clock was well into the final quarter, and I was stupid enough to let myself believe that a forty-three-year-old Italian who lived in a dirty garret would want a baby. I was that duped by his passion for Titian and especially by the way his full-lipped mouth cooed "bella" and "cara mia" and all sorts of enticing but ultimately meaningless names. I'd worn that white slip of a dress to many, many parties and dinners, not letting myself consider that the other women dressed like me weren't painters or photographers or critics. They were models, waitresses, girls. No wonder Thomas brought up Elizabeth Siddal in relation to me— *stop it,* a voice inside me bleats.

Sebastian's arms encircle my waist, he nestles his chin against my neck and shoulder, and I breathe in his scent—tobacco, the musk of aftershave, and sweat—and grief stirs deep inside me. When I left Giovanni, I left the white dress balled up in the closet beside the bloody underpants, and I never told a soul about that parting gesture, not in all these years.

Thankfully Sebastian doesn't say a word, and the sunlight—it won't be dark here before ten this close to the solstice—makes patterns on the walls and ceiling. If I'd had the baby, he—or she—would be nearly fifteen, just a year younger than Thomas's daughter. And if I'd carried that pregnancy to term, what would my life be like now? Would I have hung on at that girls' school in Lowell if only for the health care and the top-notch education? Would I have even come to the desolate high plains of West Texas?

"Renata, my dear," he says. "You're so quiet."

I turn to him, realize how much I prefer "dear" over "darling." The moment almost feels like the climax of a novel or one of those romantic period films that I'm embarrassed to say I'm a sucker for. *Helena Bonham Carter and Polly Walker trump Julia Roberts and Gwyneth Paltrow (never mind the token Emma) any day.* As I told Alicia after Thomas dumped me and I decided to leave West Texas for good, "There are no do-overs in this life. If there's one thing I've learned, it's that." Alicia just looked back at me for a long time when I said that, and I sensed she understood, at least a little, of the grief I felt over losing her.

"Please," Sebastian says. "Tell me."

And soon I hear myself telling him about the solid row of oak trees at my childhood home and all the dinners that my father, my sister, and I ate off the Spode china in the dining room in the years after my mother died. I tell him about the beef bourguignon and the other complicated dishes my father learned how to cook by studying my mother's copy of Julia Child. Mostly, though, I tell him that my father said he loved me—"a handful of times, but he never told me that he was proud of me."

"He must have been proud," Sebastian says, tracing my collarbone with his fingertips. "He must be proud."

I shake my head. "No."

Sebastian doesn't press me, just strokes my shoulder. It's July now, so if Thomas's bride is a good four months along—and she's at least that—the baby will be born before Christmas. She's tenured, so she'll take maternity leave, and she and Thomas will play house with their child. *Why are you doing this to yourself, Renata?*

It takes me a few moments to realize it's Sebastian who's speaking. He kisses my forehead, an almost chaste kiss, and runs a finger down my cheek. I'm afraid—or maybe relieved—that he can see my thoughts, but then I get it: he's talking about my father, not Thomas.

His hand cradles my cheek. "You know," he says, "not since I first came to the States, to New York, have I lived in a place where it really snows."

"I didn't know you lived in New York."

"Stonybrook. I'd never seen such snow. At Goodwill, I bought an old army coat and my mother knit me two alpaca sweaters. They arrived in time for my first American Christmas." He strokes my collar bones, my neck. "I'm about four years away from retirement. I imagine I won't be too decrepit by then to shovel snow, plow a driveway, especially if I keep taking my vitamins and playing tennis."

His body feels warm, substantial, and despite all the wine I drank, my smeared makeup, the problems with my father, and the crappy bungalow in which I've spent the last twenty months—or perhaps because of all of these—with Sebastian I feel, well, happy.

"Stay," he whispers into my hair, and I lean into him, breathe in his scent. "Stay with me."

More than thirty years ago, one of my first art teachers, a white-haired woman with skin like crepe, said, "There are no mistakes in painting, only possibilities to look at your work from a new angle."

With Sebastian's voice in my ear, I close my eyes, imagine him as he was more than thirty years ago, dressed in that coat from Goodwill and one of his mother's hand-knit sweaters, the stitches effortlessly precise in the way that comes with a lifetime of practice.

He would have been slighter than he is now, though his habit of carrying a worn leather satchel weighted with art books and sketch pads would already have been in place.

I rarely think about it anymore, the fact that my mother used to knit, though I remember her sitting beside the bedroom window with an ever-dwindling skein of pale blue yarn and an ever-growing scarf. Not yet thirty-five, she was already sick. Not that I knew it yet; no, I just wondered why she was spending so much time on a scarf when the autumn weather outside was so fine. What a terrible thing, I realized much, much later, for a woman to have to come to terms with leaving behind her two small daughters. To know that she will not be present for their growing up. And all the joy and suffering and in-betweens.

At least, I tell myself, *that will never be a part of my story.*

"Renata," he says, his arms as warm and soft as that pale blue scarf I wore all through that winter and many more winters after that, long after my mother died. "Where are you? You seem far away."

I try to remember what alpaca feels like, imagine it must be soft as the llamas who source it, and soon I'm reaching up, my hand luminous and pale in the end-of-day light, yet nothing like the sickly pallor of Millais's *Ophelia*. I touch Sebastian's cheek, now rough with evening stubble. "No," I reply, aware of the ripe, late sun on my skin. "I'm right here," I tell him. "Right here."

SOLSTICE IN THE JARDIN DU LUXEMBOURG

A wood pigeon alights on the forehead of a stone nymph and lingers there, cocking his head as if in consideration of some momentous thought; or perhaps just to watch a nimble spider cast an iridescent web from the tip of the nymph's ear to her shoulder. The spider's glossy black eye is part of her camouflage, but the pigeon's jet eye is ringed with an orange as vibrant as a gypsy's sash, and so compels attention. The bird's song is a muffled, almost humming *bru-u-oo*, followed by a series of low hoots. Spreading his wings, the pigeon, who years ago escaped a bamboo cage at the Paris bird market and found his way here, lifts into flight.

About this same time, just after four o'clock on the longest day of the year, Amelie Garnier steps through the high wrought iron gate that leads to the garden, the noise of heat-soaked concrete almost immediately giving way to the emerald cool of lawn and to the water lily shadows of the chestnut trees. And everywhere she looks, glowing beds of peonies, clematis, petunias; even lacy, delicate verbena, her favorite flower.

For almost a week now, the city has been steeped in sun and high temperatures, transforming the always-refreshing garden into a refuge. Today, almost every chair is occupied by someone reading the newspaper or a frayed paperback or simply dreaming. Why, within this corner of the garden alone, nearly a dozen well-dressed mothers sit beside babies drowsing in canvas-hooded carriages or more modern strollers.

Just before she reaches the sunny courtyard with its boat pond, Amelie notices a woman unlike the exquisitely dressed Parisians in their pleated skirts, summer blouses and pearls, and the tourists wearing creased shorts and cotton tops, their shoulders rounded beneath the weight of cameras and rucksacks and fatigue.

This woman wears a navy baseball cap paired with a paint-flecked white oxford and jeans so faded the blue is nearly gone. She has set up an easel and balances a tray of watercolors on her lap. Although there is always someone painting or sketching in this garden with its endless play of light and subject matter, something about this woman—perhaps it is the way she frowns and bites her lower lip, as if in deep concentration, or perhaps it is the arabesque lightness of the long-fingered right hand holding the brush—

compels Amelie, who draws closer, only to realize the paper is still pure white. The woman looks up, and their eyes meet.

"Commencement." The woman's voice betrays a foreign accent. "C'est toujours difficile."

Amelie smiles and contemplates a reply, but the woman is already turning back to her paper, her face once more assuming that curious focus. Besides, Amelie has a purpose in the garden today. She has come to talk to her mother.

"Keeper of the Teahouse toilettes," Amelie sometimes says, no longer ashamed of her mother's job so much as resistant to it. For forty cents, any man or woman can step into the meticulously cared for toilette decorated with yellowing prints by Renoir and Monet, and bouquets of the scarlet or pale pink roses her mother always places beside the sinks. In a public place hundreds of adults and children visit on a typical day in summer, Odette Garnier's toilette is quite possibly the most necessary of all the garden's services, especially when one compares it to the chain-smoking Sylvie Maulpoix's slatternly stalls on the other side of the tennis courts. Still, Amelie harbors the wish that her mother could at least have cultivated a slightly more adventurous position—why not a dancer in Pigalle or Montmartre, or a waitress in one of the grittier bars? Even a baker's assistant or a saleswoman at Bon Marché would have been preferable to the interminable days Odette Garnier spends behind a neat wooden table at the toilette's entrance, counting out change as she greets every man and woman with "Bonjour," sending them on their way with a smiling "Merci" followed by "Bonne journee."

Accompanied by her eight and six-year-old charges, Paul and Marie Claire, Coquelicot is just leaving the toilettes when Amelie draws near its stairwell directly behind the teahouse takeout stand. Marie Claire stops to stare, obviously captivated by her vivid clothes and hair.

But it is her brother Paul who singles Amelie out. "Why is that lady's hair pink?" he asks, speaking with the meticulous attentiveness with which he notices everything, from his mother's irritated sighs at dinner to the grief that has been tugging at the corners of old Madame Boucher's mouth since her bulldog Maurice died in April.

Coquelicot's cheeks redden, but Amelie just laughs and says, "Because I wash my hair with geranium petals every night."

"You're not to pick the flowers in the garden," is Paul's only reply.

Again she laughs, and Coquelicot, holding the children's hands a bit more tightly, hurries them away, asking herself if such stories are harmful or simply fanciful; for she knows that Paul will eventually extract the truth from the woman's words while Marie Claire, in the hopes of adopting some fanciful look all her own (for she is always sticking stray flowers in her jumper pockets, and likes to color in her fingernails with magic markers), will most likely beg Coquelicot to wash her hair with the harlequin-striped petunias that fill the window boxes outside the family's apartment.

But Paul does not pursue the subject, nor does Marie Claire, because just then an older boy of ten or maybe eleven, a boy burdened by an immense toy boat in his arms, walks past. Unlike the simple white and black boats available for an hour's rental, this one has been painted an exuberant cerulean blue, and its crisp sails are alternately yellow and red. "Magnificent," Paul pronounces, in that moment sounding exactly like his father.

Marie Claire jams her thumb into her mouth and looks longingly at the boy with the bright boat. "How about a nice glacé?" Coquelicot says, already steering them towards one of the ice cream vendors before they can begin begging her to rent a boat; for despite the shallowness of the boat pond, Coquelicot, who never learned to swim, is terrified of any body of water larger than a bathtub.

"Ice cream!" Their voices turn giddy, and soon they are on tiptoe in front of the vendor's cart, absorbed in the choosing of flavors and colors—pistachio for Paul, vanilla topped with a dollop of cassis for Marie Claire.

Ten years ago, thirty-one-year-old Coquelicot did not see herself as a nanny to two privileged children who live a ten-minute taxi ride from the Jardin du Luxembourg in one of the elegant, stone apartments that share space with embassies and other government buildings on the Rue Grenelle. No, ten years ago, Coquelicot believed she would find an apprentice position at one of the fine old bakeries in the city where egg-glazed bouquets of warm, buttery brioche and trays of crispy baguettes steam the glass, and row upon row of macaroons, meringues, petit fours, flan, and half a dozen varieties of tart fill the shelves.

But then her mother's heart stopped beating while she sat beside a stranger on the metro. Six months later her father remarried, and the support Coquelicot counted on vanished. No longer was it possible for her to consider living at home while earning an apprentice's salary, not once her stepmother and her stepmother's son, Jin, laid claim to the apartment. As for her father, it was as if he now forsook all ties to Coquelicot's mother, the woman he'd married nearly three decades earlier when they were both students in Bejing.

On those rare occasions when Coquelicot does return home, she finds no sign that her mother has even been there. Her mother's lace curtains have been taken down, and the silk pillows she embroidered with peonies and dragons and sun-colored carp have disappeared. Even the kitchen garden of herbs and Chinese vegetables her mother cultivated on the terrace has been replaced by her father's second wife's stunted roses and cramped pots of scentless jade.

Although a nanny's salary is not ample, it comes with room and board. Coquelicot's first employer had been difficult, but the DuPlessis family, with whom she's been since just after Marie Claire's birth, is generous and appreciative of her, especially Olivier DuPlessis, who pays Coquelicot extra to cook bouillabaisse or one of her delicate soufflés for dinner a few times a week, clearly understanding what satisfaction she finds in the kitchen. 'No,' she often tells herself. 'I can't complain.'

Still, Coquelicot feels a little stab of loss whenever she passes one of the grand old bakeries in Saint Germain or along the Rue du Bac; for ever since Coquelicot and her mother joined her father in Paris when she was a child of about Paul's age, Coquelicot believed she would have a patisserie of her own one day, a patisserie she would keep filled with boxes of the wild poppies she and her mother first glimpsed from a train window en route to Paris.

As she and the children make their way towards the carousel in the center of the park, they pass a woman whose narrow face and long stem of throat remind Coquelicot of a woman in a painting by Modigliani in one of the DuPlessis's art books. The painting always makes Coquelicot think of rain in January, and the artist's style inevitably brings to mind the madonnas who bow their heads in any one of Paris's soot-stained churches. So Coquelicot avoids this artist's pictures, preferring instead the fairy tale magic of Chagall, whose flying roosters and rose-decked goats bring to mind the stories her mother told her when she was a child.

"Nounou," Marie Claire whispers, tugging at the dotted swiss blouse the child's mother gave Coquelicot from a pile of fashionable cast-offs. "That lady's *crying*." Her voice rises with this last word, and Coquelicot fears the other woman has heard. "Why is she crying, Nounou?"

"Because something has made her very sad," Coquelicot says quietly.

"What a beautiful child," Susan catches herself thinking, captivated by the way Marie Claire's honey curls escape from her neat plaits. Immediately, Susan finds a picture of her own daughter at this age. Until Madeline turned seven and allowed Susan to braid her hair, the child's thick red locks were even more unruly than this girl's. At night, Susan used to rub olive oil into her hands, then run her fingers through Madeline's hair, gently teasing out the tangles before she turned to comb or brush. Until a few months ago, when Madeline awoke screaming that she couldn't see, her vivacious hair seemed a sign of her relentless good health and capacity for mischief.

"Mon esprit follet," Pierre often called their daughter, always remarking on the way Madeline's cheeks glowed like fresh strawberries, and wondering if she would prove to be as athletic as her mother, whose American love of sport—Susan continued to play a fiercely competitive game of tennis well into the eighth month of her pregnancy—caused Pierre's own mother to gather her eyebrows and frown throughout their first two years of marriage.

Watching the Asian woman's black hair fan across her face as she stoops to wipe ice cream from the girl's chin, then gives her a worn rabbit to hold, Susan feels thankful that she and Pierre never left Madeline with a nanny. Not that nannies like this one don't provide expert and often loving care (Susan notices how fervently the little girl clings to the nanny's hand). It's just that the parents who turn their children over to other people during the very early years miss so much. And how can anyone afford to miss out on a bedtime story or a mushroom hunt or a few hours playing

115

beneath the plane trees when no one knows what the future has in store?

Until Madeline began primary school two years ago, Susan arranged her classes at the English Institute around Pierre's work schedule and his mother's free Monday and Friday afternoons. Despite the tensions between the two women, Susan's mother-in-law remained devoted to Madeline, her only grandchild; and seemed to secretly revel in the tricks the little girl played on the people in their building.

"Look out," a voice cries, just in time to prevent Susan from tumbling into a watercolorist beneath a canopy of chestnut trees.

"Oh my god, I'm terribly sorry," Susan says, knocking over the watercolorist's pitcher of water and reverting back to English.

"It's alright," the other woman says, also in English. "No harm done."

Susan registers the New York Yankees insignia on the cap and the wide-planed features of the other woman's face. "You're American."

"Yes." She smiles.

"Me too," Susan hears herself say. "Where are you from?"

"Chicago, and you?"

"New Jersey, though I've lived in Paris for years now."

The other woman holds out a hand. "Katherine Pushkin— Kate."

"Susan Sunier." Susan's eyes flicker over the paper, and she feels an unexpected flutter of happiness at the way the garden's chestnut trees have been loosely rendered in cool greens and browns with hints of amber and lemon-yellow sunlight. She admires the way the fuzzy-edged stone urns filled with pink geraniums cast shadows along the garden's walls. Just to the left of the geranium border, there is the water-light silhouette of a child washed through with sapphire. This image makes Susan's heart beat fast. "Will you let me replace your water?" she asks, meeting the other woman's gaze.

"No need." Kate smiles. "I was ready for a break anyway. Care to join me for a coffee?"

Susan doesn't answer right away. She always comes to the Jardin du Luxembourg alone from the hospital. Almost every day, she buys a falafel sandwich at the Lebanese market across the street, and eats it so quickly that it sears her tongue. She never buys a drink at the market, choosing instead to dwell within her thirst during the first part of the mile-long walk along the wide Rue de Sèvres, with its traffic and its petunia-filled window boxes. Only when Susan is halfway to the garden does she buy a half liter of Vichy water. This, too, Susan swallows quickly, aware of the way her thirst makes her gasp. These days, the walking feels absolutely necessary, the rhythmic action of putting one foot in front of the other keeping her focused on the sounds and what she sees around her.

"Well?" Kate repeats the question.

"I'm sorry, I can't." The idea of sitting down and making chit-chat with a stranger, even with one who has, with water and color, captured something so essential in this garden, seems unbearable beside the image of Madeline's small white moon of a face beneath the blankets.

"Are you alright?" Kate reaches for Susan's hands, which are shaking.

"My daughter's not well," Susan says, unable to hold back the words. "I've just come from the hospital. I'm—I'm not thinking clearly."

Kate's eyes are a pale green flecked with gold, the corners creased with laugh lines deeper than Susan's own. "Sometimes a stranger can be the best sort of listener," Kate says, so gently the words are not invasive. "If you need to talk."

Again, Susan finds herself drawn to the light-filled vision before her.

"Come on," Kate says. "Just a cup of coffee."

The stairwell leading to the toilettes is a bit steep, and as Amelie makes her descent, she nearly loses her balance, and pictures herself falling. What would have happened then? She does not pursue the thought, promising herself instead that she will wear flat-heeled shoes from now on.

Her mother's jet eyes glitter when Amelie enters the toilettes, and then she frowns, her fine-boned face taking on that familiar, imperious look. When Amelie looks at her slim mother, who is still beautiful despite the way the difficult years have imprinted themselves on her features, she can find no trace of the butcher who brought her up. No, in her mother's face, Amelie

117

believes she can see the mark of the penniless Italian artist—now hailed as a genius—who was Odette Garnier's real father.

"What have you done to your hair?" her mother asks, instantly drawing the attention of the half a dozen other women and a very small girl who shifts her weight from one foot to the other, obviously anxious for an open toilette.

"Do you like it, Maman?" Amelie asks, touching her asymmetrical pink bob and trying to keep her voice neutral, for she knows there is only one way for her mother to respond.

"Only in the boutiques could you get away with hair like that," Odette says, even though they both know the metros are filled with young women with wildly colored hair. Even among the pollarded rows of chestnut trees and the historical queens and saints of the Jardin du Luxembourg, there is inevitably someone with burgundy hair, sometimes even electric blue.

"Maman," Amelie says, lowering her voice. "I need to talk to you. Can you take a break soon?"

Odette glances at her watch. "Not for twenty minutes. What's happened?"

"I can wait that long," is all Amelie says. "I'll find a seat not far from Saint Genevieve."

Odette nods, and for the first time she actually smiles, for Amelie has been fascinated by Paris's female patron saint ever since she heard the story of this woman of unshakeable faith and courage who saved the city not once but twice: first when Genevieve and her followers found grain for the starving citizens during a siege by the Franks; and again later when she rescued them from Attila and his invading Huns by asking them to pray. Once Amelie's primary school teacher told the class where Genevieve was buried, Amelie began begging Odette to take her to visit the saint's remains, which are kept in a marble tomb within the light-filled walls of St. Etienne sur le Mont, a short walk from the garden. To this day, Amelie always brings a bouquet of peonies or tea roses to the church on the saint's day. ("And you say you are not a creature of tradition," Odette always says.)

"Twenty minutes, okay?" Amelie says, for no matter how tolerant her boss at Sonia Rykiel Ready-to-Wear may be, she has to get back in time for the evening rush. Today, the solstice sale is on, and after seven years on the floor, she has at last been made assistant manager.

118

"It's Marcel, isn't it?" Odette asks, the seam in the center of her forehead deepening.

Aware that the toilette's patrons are listening, Amelie holds her voice to a murmur. "Yes."

Outside, Amelie walks over to the teahouse and orders a demitasse of espresso with a side of frothed milk. She has a croissant in her purse, and although she is still nauseated despite having reached the end of the first trimester when morning sickness is in theory supposed to end, she knows she has to eat.

Amelie expected only disapproval from her mother when she announced her pregnancy a few weeks earlier. Instead, Odette took her daughter's hands between her own, and wept, whether with joy or with sorrow Amelie could not say, and somehow did not dare to ask. Since then, Amelie has become more curious about that shadier chapter in her mother's history: her alliance with a gypsy guitarist known only as Ruse, the father of Amelie's half brother, Marcel. Despite Odette's marriage to Amelie's father when Marcel was still a toddler, despite her weekly attendance at Mass and her faithful keeping of the privileged Jardin du Luxembourg's toilettes, there was that bird of paradise span of months when Odette lived in a riverboat on the Seine with the auburn-haired, eight-fingered Ruse, who disappeared, leaving behind no clues as to how to find him, when his son was three months old.

"Marcel never knew his father," Odette used to tell friends and neighbors, as if this single statement—and the unspoken history it hinted at—were explanation and justification enough for Marcel's troubles and for his criminal record.

This time, however, it is worse than before. This time, when Marcel was allowed his single phone call from the police station, he phoned Amelie at Sonia Rykiel to confess that not only had he been arrested near Notre Dame for dealing cocaine, but he had been diagnosed with AIDS.

With his long, dark fringe of lashes and his absent father's sharply angled, North African features (he never inherited his father's bi-colored eyes: one gold, the other ice blue), Marcel has always been far too beautiful for his own good. Not only the girls, but some of the men in the clubs Marcel began hanging out in during his teens, took an almost obsessive interest in his feline body shimmering with sweat on the dance floor. And then there was that night, more than twelve years ago now, when Marcel came home smelling of musk and cigarettes, and climbed into bed beside Amelie, and told her how much he had been paid to crouch at the edge of the bed and let his boss fuck him from behind. "Maman mustn't know"—these were the words that formed unbidden on Amelie's tongue.

Amelie considers the irony of her reaction now as she sips her demitasse of taboo coffee and strokes her growing mound of belly, for in the years that followed it has always been Amelie who has broken the news of Marcel's affairs, arrests, and illnesses to their mother. Maybe if Marcel could have seen what his actions did to Odette, he could have changed. *Reformed*—that was Amelie's father's word. But Amelie knows that change would have had to come long before Marcel developed an appetite for cocaine, and now heroin. And long ago, Marcel was a cocky, gorgeous boy who believed his looks and his charm would take him as far as he wanted to go. By the time he discovered the necessity of education, money, and family connection, he was already getting stoned in the Latin Quarter and sleeping with men who could pay, and the occasional woman.

Absorbed in these thoughts, Amelie becomes aware of the nausea flushing through her. Although the pregnancy book says this symptom is a product of her elevated metabolism, she's sure that anxious thinking makes it worse. If she doesn't stop soon, she will feel faint and vomit-y and need to lie down on one of the benches, inevitably drawing the attention of one of the gendarmes who, no longer recognizing her as Odette Garnier's little girl, will suspect drugs. *Breathe*, she tells herself, counting both her inhalations and her exhalations. *Breathe*.

Trying to move her thoughts away from Marcel and her mother, Amelie's gaze flickers over the middle-aged lovers with their tongues in each other's mouths. Although the woman is dressed conservatively in navy blue skirt and white blouse, her companion wears mint green and white seersucker trousers, and there is a diamond stud in his left ear. *Get a room*, she thinks, then turns toward a matron in beautiful purple pumps, definitely Italian given the craftsmanship. While eating her way through a gold foil box of chocolates, the woman is reading a dog-eared novel depicting a busty heroine in futuristic clothes on the cover. And not far from the woman, an African man with a tangle of braids strums a guitar. Beside him, a cinnamon-colored poodle sleeps within a hat, occasionally raising its head to yip at the man, as if critiquing his music.

Soon, the watercolorist Amelie remembers from earlier approaches with another woman. They seem unlikely companions, for unlike the artist in her paint-stained shirt and faded jeans, her companion wears a silk blouse of seashell pink, pearls, and a taupe linen skirt with matching shoes. The two women come closer, and Amelie hears them speaking English. Are they old friends? Or did they just meet in the garden?

Even after she agreed, Susan felt unsure about joining Kate for a cup of coffee. But once they sit down at one of the wrought iron tables close to the boat pond—the voices of the children reaching out to Susan even from afar—she feels the tightness in her neck and shoulders give way.

Kate's voice and her gold-flecked green eyes seem both comforting and familiar, and soon Susan is speaking more freely with her than she has with almost anyone else, at least for a long time, even longer than Madeline has been ill. "My husband's family is very formal, very self-contained. Even now they cannot really talk about Madeline's prognosis, preferring instead to discuss orchids and art openings with such seriousness that I feel I'm meant to find a hidden meaning. Either that, or I'm going insane."

Susan's hand quivers as she sets her coffee cup down in its saucer, and a woman seated nearby, a woman with in-your-face-electric-pink hair zeroes in on the movement. Susan frowns at her, eager to will her away.

"What's wrong with your little girl?" Kate asks.

"A brain tumor," Susan says. "At first the doctors believed they could stop its growth, but that hasn't happened. And surgery," she says, as if anticipating Kate's next question, "just isn't a possibility."

"Is Madeline your only child?" Kate asks.

"Yes." Instantly, Susan is reminded of the second pregnancy, the one she'd terminated during a particularly rough period with Pierre. When the doctors gave her Madeline's diagnosis, she struggled against the conviction that she was being punished. She, the daughter of biochemist who'd been raised to mistrust all forms of superstition, now fights the belief that the gods are visiting judgment on her.

121

The two women sit, hands cupped around the cooling coffee, the voices of lovers, friends, parents, and children surrounding them. The matron returns her novel to her purse, slips the last truffle into her mouth, and gets up to leave. The man with skin like toffee secures his mane of braids with a red ribbon, then stretches out along a bench, resting his guitar on his belly. The poodle climbs out of the hat and nestles itself within the crook of his arm. The woman with the bright pink hair suddenly stands, sways for a moment, then waves to a woman who has just emerged from the toilettes, a woman Susan knows she has seen before. But of course, she runs the toilettes.

Three glove-gray pigeons with white necks now gather at their feet. Someone has dropped a sandwich there, and the birds begin pulling at the bread, breaking it off in big chunks, and struggling to fit the pieces into their beaks, with what looks like great effort. "Do you know what they're called?" Kate asks, motioning to the birds.

"*Pigeon ramier*—wood pigeon," Susan says. "I've seen them along the cliffs in Brittany. They're so wild there, so aloof. Here, it's almost impossible to believe they're sea birds. Still, they're lovely."

"Remarkable thing about animals," Kate says, her attention turning from the bird to the toffee-skinned man who has picked up his guitar once more and begun to play. "The way they manage to adapt to their environment."

Susan tenses, gripped by the image of Madeline stepping out of church on Easter Sunday and hurrying after these same birds, her feet clad in black patent leather, her white socks slipping down around her ankles. How lucky Susan had felt that day, how blessed, and how many promises and plans for her daughter's future danced through her as the Easter frock billowed up around Madeline.

"What are you doing here?" Susan now asks, her voice coming out clipped, as the ebullient Madeline in the joyful frock is replaced by the still child in the hospital bed. "Are you a tourist? Or are you here to work?"

Startled, Kate replies, "Neither really."

"Then why are you here?"

"I came to Paris to think. I teach art history at a private college in the States. I've had a proposal of marriage." Kate speaks these words softly. "When the semester ended, I bought a cheap-enough ticket to France. I lived here for a year when I was younger. I made some important decisions then, so it made sense to come back now."

"A proposal of marriage," Susan repeats the phrase, surprised by its formality. "Does that mean you haven't said 'yes'?"

"Oscar and I are good friends," Kate says. "But we aren't really in love."

"Then why marry?" Susan asks, reminded of Pierre's slope-shouldered figure in the hospital chair.

"My mother had a stroke last year. I realized, then, that I wanted—that I needed—to have a child. I've known Oscar for years. We always joked that if we hadn't met anyone by the time we were thirty-five, we'd marry. Next month I'll be thirty-nine."

"Ah," Susan says, oddly certain this Oscar must share Kate's desire for a child. Middle-aged men, Susan has found, make particularly dedicated fathers. Forty-five-year-old Pierre, who used to travel to Belgium, Austria, and even Turkey and Morocco, easily surrendered his wanderlust with Madeline's arrival, something that disappointed the twelve-years-younger Susan who'd always wanted to see more of the world.

"It's possible to have a child on one's own," Susan says. "But it's much easier to share the experience. People always talk about the demands of infants and toddlers, all those sleepless nights, the hours of nursing; but in my experience the real work begins when they're older. Suddenly everything prompts a question." She laughs, giddy, nervous. "It's like looking through a kaleidoscope. Living takes on a glow you remember from your own childhood. But you're tired too," Susan adds, "especially if you're older. And there's so much you can't control."

Kate is on the verge of taking Susan's hands again, but something about Susan—the taut line of her spine, perhaps, or the edges of her mouth—holds Kate back. "I couldn't do it on my own," she says. "I'm too selfish, too self-absorbed."

"You don't strike me that way."

Kate shrugs, smiles. "We just met."

Having talked to her favorite friends on the carousel—the white pony with a chipped golden tail, and the vividly-painted rooster who always waits for her and is disappointed when she doesn't ride him while trying to grab the carousel operator's brass ring—Marie Claire wants to go home. But Paul is climbing on the jungle gym—his neat blue shirt riding up over his belly in a way that would annoy their mother—and he will continue to play there until Coquelicot checks her watch again, then tells him it's time to leave.

Marie Claire finds her nanny's face pretty, though it is very different from all the other faces she knows. All the people in Marie Claire's family have blue or pale green eyes, but Coquelicot's are almost black. Sometimes, Marie Claire believes Coquelicot's eyes are dark because they are like the poppies for which she was named. Believing this, Marie Claire sometimes looks at the flowers and almost expects a person to climb out, or perhaps a human eye will emerge where there is now only stamen. She once asked her father about the reason for Coquelicot's slanted black eyes, her wide-planed face, and ink-dark hair, and he took her over to the globe in his study. Pointing out a bumpy country far from France, he said, "China. This is where Coquelicot was born. In China, the people look like her." At first, Marie Claire had a difficult time understanding what he meant, but when she began searching for and finding people whose eyes and noses and hair resembled her nanny's, she thought *China*, and pretty soon she could picture all of them climbing into bright boats (like the one with the bold red and yellow sails the older boy was carrying, she realizes now) and making the long journey to France.

"One day I will go to China," Marie Claire told her father, "and people will wonder about me there." Her father told her that this was a good idea. He also told her to be sure to pack enough warm clothes. "And *Lapin*," she reminded him. But when she brought up the poppies, he seemed puzzled by her need to find a flower that somehow contained her story. And Marie Claire could not possibly explain a connection that felt very real to her—the way the crescent moon birthmark on her forehead feels real, or their bristly-coated terrier Gericho's sharp bark. So she just said, "Oh Papa, you silly," words that left her feeling unsatisfied.

With Marie Claire seated beside her, Coquelicot watches Paul scramble up the rope jungle gym, and hopes she will not have to remind him to stop when he reaches the sixth rung.

"Nounou," Marie Claire says, fitting her small body against Coquelicot's. "Is it almost time to go home? I miss my room. I want to lie down."

"Yes," Coquelicot says, wrapping her arm around Marie Claire's shoulder. "But for now, why don't you pretend I am your bed. Imagine my arm as your pillow."

"Okay," Marie Claire says, squeezing her eyes closed and giggling.

It is moments like this one when Coquelicot most enjoys being a nanny. Compared to so many of the other nannies who come to the garden with demanding or simply overindulged children, she knows she is lucky to have Marie Claire and Paul, who are clearly grateful and happy in her care, almost always turning to her with their cuts and bruises, and never forgetting to include her in their discovery of a butterfly or a violet growing in the sidewalk's crack.

True, their father adores them, but he works long days in the family's wine export business. As for their mother, Juliet DuPlessis routinely disappears for long shopping excursions with her friends on her days off from the publishing house and often finds reasons—a novel she wants to read, a prospective client she needs to meet for lunch, a hair appointment—why she cannot take them to the garden or to the petting zoo at the Jardin des Plantes. This is why both children always insist that Coquelicot help tuck them in at night; and why Marie Claire now wraps her ice cream-sticky hands around Coquelicot's waist, and surrenders her weight.

"Don't be silly," Agnes, one of the other nannies, said when Coquelicot told her that Marie Claire and Paul loved her as if she were their mother. "They're dependent on you, but they know who their mother is." Agnes gestured to the group of young mothers who always, Coquelicot noticed after that, kept a safe distance away from the other nannies. "And if they don't know the difference now," Agnes added, "they will in a very few years."

Having been a nanny for fifteen years, Agnes Corot claimed a good deal of authority with the other nannies. Still, Coquelicot never quite believed Agnes's words. And although she never said as much, she looked to her own childhood for the internal proof she required. For it was with her own mother that Coquelicot had done the sort of simple but undeniable things that Marie Claire does with her now. She still remembers the first months in Paris when she would sit beside her mother in the cool summer mornings, her mother's skin pressed against her own. Holding her hand to her mother's heart, Coquelicot listened to the steady rhythm and believed the beating of her heart and that of her mother's were one and the same. *Didn't Marie Claire do much the same thing? Didn't she often ask to listen to Coquelicot's heartbeat?*

"Paul, don't climb any higher," she calls out, hoping Marie Claire, who is now sleeping against her, will not wake.

Although Olivier and Juliet DuPlessis seem to take it as a given or at least as a possibility "when you are so good with children," Coquelicot doubts that she will have children of her own one day. She is over thirty and hasn't had a serious boyfriend in several years. Where would she find a man who would want to marry her? Seven days a week, she lives in the small bedroom sandwiched between the children's rooms in the DuPlessis apartment. Everyone in the building is French and Caucasian with the exception of the Egyptian diplomat and his family who live on the floor below; and the American filmmaker, a Japanese who occasionally comes to dine with the Dubonets next door. Coquelicot has kept a few ties to the Chinese community in Paris, but even these have grown tenuous since her mother's death and especially since her father's remarriage. True, France is becoming more progressive. Every day in the Luxembourg Gardens, she sees a mixed-race couple or a Parisian family with a small Chinese daughter in tow. Still, there is a shyness within Coquelicot and a self-containment that prevents her from opening up to other people, especially men. She feels the most comfortable with Marie Claire and with Paul, and occasionally with their father, Olivier.

One night, he came into the kitchen after his wife had gone to bed to find Coquelicot experimenting with a soup recipe. The children had colds, so she was adapting a traditional carrot soup by adding more ginger and a hint of orange. She was in the process of stirring these ingredients into the mixture when she heard Olivier's slippers on the tile floor. "I don't know what we'd ever do without you," he said, laying a hand on her forearm, after asking her to let him sample the soup. "We'd—I'd be lost without you." From behind his wire-rimmed glasses, his blue eyes met hers, and for a fleeting moment Coquelicot allowed herself to believe he was sending her a message.

In bed that night, she replayed the scene, prolonging the amount of time his hand lingered along her skin, hearing hidden notes of tenderness in his few words. Of course, she knew she couldn't continue the fantasy, or she would begin blushing when he came into the room, and pretty soon Juliet would catch on, and no matter how good a nanny Coquelicot was, she would lose her place. Coquelicot knows this, for it's happened before. Not to her, but to two of the other nannies she'd met over the years: the first time, a girl from St. Petersburg fell in love with her French employer and began telling all of the other nannies that she was pregnant with his child (a circumstance that seemed to be untrue). The second nanny was a Chinese immigrant like herself who developed such a crush on their charges' father that her own fiancé broke off their engagement. "Always best to know your place," Agnes Corot advises whenever one of the other nannies seems in danger of crossing a boundary. "Know your place, and use it to your own advantage."

Yes, Coquelicot recognizes plenty of truth in Agnes's words. But she also knows that she could never have survived the loneliness of her mother's death—the pungent absence she can sometimes still taste in the air or in her food—had it not been for Paul and Marie Claire. With them, Coquelicot believes she has secured a small portion of the happiness that would have been hers had she spent her mornings kneading loaves of bread, then watching the crusts bloom golden-brown in the ovens, a line of hungry customers dependent on her *pain ancienne, pain aux cereales* and airy brioche to sustain them throughout the seasons and the years.

"Yes, Maman, I've told you all I know," Amelie says, holding her mother's rough, left hand between both of her own as they sit beneath the statue of Genevieve, whose outstretched hands seem to promise a kind of comfort, if only Amelie could figure out a way to unlock the saint's secret.

Perhaps, if Amelie were a woman who'd known her calling from the time she was a small child, like Genevieve—singled out of a crowd by a visiting bishop when she was only eleven—perhaps Amelie, too, could find the strength to handle this situation better. Perhaps she could even have prevented it. If she'd always known she mattered—if she'd known her life would make a difference to the lives of others—she could have…

What? Amelie finds herself asking, now. And how absurd, to compare oneself, especially one's pregnant self, to a saint who committed herself to chastity before even knowing what sex was about. A woman who never had any doubts about God or the inequalities in her world. And then, Amelie realizes, there was the way Genevieve's parents helped her to realize her potential.

"Daughter"—as a child, Amelie had read the story hundreds of times, so the words easily returned to her— "rememberest thou the promise thou did make to God yesterday?"

"I do remember," replied the holy child. "I remember my promise, and I will be faithful to it."

"Will Marcel receive medical attention?" Odette now asks. Amelie squeezes her mother's hand, hungry for Odette to squeeze back.

"It's not like in the old days, Maman. Marcel may have a criminal record, but that's not the only way the law sees him. He's only thirty—young enough to be rehabilitated."

"But AIDS." Odette shudders, and the lines around her mouth deepen. "He won't be rehabilitated from that."

"We can't know that yet, Maman," Amelie says, unsure if she believes these words, even as she speaks them.

"There was a time when I saw what was happening to Marcel," she tells Amelie now. "After that incident with his boss at the bar. I think I knew even then that things would not come out well. Is it possible I gave up on your brother too soon?" Odette's eyes are wide and afraid.

Amelie does not know how to reply when her own memory of that period in their lives has grown faint. What she most remembers is her own father's rage, his sense that Marcel had shamed them, and his fear that his stepson's homosexuality and "debauchery" (another one of Peter Garnier's overblown words) would ruin his business.

"Maman, you loved Marcel. You did your best for him. At some point—" And here the queasiness rises from Amelie's gut to her throat, and heat fills her face, and she knows the nausea is right behind her tongue, just waiting. "At some point, Marcel has to take responsibility. I know you've always hinted at Ruse, the fact that he wasn't around. I know you've found reasons. But honestly, Maman,

Marcel is thirty years old. He could have found a way to take another path."

"Do you honestly believe that, Chat?" Odette asks, returning to the much-beloved nickname.

"I have to," Amelie runs her fingertips over her belly. "Otherwise, I wouldn't be having this baby on my own."

Odette purses her lips and nods, and Amelie feels both grateful but also a little sorry that her mother refuses to pursue the father's identity. Amelie's sexual history, unlike her so-called outrageous hair and clothes, is not of interest to her mother.

"Will you go and post bail?" Odette asks after a while.

Amelie slumps along the bench. She doesn't even glance at Saint Genevieve, though she remains aware of the statue's presence. No, suddenly Amelie is overwhelmingly tired and unsure of how she will ever manage to find her way back to the boutique on the Rue des Quatres Vents when what she really wants is to go home and sleep for a very long time. "I told you," she says, more sharply than she would have liked. "There is no bail this time. There's only a term to be served. Two years."

Odette nods. "That's right. You did tell me. I'm sorry."

Seated beside her mother, who will be fifty-two in July— just a year older than her own ultra chic boss Charlotte, yet what a lifetime's difference in the way age has worn patterns into the two women's faces and lives—Amelie finds herself longing to ask Odette about her life with Ruse. She longs to understand what compelled her mother, once a beautiful woman with a singing voice so lyrical it earned her the nickname of "La Petite Merle," to take up with a man who promised her nothing (or so Amelie has always believed); a man who ultimately abandoned her and his child. Why, Ruse even went so far as to steal the rose gold and ruby ring from her finger before he left.

Although Odette never said so, and rarely speaks about the period when Peter Garnier, Amelie's father, courted her, Amelie feels sure the reason her mother married him was because she was tired. It is a suspicion confirmed by the few surviving photographs of her mother from that time, photographs in which the resilient Odette looks gaunt and afraid, her shoulder blades two sharp wings beneath her clothes. And Peter Garnier had a grocery with a small apartment above it. He seemed safe, and he has proven to be safe, even if that safety brings with it a sort of skin-crawling provincialism, at least in his daughter's eyes. Did you know that Ruse would leave you? Amelie wants to ask. Or did you believe you could hold him with a child?

Amelie never believed Jean-Michel would stay with her, and perhaps she would not have wanted him to—why she let him slip back to Marseilles and his wife without telling him about the pregnancy. Initially, when the home test told her she was pregnant, Amelie believed she would have an abortion—something she has not told her mother. Once she made up her mind not to continue the pregnancy, she came to the Jardin du Luxembourg. Yes, it was the place that first reminded her of that painful difference—that feeling of not belonging that shadowed her for years, even in her parents' home. Yet the garden simultaneously seemed to know her life story as intimately as it knew the seasons and the light.

Believing she would terminate the pregnancy, Amelie came to the garden. After wandering its many paths, she stopped and sat down not far from where she and her mother are sitting now. It was a drizzly late afternoon, and there were very few people here. Eventually, she caught sight of a woman with a little girl. Unlike so many of the families who patronized the garden, this pair spoke rapid, guttural French very like the language Amelie had spoken growing up on the Rue Cler.

What attracted Amelie was the happiness this mother and daughter so clearly found in each other's company, for the mother was telling some sort of story, and the little girl would ask for more details, or she would fill in a part of the story that the woman had overlooked, so that it seemed to be a long-established routine between them. Watching them, Amelie felt a sudden gurgle of joy—and of longing—for there had never been that kind of closeness between her mother and herself. No, despite all of Marcel's problems, she always knew that Odette loved him more. Odette loved him regardless of how well or how poorly he did at school, regardless of how polite he was, or how rude. Marcel was her wild child, her boy. Amelie was the grocer's daughter. With a child of her own, would Amelie at last be able to redefine the terms?

"Maman," she says at last. "I need to go back to the boutique. I've been gone too long already."

The older woman nods, strokes Amelie's fuzzy, pink hair. "Your haircut," she says.

130

"What about it?"

"It's not as bad as all that."

Amelie smiles. "You mean you like it?"

Odette shrugs. "It becomes you."

It's nearing seven o'clock before Kate and Susan part. The two women exchange addresses in Paris, and Kate even gives Susan her address in the States. Still, Kate senses Susan will not get in touch with her again. Susan has told her too much about her life, as people in need sometimes do with strangers for whom they feel an affinity. It works both ways.

"I studied art in college," Kate finally explains when Susan asks about the watercolors. "It's the work I most love, the meditative rhythm I can climb inside when the painting is going well. I thought painting here in the gardens would help me to see more clearly. Not necessarily the individual people, or the landscape, though they are important."

"What about the children?" Susan asks.

"The children are the creatures with the most energy," Kate says, reminded of that joyful silhouette awash in sapphire blue, a figure that had come to her in two clean strokes of the brush—pure Zen—and smiles. "Oh," Kate adds, realizing the stupidity of her words, "I'm so sorry."

"No," Susan says, leaning closer. "It's okay. Children are light—*life*. How does one separate them? How?" Her voice quivers, but when Kate tries to comfort her, Susan just shakes her head, whispers, "No, this is good. Talking this way is good."

Kate feels it, too. "I think that's why I've become obsessed with the way the light moves through the chestnut trees and changes the way the various points in the garden look at different times of the day. That corner with Chopin's statue," she signals to a particularly lush spot in the distance. "Mornings it is a cool grove of shadow, but come mid-afternoon the light has exposed a mystery it will not recover until dusk."

"I see it," Susan says, with such clarity Kate believes that the other woman must come to the garden for much the same reason as she does, to see.

"Every year," Kate says, "I start with the Etruscans. When I teach Intro to Art History. I tell my students these ancient people, they understood something."

"What?" Susan asks. "What did they understand?"

"The sun, the darkness. We have to learn it all over again. I always spoke as if I understood. Only I didn't."

Susan reaches for her hand.

"Will you tell your husband of your visits here?" Kate asks, just before saying goodbye.

Susan shakes her head. "I couldn't. It just wouldn't make sense to Pierre."

Kate does not say anything after that, and yet she feels oddly certain that Susan Sunier's husband must also be among the other visitors to the garden. And once Susan has gone, she begins to imagine him—a lean, solitary figure with fine, dark hair and dark eyes made more luminous by suffering—walking quietly down the gravel paths. Every once in a while, he pauses, struck by the way the leaves of the chestnut trees seem not just to hold, but to prolong the light as the sun wanes in the sky, or he finds himself drawn in by the dignity and calm of two old women, two old friends, sitting close together. Surely there would be answers here for him also. Or at the very least comfort.

Once Kate returns to her painting, she realizes that a figure like Pierre's must enter the scene to balance that ebullient silhouette of child. A figure to be rendered in a wash of violet, the last color in the rainbow spectrum; a figure whose shoulders may round towards the earth, who may not walk straight-backed; but a figure who, like the sapphire child, must be bathed in light.

ELEGY FOR A FAIRY TALE

I.

My grandmother left me many gifts including a pastel landscape of birch trees in winter by a long forgotten Russian artist and a ruby ring she once buried in a wartime garden, but her greatest gifts were her stories.

Before she died, I spent countless afternoons at her bedside listening to her spin worlds embellished with the gold of fairy tales. There was one story in particular I longed for, the one about the little girl who, accompanied by her faithful dog, is sent out to do some errand for her own grandmother in the woods. Usually, the girl is sent to pick blackberries, or to forage mushrooms, and inevitably she loses her way while following a fleeing deer or some vivid, elusive bird. As day gives way to night and shadows accumulate beneath the hollows of trees and in the crevices of rocks, the sounds of the forest creatures take on ominous tones, and the girl begins to feel the damp burrowing into her skin. (Having spent many summers in an ancient Siberian village, my grandmother was especially skilled at describing the chill of a Russian forest at twilight.) Just when the girl is about to give up, her faithful dog—a collie, wasn't it? or perhaps a German Shepherd?—nudges her away from the leafy arms of the oak tree beneath which she is sheltering, and convinces her to follow him. Somehow that dog always knows the way home, and it is at home the girl finds her mother or her kerchiefed grandmother waiting, hands clasped in her lap, face pinched with concern.

Why these adults who have sent her out don't go and search for her, I never asked. Why the dog waits so long—usually until the girl has exhausted herself crying—didn't preoccupy me either. Why would logic intrude when this journey through a pine forest mesmerized? Especially given my grandmother's powers of description and her ability to create suspense like a body of water I could dive into, plunging down, down, strangely buoyed…

Thirty years have passed since we buried my grandmother; twenty-two since you and I said goodbye for the last time. Yet it's only now, when I think back to my own life's beginnings, that I begin to understand why I fell in love with you whose life seemed to hold so many unopened stories. The day we met remains etched into my memory as sharply as the lines around my grandmother's eyes—their cause, she once told me, both laughter and sorrow.

Return with me then to the summer I turned fourteen, the summer I was new to Maverick, my family having just moved from Chicago to Texas where we settled into the rambling white-washed brick house. When we arrived, the house had been uninhabited for years. In the garden, wisteria webbed the elms and scarlet roses overreached the crumbling fence. In the garden in south central Texas in summertime, the mosquitoes, the bitter weed, and the wild garlic reigned.

Into this world you stepped one hot day in early July, having been called in to salvage the fence and the gazebo where the weeping willow trailed its long arms through an algae-rich pond, where after dark I liked to sit (in long-sleeved shirt and pants, brown soap coating my exposed ankles and hands) and listen to the frogs, crickets, and other night sounds.

On that second or third afternoon, you perched high on a ladder where you'd just managed to separate the climbing roses from the vines and said, "Think you can fetch me that twine from my satchel? If I move, I'm going to have to reconfigure everything."

"Of course." Since your arrival I'd been matching my sandaled feet to the prints of your boots as you hacked your way through the knee-deep tangle of brush at the back.

When my older sister Jenna teased me about you, I reminded her that I'd already read *The French Lieutenant's Woman* and *Summer of My German Soldier* while she wasted the honeyed days pouring over *Vogue* and *Vanity Fair*, so what could she possibly know that I didn't?

Though it darkened later, your hair that summer was precisely the shade of the meadow grasses I used to gallop through (playing horse) at my grandmother's. You wore it short the next time we met, but back then it curled around your ears and forehead and formed small ringlets at the nape of your neck.

"Don't you have better things to do?" you asked, as I tucked into the window seat of the gazebo, peering over at you from behind my book, while you checked for rotting wood.

"No," I said. "I told you so already." How I was drawn to you, to your voice that held within it the rush of dragonflies, the pull of river water.

Your hazel eyes were flecked with gold, and when you looked at me, I was reminded of the owl that roosted in the willow tree some nights, the one whose call seemed to contain some message, if only I'd known how to decipher it.

Not long after I began to spin stories about you, though in the end everything I imagined proved far less interesting than the truth, or the version of it that had escaped into the world. Soon I, too, knew that your father had run off when you were not much older than my brother Sam who loved to build towers and cities out of the battered wooden blocks we'd carried from house to house during our moves.

Your father had run off, my mother said, stranding your own mother with two boys, one reason why my mother hired you to do the work and not a more experienced carpenter-handy man.

"Don't romanticize things, Anna," my father said to her. "We need to economize, and that's why Seth is here. Did you see how long it took him to assess the damage in the gazebo?"

"So?" Mom said. "We're paying him by the job not by the hour. He's careful. You should appreciate that."

"He strikes me as someone who gets lost in his head," my father said. "Didn't he drop out of school for a while?"

"He's had a rough time," my mother said.

"Is it true you haven't seen your dad since you were really young?" I asked you the following afternoon, sure this absence must have something to do with your "rough time."

You glanced up at me, smiled your crooked smile, and the crescent-moon scar tracing your left cheek diminished a little. I was dying to find out where that scar came from. "He left when I was six," you said, "but it's not like he disappeared. I visit him in L.A. every once in a while."

"That's where he lives?" I said, picturing orange trees, Mickey Mouse, traffic.

"He wanted to get into the movies as a stunt man."

"So he jumps out of moving cars and stuff?"

You laughed. "Sometimes. He specializes in heights."

I laid my book face down at my side. "Heights?"

"He's fearless about them, stood on the roof a lot when he was still around, and there were days he'd string up a rope between our house and the neighbor's and practice walking across."

I pictured the tightrope walker at the circus, and the back of my throat went dry. "Isn't it dangerous?"

"Sure. That's part of the thrill. When I was six, maybe seven, he walked that rope between us and the neighbor's. It was around December I think, because I remember the lights and the wind; but he stayed out there for God knows how long in a turtleneck and some thin pants, his arms stretched out at his sides."

I leaned closer, my throat tight. "What did you do?"

"What could I do but stand there watching as he placed one foot in front of the other? He was barefoot. I think I knew then that he wasn't going to stick around."

You spoke without bitterness, which amazed me then and now. My girl self just asked, "So, has your dad made a lot of movies?"

"A few. He had a part in a James Bond film a while back. I went to see it. He jumped from one building to the next, told me they strung a huge net underneath."

I shivered, unable to imagine what it would feel like to fall from such a height. "Wow."

"Yeah well, since then he's been doing pretty much the same kind of work as I am." You laughed. "Not bushwhacking through yards, but he does a lot of carpentry. He's good with his hands. When I went out there, he built a tree house."

"For you?"

"For his other son and daughter."

I stared at the muscles threading your arms, scratched now from the roses' thorns. "Do you like it," I said, "bushwhacking through yards?"

"It's alright. It gives me time to think. Some days, my mind seems to race so hard I have trouble keeping up. When that happens, I'm glad for the steadiness of digging, planting, bushwhacking. But it's only for the time being. See," you smiled. "I'm going to go to college in the fall."

You might have said such a thing very naturally to someone else, but with the bees circling the black-eyed Susans and a unicorn-shaped cloud overhead, I felt as if you'd told me a great secret.

"So," I said, drawing closer, "what do you want to study?"

"Literature, what else? I read Hemingway and Fitzgerald in high school. After that," you grinned, revealing a chipped front tooth that complemented your scar, "there was no turning back."

"What do you like about them?"

You squatted, your knees poking through the holes in your jeans. "The places they take me, the way they reveal my own life back. A character might stand there, like in *Gatsby*, looking out at a green light on a dock, and feel that light makes all his hopes and dreams real. Does that make sense?"

It wasn't until my senior year that I read *Gatsby*, but the focus in your eyes just then, and the way your voice became taut, rather like that tightrope your father walked, tugged at something deep within me. "Yes."

"Good." You looked away then, so that I felt sure you'd shown me something no one else had seen before.

That night when I settled against the pillows determined to make a start on *Jane Eyre*, it was you I pictured beside me. I'd stop to think about the meaning of a word, and even though I could have looked them up, the next day I asked you to tell me the meaning of "opprobium" and "ameliorate" and "ambrosia."

"Where did you find those?" you asked, working out the sentence despite the nails between your lips.

"Charlotte Brontë," I said a little slyly. "I'm reading *Jane Eyre*."

My confession seemed to crack something open, and I could have sworn I heard the break, like the opening of the pecans I shelled by the dozen on lazy afternoons. After that, you seemed to welcome my reading to you while you worked. I read *The Sun Also Rises* aloud, imagining I was Brett Ashley to your Jake Barnes.

"This was the Brett that I had felt like crying about. Then I thought of her walking up the street and stepping into the car, as I had last seen her, and of course in a little while I felt like hell again. It is awfully easy to be hard-boiled about everything in the daytime, but at night is another thing."

Did you catch on to my imaginings? I wonder now, picturing the two of us in that humid gazebo, me curled on my stomach, perspiration dotting my forehead and gathering in the hollows of my arms as I read and stole glances at you sanding, hammering, then painting the wood, until the once ramshackle gazebo looked like the set from *The Sound of Music*.

Your last day working on our house drew near, and I willed my parents to find some job to keep you with us just a little while longer. And when that didn't happen, I stayed up until dawn writing you a story about my grandmother using my father's fountain pen.

Once upon a time… *This is how my grandmother always began her stories, weaving together fairy tales and memories that journeyed back to the Russia where she was born. If there'd been more time, if I was older, if if if any number of things… I would have recounted my favorite of her stories—the one about the girl who gets lost in the woods with her <u>venturesome</u> (from* Jane Eyre*!) dog. Most of all, I would have told you about her.*

Maybe one day I'll have that chance. Maybe I'll be traveling through Spain like Brett Ashley, and I'll step into some smoky bar, and you'll look up and smile, and I'll know you've been thinking about me, too, maybe even looking for me around street corners, in shop windows. Or maybe our meeting will happen in New York at some theater or at the Metropolitan Museum, there on the steps overlooking Fifth Avenue. Or perhaps you'll come home one holiday to find me standing behind the bakery counter, my skin and hair dusted with flour. "May I help you?" I'll ask, looking up to meet your crooked smile.

Wherever it happens, if it happens, I'll have to tell you about my grandmother because she was the most important person in my life, though I'm beginning to believe that you're going to be important, too. She was the one who sat beside my bed on too many afternoons when my temperature pitched over 102, and my mother had to go into work. (She quit only after Sam was born.) My grandmother would lay a cool cloth on my forehead, stroke my hand, and sing to me in Russian.

When my parents went away on a holiday, Jenna went to stay with my father's parents, and I stayed with her. In summertime, she and I drove the old blue Nova to her cottage in Michigan, sat outside on the porch swing all through the long afternoons eating blueberries. In winter, we tucked into her sofa. I held her yarn as she knit and talked. Our time together was a gold-leafed story book, the illustrations all hand-painted, her words light as butterflies, others weighty as stones falling through deep water.

In the morning, the kitchen smelled of the ambrosial lemon cake my mother had baked in your honor. Jenna turned up wearing a strapless sundress the color of ripe melon, her ginger hair teased into a high ponytail. I wore the same white shorts I always did, though I chose a pretty white eyelet blouse and left the top two buttons undone.

"You've been a godsend," Mom said, as we sat at the picnic table that you carried into the gazebo, so we could celebrate there.

You laughed and wiped those damp blonde tendrils from your forehead—how I longed to touch them, to brush them up and away. "A pleasure," you said, turning your hazel eyes on me. "Besides, I had Nadia here to keep me company." My cheeks must have turned flamingo pink, but thankfully not even Jenna said a word. "How many books do you think we read this past month?"

"Let's see," I said, closing my eyes, as I tried to bring each and every one of those days back. "*The Sun Also Rises, Tender Is the Night,* one two three four stories, and the first eight chapters of *Jane Eyre.*"

Mom's eyes settled on mine. "Yes, my Nadia is quite a reader. I expect she'll be studying English one day also."

"Is that what you're going to study then?" Jenna said, frowning a little.

You leaned forward, your forearms hugging the tabletop. "I'm going to study everything I can," you said, and suddenly a picture swam up of you driving off in your ancient Ford truck, the bed filled with boxes of clothes and books and bedding instead of garden tools, and I was unable to finish my cake. Sam scooped up the sweet bits in his chubby fists and pushed every last mouthful between his cupid lips.

"Here," Mom said, sliding an envelope across the table. "You'll find the contracted amount here, plus a little extra, to help buy the books for those English classes." She smiled, then gathered up the china plates and glasses as Jenna lingered for a while beneath the willow tree. I knew she was waiting for me to leave, but I planted myself at your side while you took one last look at the gazebo.

"I wrote this for you," I said finally, handing you the story I'd tied up with a pink silk ribbon, like some secret scroll.

Did I imagine it, or did the gold in your eyes deepen to amber?

If my grandmother had told this part of our story, she would have had you dressed in a white shirt of fine cotton and a pair of crisp twill pants like the ones she used to iron for my grandfather. Your blonde hair would have been carefully parted, and you would have scrubbed the dirt from beneath your nails.

But would you have taken my hands between your own, holding them so tightly I'd feel your calluses pressing into my own skin?

Once upon a time, my grandmother was a girl in a navy blue dress and shoes with navy blue ribbons in her hair. She wore pigtails because her hair, dark like mine, was thick and tangled, and she attended a school named for Russia's Catherine the Great, who'd apparently had a love affair with one of my ancestors and ordered the court marshal of another.

Grandmother's father was a three-star general under the last czar, but he wasn't around much, always organizing soldiers and sometimes traveling to other countries, like the time he went to Japan to negotiate for prisoners. I have his camp mirror in my room. It's got a long crack running down the middle, and I sometimes think about when and how it must have happened; and why, of all the things my grandmother salvaged when she came to the States, it was her father's camp mirror, an object now empty of his reflection, that she chose to tuck in to her great trunk among the photographs, the few bits of porcelain, the pastel of the birch trees, and her remaining jewels. My grandmother's name was Nadia, too. Nadia Maria Petrova. I was named for her. In Russian, Nadia means hope...

She married my grandfather when she was twenty-three, but he wasn't the man she loved, not that she told me this. I knew it from the album she kept from her youth, an album full of pictures out of which she'd spin stories. Whenever she spoke of her true love, the timbre of her voice deepened, as if she were tunneling into the past, trying to hold it there, the way amber preserves lost time.

My grandfather's name was Viktor, and he was a railroad engineer fifteen years older than she was. She married him, she confessed once, because he had a good job under the new government, and she had to take care of her mother and her younger sister Katrina.

My grandmother's true love was Misha, the caretaker's son. His eyes, she said, were as blue as the cold lake in which they swam together each summer; his hair, blonde like yours. Misha was lean and catlike, and when he ran, it was fleetly, with the silence of a deer. He wanted to train as a dancer, but my great-grandfather convinced his father to send him into the army instead. Because my great-grandfather loved Misha's family, especially his mother, whom he nicknamed the good shepherdess, he promised to find a high-up place for Misha, and so at eighteen off he went. A year later, the revolution broke out and Misha, a soldier in the White Army, was sent off to fight...

140

II.

Four Augusts later, my mother loaded up her Volvo and drove me back up north; our destination: the University of Chicago. Jenna, who went to the University of Texas at Austin and majored in fashion merchandising, and her friends, would once have called it a geek's school. But not once she became engaged to a patent lawyer with a six-figure salary whose glasses were black and much thicker than my own.

The University of Chicago's gothic buildings seemed the architectural counterpart to the rich inner life of Jane Eyre, whose voice echoed through me as I made my way across the quadrangle flanked by the high, white stone. It was a matter of days before I'd made a home for myself at one of the wooden tables in Harper Library, where the light sifted through the lead-glass windows, casting patterns on tabletops, on floors, and on the seemingly endless aisles of books.

Mid-October—the leaves outside a kaleidoscope of reds, oranges, yellows—and midterms were upon us. At the tables, students sat shoulder to shoulder, every seat filled. "Excuse me—"

I looked up, blinked once, then stared into your grinning face. "You," I said. "You."

A dozen heads looked up from their books. Several whispered, "Ssshhh."

Your crooked smile. "No, you."

My limbs turned to honey. "What are you doing here?"

"Grad school."

"English?" I asked.

"What else," you said, then took my hand and led me out of the reading room, down the marble hallway, and into the autumn light.

With very few people in your life, my grandmother told me once, will there be no need for explanations, that long filling in of the gaps that are years. Misha was that person for her. She met him again after the revolution, once her father had been shot into an open grave with his fellow officers, and she and her mother and younger sister were sharing their house with four other families, the few remaining jewels she'd held onto buried in the kitchen garden.

141

Misha looked at my hair, once so dark and curly, now threaded with silver though I was only twenty-one. He took my hands, callused from harvesting vegetables and washing clothes, and he didn't ask if I still played Mozart and Chopin on the piano come nightfall. Nor did he ask if my mother had managed to keep the black pearls Father had brought back from Japan. Perhaps he knew that she'd had to sell them to bribe the officials to allow us to stay in our home.

I tell you all this, but what mattered was that Misha remembered me, my grandmother said, the shadows behind her eyes, those two violet curtains, vanishing for just a moment, so that the light shone through. There was that kind of recognition between us. And when he took my face between his hands, which were far rougher than even I could have imagined, I kissed him, and it was as if the two of us were meeting as we had in the cold mountain lake all those summers ago, summers that belonged to another world, one we'd never known we'd lose. No need for explanations, Nadia, she told me, almost fiercely. Remember that.

I'd always imagined I understood what my grandmother meant, but I didn't, not until you led me out into the sunlight, tucked my arm within the crook of your own, and drew me inside your overcoat which smelled of pine needles and smoke.

I leaned into your warmth, matched my footsteps to yours, and we crossed the long length of the quad, past the students playing hacky-sack and the others smoking or talking over their books. We kept walking past the bright-lit windows of the Regenstein Library, down Fifty-Seventh Street, all the way to the lakefront, stopping only once to buy coffees in Styrofoam cups and sticky-sweet rolls scented with cardamom from the Middle Eastern grocer.

The lakefront where we sat on a bench marked by the stories of other lovers was called the Point, but I didn't know that then, so for weeks I came to think of it as simply our place: yours and mine.

"I'm studying literature, too," I said, as we sipped our coffees and licked the honey from the sweet rolls sticking to our finger tips. "My father wants me to study languages, pictures me in some international office someday."

"Is that how you picture yourself?"

"No."

You smiled and stroked my face with such gentleness I believed you understood me completely.

"I thought I'd study Russian after taking a class with Edward Wasiolek," you said after a while. "I wanted to read the novels in the original."

"So can you speak Russian now?" I asked, the few words I'd learned from my grandmother—*zolotoi* for gold, *sobaka* for dog, *volk* for wolf—blossoming on my tongue.

"I gave up, too difficult. And then," you grinned, "I found the poets—Rilke, Celan, Eliot."

I smiled, then waited, my heartbeat thrumming in my ears, for you to say something—anything—about the story I'd tied up with pink silk ribbon, all those years ago.

Instead, you drew me to you, holding me so close my heartbeat dissolved into yours. I'd kissed a couple of boys by then, boys with glasses and braces on their teeth whose hands sweated when they held mine. Their kisses were nothing like yours. When you kissed me, I understood what Thoreau meant when he said, "There is no remedy for love but to love more."

It was nearing dusk before we left the lakefront. You held my hand, and when you tucked it into your coat pocket where it rested among the pennies and the single, stale Life Saver, I matched my step to yours. Along the way, every landmark suddenly stood out in bold relief. We passed the lab school where children in red, blue, and yellow parkas scampered on the playground. Then we continued on past stately Ida Noyes where I sometimes swam alongside the old women in their black bathing suits. Next, we passed the Reynolds club which smelled that afternoon of strong coffee, until we arrived at a high, stone building on Blackstone.

You led me inside, and we stepped into the wrought iron elevator and pushed the button to the eleventh floor. You kissed me again then, whispering that I smelled just as I had that summer in the heat of the gazebo, the wisteria and trumpet vine twining the pillars. Our kisses deepened, became hungrier, and I understood that I wanted this, too, that I had always wanted it, ever since you walked into that overgrown garden and let me walk, literally, in the steps your work boots made.

It was an extraordinary thing that my grandmother and what remained of her family managed to stay in Russia once the czar and his family were murdered, the great houses broken up, thousands of people having fled, so many others having "vanished." My grandmother and her younger sister were young enough to adapt to the new regime, but their mother, who had grown up with a French governess and studied painting, music, and dance, seemed to shrink a little bit more every day. "Like a tree that has too little light and water," my grandmother said. The once vibrant leaves yellowed, then browned at the edges, and fluttered to the ground like dying butterflies.

My grandmother continued to meet Misha in the evenings when he was able to get away, loving him with the tenderness she'd once reserved for her father's mastiff Olaf. At night, they would lie together in a gathering of horse chestnut trees in one of the great parks, marveling at the fact that the trees, like they themselves, had somehow managed to survive the war when nearly everything else had been cut down for firewood or fuel. She did not tell me that she and Misha made love, though having known your touch, your body moving alongside mine, I hope they could have shared that.

"Happiness is a strange thing, isn't it?" I said to you one night as we lay on the sofa with its faded floral slipcover that camouflaged the coffee and tea stains, the strawberry jam we ate with our scones; and even the long, gray hairs from the alley cat we coaxed inside one evening, naming her Anastasia, an outlandishly regal name for a striped tabby, why we wound up calling her Ani. We were living together by this time, a point my parents chose to overlook on their visits, though I sensed my mother secretly approved; she, too, loved you more than a little, seeing you in the garden that continued to flourish in the years after all of her children left home.

"Strange? Why happiness is the most natural thing in the world."

"Why aren't more people happy together then?" I said, scooting over to massage your socked feet, while Ani kneaded your chest and purred.

"I can only answer for myself."

"You're happy then?" I said, coming very close, kissing you on the moon-shaped scar, the ear, the wide expanse of brow.

"Happiest," you said, wrapping me up in a close embrace.

"There's something I've wanted to ask you for a long time," I began.

"Go ahead."

144

"When you left for college, I gave you that letter—my grandmother's history. You never mentioned it. All those years in between, and not a single letter: why?"

"You were fourteen, Nadia, and I was twenty."

I wondered then if we hadn't found each other at Chicago if our past would have remained just that, if our story would have ended there. And sadness seeped into me.

Around midnight it began to rain, and you opened the windows so that we could listen to its music as we lay in bed, your arms wrapped around me, your cheek pressed against my back. "Come on," you said, and I turned towards you, my uncertainty vanishing.

Soon we were outside, both of us barefoot, you in your striped cotton, me in a t-shirt and shorts. You coaxed me into a dance and we made wide, looping arcs, inscribing ourselves—our love—into the night's memory, the only light coming from a distant streetlamp.

After a while you began to sing that silly Woody Guthrie song, "Wake up, wake up, wake up..." that you sometimes played on an old guitar nights when you couldn't sleep, and I'd find you roaming the darkened rooms of our apartment, or curled onto the sofa with far too many books.

I joined in at first, but soon you were singing so loudly I was afraid you would wake the other people in the building. I was amazed by your energy at such moments, amazed and perhaps—I realized only later—a little afraid.

In my grandmother's album, there's a photograph of her standing at the big train station in St. Petersburg. I like to imagine the photograph was taken by Misha, that she has accompanied him there to see him off. It's springtime, and she wears a white hat with a single rose. The image is in black and white, but I know the rose was dusky pink because she spoke of such roses in her family's garden, and I want to believe a rose planted on the occasion of her mother's marriage would have survived the revolution. Her dress, too, is white and long, and just brushes her ankles. There are gloves on her hands, and she holds a handkerchief. It is this token, embroidered I am sure with the fanciful flowers she stitched into my childhood dresses, that tells me that Misha is going away. She told me that he was ultimately sent to the Urals to work. She will not cry in front of him, though her expression is somber, her violet-shadowed eyes which never aged, having always been old perhaps (at least since the Revolution), directed at the person behind the camera, as if to say, "How can I let you disappear from my life, not now, after I've only found you again?" The train system in Russia, my grandmother told me more than once, was always punctual, even in the midst of crises.

III.

By the end of my senior year of college, the well-established ferns and dormant geraniums and little groupings of cacti on the windowsill leaned towards the sun, and that beloved pastel of the birch trees presided over the wall of our bedroom, just opposite where we slept, so that we could always see it when we awoke and again when we went to sleep. It was during this time of making plans for what came next—for you, too, were graduating from the doctoral program—I first recognized something within you had truly altered, sped up, become brighter, bolder, electric.

"Nadia!" you called one afternoon, bursting through the front door, carrying a bouquet of yellow lilies and a single pink rose.

I looked up from the desk where I sat writing my thesis on Charlotte Brontë, and Ani looked up, too. "What's this? What's happened?" I said, as you thrust the bouquet into my arms.

"They're going to hire me." You burrowed your face in my shoulder where I breathed in the promise of lilacs and months of sun.

"Who?" I said. "Who is?"

"The department."

"I'm sorry," I took you by the hand and led you over to the sofa—its color a rich, plummy wine—that we'd splurged on at Christmas. "You need to start from the beginning."

You told me then that the department was planning to hire you as soon as you completed your dissertation on mystical experience in Paul Celan and T.S. Eliot.

I sat there for a long time, unsure if I was more thrilled or frightened. Not that I knew much, if anything then, about the academic hiring process; nevertheless, I understood that getting a job at Chicago meant you were going to join the crème de la crème.

"Amazing," I managed, convincing myself that your article

146

on Eliot in that prestigious academic journal must have really broken new ground.

"Now go and put on that gorgeous pink dress," you said, and pulled me to my feet. "We're going to celebrate."

You wore the ivory jacket that reminded me of Cary Grant and a pair of ancient jeans, and I wore the dress that same dusty pink as the roses in my family's garden. Hand in hand, we walked down Fifty-Seventh Street. You set such a fast pace that I had to match two steps to your one, me in those absurdly high heels you bought for me a few weeks before, heels I never wore afterwards. We'd almost reached the elevated train when I stumbled on a crack in the sidewalk, caught the heel, and turned my ankle. By the time we reached the tracks, the ankle had begun to throb, but your eyes and the rush of your voice told me that I couldn't disappoint you.

"Champagne," you said to the waiter at L'Escargot, a restaurant we couldn't really afford, "and ice for the lady's foot."

Glancing at my elevated leg, the ankle now the size of an orange, the waiter grimaced sympathetically.

Afterwards we'd planned to go dancing at that jazz club on Oak Street, but dancing, we both knew now, was out of the question.

Outside the restaurant, you lifted me into your arms. Limning the inside of my ear with your lips, you said, "What do you say we spend tonight at the Drake?"

My mother told me once that the Galetsin family, first cousins to the last czar, lived at that grand hotel now, occupying most of one of the top floors.

"How can we possibly?" I said, reminded of our careful budget, the shopping trips to the Co-op where we always selected the produce that was slightly bruised, the second-best cuts of meat—and this, a night out, maybe once a week, and nothing remotely as extravagant as this.

"Come on, Nadia." Already you were hailing a cab. "Just this once let's live a little."

Haven't we been living all along? I wanted to ask, amazed by your energy. But you also used a high-handed tone, one that hurt more than my ankle, which resembled a grapefruit by the time you put me down in that throne of a bed, in that high-ceilinged room, with its gilded copies of Impressionism's masterpieces on the walls.

With the curtains drawn back to reveal the street-lit view of Lake Shore Drive, and just beyond, the blackened lake, we made love, the unfamiliar sheets, surely Egyptian cotton, slick against our skin. Afterwards, you spoke far too quickly, your words bumping up against each other as you held me close, talking to me of all that lay ahead for us, so that I could hardly keep up. Before I fell asleep, I pictured your father—falling from those heights—and still you talked on.

"A memory without blot or contamination must be an exquisite treasure— an inexhaustible source of pure refreshment: is it not?"—The words come from Jane Eyre, *and though they can cut like a new razor, I keep them pinned to the bulletin board above my desk to this day.*

Were my grandmother's memories of Misha as "pure" as that cold lake in which the two of them once bathed? Did they "refresh" her? Yes, the curtains within her eyes parted when she spoke of him. Even so, I believe her love for Misha—like the sweetest, most juicy berries that are always the most difficult to reach, and usually at some cost (getting lost in the woods, for example)—must have tamped the love she felt for others, but especially for my grandfather.

I had my daughters, she said of my mother and her younger sister, Sabine. True enough. In a photograph taken just before they immigrated to the States, the two sisters stand side by side in a small public garden. There are ribbons in their hair, and their shoes have been polished to a high shine. Despite the darning of their dresses, my grandmother has embroidered flowers along their collars. There is no doubt: these girls are beloved.

But what about the nights when my grandparents lay together in a room that opened onto the Crimean Sea, the salt air and the fragrance of warmer countries wafting in through the windows? What were my grandmother's thoughts then? Did they return her to the lure of the clear water of that distant lake? Did she find herself at the station waving goodbye, Misha's face in the window receding with every breath? Did her habit of reading deep into the night, turning over the pages of her album, cooking up pots of her famous jams after midnight—did all of these ways of filling the quiet hours begin at this time?

We took the train back to Hyde Park. At the university hospital, a young resident with brillo-pad hair pronounced my ankle sprained and chastised me for not coming in immediately. The resident wrapped my ankle with tape and injected it with a

148

steroid, then sent me home with painkillers that knocked me out for some thirty-six hours. I still remember waking very briefly from that codeine-laced sleep, aware that you were not in bed beside me, not even when I woke in the tenuous midst of night, occasionally catching the drift of the guitar, the taut edges of your voice, some troubled melody.

When I finally got up, I found you sitting at the table in the kitchen, before you a pile of books set down helter-skelter; and the calendar, the days crossed out, again and again, with red x's, so that the month seemed to become some abstract design, or puzzle. "Are you alright?" I asked, sensing, even through the fog of codeine, that something was absolutely wrong.

You fixed your eyes on my own, said, "I'm trying to figure out the time."

"Late morning," I said, looking at the clock. "Ten past eleven."

"No," you said, knocking the calendar to the floor. "The year, Nadia: what year is it?"

Am I dreaming? I thought, *for what else, other than a dream, could such strangeness be?*

"Nadia," you whispered, tilting away from me, "what year is it?"

At my feet, our tabby cat sat there motionless, the only movement, the metronome beat of her tail. I stared at her, tried to swim up into the air, a frantic new terror coursing through my body, though I, too, was still. I still don't know if I ever answered you. What I remember, with Technicolor precision, is the fevered way in which you rambled on about the passage of years we would live, countries we would see, the many children we would have…

IV.

Twenty-two years have passed since then. I've married again, not with the giddy happiness we once knew, but with the grace that comes with a good man's arms around me each night, the stable eddy of our conversations, plans for travel and our home, friendships, and especially the twin daughters to whom I've begun to tell my grandmother's stories, but never the stories about you.

Even so, you appear in my dreams, and sometimes a song will come on—Bob Dylan's "Tambourine Man" and anything by Woody Guthrie—or I'll turn the corner on a street, struck by something familiar—a loping stride like your own, the scent of wild garlic—and I'll almost expect you to step through a doorway and greet me, as in that Rilke poem you would recite to me nights when we would not sleep. *"Streets that I chanced upon—/you had just walked down them and vanished…"*

When I think of the spiral of years that followed, years in which neither one of us could find our footing, when I, too, curled up in bed until mid-afternoon, paralyzed with fear, I find myself asking what if our story had ended that morning when you awoke to the belief that too many years had passed. What if, instead of wading through the next seven years and two more hospitalizations, and in between a brief, blissful year of marriage, I'd left you after walking away from the psych ward at the university where another young resident, this one with bobbed blonde hair that didn't suit her grave voice, concluded manic depression or bipolar disorder, a disease of terrifying highs and even more debilitating lows. "How is it that you didn't see it coming?" the resident with the blonde bob asked me after delivering the diagnosis.

My grandmother would have reminded herself, and me, of the futility—the absurdity—of trying to rewrite what has become history. As for recognizing the signs, how could I possibly, not knowing what I should be searching for? As for leaving, how could I have left then when you were the sun to my moon?

That morning at the hospital, I lingered until the young resident came out to see me, her face pale when she fetched me from where I sat in the sticky vinyl chair in the waiting area. "But it's controllable, isn't it?" I asked, after we sat in that quiet, brightly-lit consulting room where all I could hear was the iridescent hum of the fixtures above.

"With medication, yes, but there will be side effects. We'll have to see how he responds. The immediate priority," she said, her own eyes masked by her silver-framed glasses, "is to bring Seth down from this mania as safely as we can."

Ten days later, the mania a surreal memory, I came back to the hospital to find you seated at a bright blue table by the window, the kind you find in a kindergarten classroom, your beautiful, tawny head between your hands. I stayed through all three visiting hours as you sat in silence, speaking only when I pressed you again and again. Depression, I learned then, was far more terrifying than mania, and one that endures like a long, cloying illness, a claustrophobic white fog.

Nearly a month before they allowed me to bring you home, and I dressed as if for a party, not in the dusty pink dress, which seemed bad luck now (though I hung onto it for years), but in the forest green silk that still lingers in my closet, delicate and fragile as memory.

Holding your hand, we walked the six blocks back to the apartment I'd filled with yellow and pink roses and as many lilies and yellow-throated irises as I could afford.

"I made dinner," I said, leading you to the table where I lit the candles, poured us sparkling water, for you were no longer allowed wine. All your favorite things: stuffed artichokes, poached salmon, rice with almonds and saffron. And we sat, but I alone ate.

In the weeks that followed, your medical cocktail kept changing, and still you could not concentrate on the poets you so loved to read. "It's like the page has become a Pollack painting," you said. "I get caught up with the colors, the design, but what it means doesn't stay with me."

More drugs: anti-depressants and anti-psychotics and anti-god-knows-what-else, and what did it matter when too many mornings you continued to sit beside the window, your head in your hands, until I believed the grandiosity of mania—two thousand dollars on your credit card that first time—was better, oh so much better, than this.

"I'm more like my father than I realized," you told me when I sat beside you in yet another hospital some three years later, this one in New York.

"Those heights?" I said, and you nodded.

You were speaking figuratively then, though the lows were anything but metaphoric. Even now I remember the sour smell of unwashed skin and sheets, the piles of books you could not read, your beautiful mind a dark cave I could not enter.

In the last two years of my grandmother's life, she and I watched Dr. Zhivago *perhaps half a dozen times. I'd lay my head on her lap, relishing the feel of her fingertips in my hair, the rose gold of her wedding ring occasionally snagging on a tangle. Entranced by Omar Sharif's Zhivago, I fell in love with him; for me, always, Zhivago was the pale, coffee-eyed Egyptian actor; and Julie Christie, Zhivago's beloved Lara.*

When you and I finally sat down to watch the film, you preferred Geraldine Chaplin's Tonya to Christie's Lara. And really I should have been flattered, for ultimately I am much more like the good, mild Tonya than fiery, passionate Lara. I could never have plunged a knife into a man's heart. I could never have continued to stand by Pasha with his coldness, his scarred revolutionary ideals. Loving Zhivago, though, well, that's a whole different story. And besides, Tonya and Lara both loved him, and Zhivago loved them back, though it was Lara whom he could not live without.

At the very end of the film, no matter how many times I watch it— that moment Zhivago recognizes Lara in that crowd of workers so many, many years after they've been separated—I still keep hoping that he will reach her, that she will turn around, that she will rush into his arms.

Instead, Zhivago chases the streetcar onto which she steps, and as it pulls away we see his face reflected in the glass, and just beyond, Lara, staring straight ahead, her golden hair covered with the requisite blue kerchief. His heart is breaking—literally—and she doesn't even know he is there. Yet we know that her straight-backed, forward gaze and the gray-blue of her clothes are proof of the half life she is living without him.

V.

Last Wednesday, a day I still think of as our anniversary, my mother, on the verge of her eightieth birthday, telephoned to say that while going through my grandmother's things, she found a shoebox filled with letters. "Most were written after she escaped to Lithuania," she said, the papers ruffling in the background, "and they seem to be from friends who managed to get their letters out—Anya Prisekin mostly, a few from her cousin Helenka."

"And the others?" I asked.

"A very few were written during the years just after she married."

"Are there any from Misha?"

"Just one," my mother said.

"Send it to me, please."

152

"Oh Nadia, it isn't much. I'm afraid you will be disappointed."

"It doesn't matter. Please," I said, "just send it."

Dearest Nadia,

Boris wrote to tell me of your marriage. How could I possibly hold onto the hope that we would find our way back to each other again? History is against us, the age in which we live. Even so, in sleep sometimes when I dream, we are together again on that northern lake surrounded by purple-hued mountains. We are sixteen and strong swimmers. The gold bellies of kingfishers could not be brighter than our laughter.

Misha

Often, when I dream, I'm back at the gazebo you repaired, wrapped in the purple mist of wisteria and the surviving trumpet vines. I am fourteen years old, and I am reading aloud to you as you work. Sometimes, I stare at the crescent moon scar on your cheek, shiny with sweat, and I wish I had asked then what had marked you.

Not until Chicago, in the weeks after we became lovers, did I learn that you were scarred by the heel of your father's shoe. It fell from the rope that time he was out on the high wire in the midst of winter. You told me that you were looking up, not yet dazzled by heights, not yet dreaming of stories and literature, not even feeling the pain of the blow. No. All that time you kept looking up, amazed by your father perched on that homemade tightrope, arms outstretched as he tried to regain his balance. "Yes, he swayed, and something inside me seized up. But he did not fall, Nadia," you said. "Not that time anyway."

LITTLE ONE

Once the last car turns around the corner, Stephen walks back to the house, the stout corgi, Toby, following. Six days since Milly's funeral, and the first time in months that Stephen is alone in the white-washed brick colonial that he and Milly shared for twenty-one years.

In the rose-colored living room, which houses a blown glass chandelier they found in Venice more than a decade earlier, the carpet still holds the imprint of Milly's hospital bed. Some four months ago, after returning from the cancer center in Houston where she was told that the tumor in her uterus had grown back—*"I'm sorry, but there's nothing more that we can do"*—Milly took up residence in this room with its two walls of floor-length windows overlooking the garden she so loved, one that housed bougainvillea and mandevilla and endless pots of hibiscus; a garden that they both knew she would never again see in bloom. Round-the-clock hospice care followed, ever-increasing doses of morphine, a gradual, needle-sharp slipping away.

It's been ten days since Stephen came downstairs to check on Milly, taking note of the lights of the Christmas tree which they'd kept on during the night so that she could see them. The nurse, Hilda, was lying on the sofa beside Milly's bed, dozing. Stephen had only to look at his wife to realize that she was gone. Yes, it had been inevitable—imminent—yet her dying surprised him, for she'd managed to drink a toast the previous afternoon, even talked about a childhood Christmas until the pain reared up, and Hilda brought out a glass of water and the morphine.

Stephen stands beside one of those windows now, staring out at the gray-white light of early January, the inky branches of the live oaks sharply etched against the sky, still amazed that it has worked out this way. In two weeks, he will be seventy-four-years-old. And Milly would have been sixty-one, the two having been born thirteen years, four days, and some six hours apart. Until Milly's diagnosis, Stephen believed that she would be the one to inherit the burden of his aging.

Late afternoon sinks into evening, and the West Texas sky turns that gorgeous coral pink that almost makes the dust storms on these high plains worth it. Stephen resolves to clean out the refrigerator, laying out dozens of tins and foil-covered dishes until the granite counters are full. Since October, friends and neighbors and former colleagues have been bringing food, everything from casseroles and roasts to gaily-decorated Christmas cookies and pan after pan of oatmeal bars, brownies, even Rice Krispy treats. While Milly's grown sons were here, and later the three grandchildren, the food was eaten, some of it anyway. These days Stephen lives on canned soup and fruit, cereal, and ice cream eaten straight from the container, a ham and cheese sandwich when he remembers lunch.

By 9 p.m., he is scouring the shelves and storage bins. An hour later, staring at the now pristine interior, empty save for a carton of milk, butter, a loaf of sliced whole wheat bread, some packaged cheeses, and a bowl of artificially red apples, Stephen feels a disproportionate sense of accomplishment.

Four days later, Stephen is back at the faux adobe building surrounded by yucca and ornamental grasses that houses the South Plains Medical Center. After his stroke the previous winter—a mild one—but still his colleagues had expected Stephen to retire, never believing that he would make what seemed a miraculous recovery. "I plan to work until I'm eighty, or until they force me out," he used to tell Milly when she fretted over a cold that would linger well beyond the normal time, her worry a sign that she, too, would like him to step down or at least cut back. Since Milly's diagnosis, no one awaits Stephen's imminent retirement anymore.

Late that morning, while Stephen is in the midst of seeing a new patient, a frail, eleven-month-old boy with Down's Syndrome, accompanied by his twenty-six-year-old mother, the doctor looks out the window and spots his stepson Leo walking over from the parking lot. Leo, the youngest and the most troubled of Milly's three sons, has never been on the best of terms with Stephen, who hasn't seen him since the funeral. So what is Leo doing here of all places?

On the examination table, the tiny patient's ribcage protrudes, and his skin is dry, even scaly, but not once does he cry or fret. No, he just lies there staring up at Stephen and his mother. "We're going to need to assign some specialists to your son's care," Stephen says. "And we'll need to run some extensive tests."

"What's wrong with him?" his mother, Lena Sanchez, asks, brushing her long, black hair away from her face. Like so many people who come to see Stephen, Lena Sanchez's features are pinched with strain.

"It's too early to make a definitive diagnosis," Stephen says, "but it's clear that your son isn't getting the nutrition he needs."

Lena Sanchez's thin body stiffens. "I take very good care of my son."

"Ms. Sanchez," Stephen says as gently as possible, "children, especially those with Down's Syndrome, often do not chew and digest their food properly. It's possible, too, that Marco is missing a digestive enzyme. We won't know any of this until we do some blood work and other tests. What I want you to understand," he makes sure to hold her eye, "is that none of this is a judgment on your care. Your son is going to require medical intervention. We'll need to assign a dietary consultant, a physical therapist. The fact that he's still not crawling remains a problem."

She nods, bites her lower lip. "He'll be okay? No one will take him from me?"

Stephen restrains the impulse to reach out and touch her arm. "We're going to do everything we can for him," he says. "And no, no one will take him from you."

"Hey," his stepson Leo says, when Stephen steps into his office, drained from the appointment with Lena Sanchez and her child, for despite his words of reassurance, he does not believe the outcome will be promising. He takes in Leo's tight black t-shirt, in particular the way his stepson's bicep flexes when he raises his hand in greeting.

"I thought you'd be at the restaurant," Stephen says.

"I'm working the dinner shift tonight. I don't need to come in until 4:30." Leo, who is dyslexic, has a bachelor's degree in Fine Art and is a good, if undisciplined, painter. Thanks to Milly's efforts, two years ago he earned a Masters in Education. Why, then, is Leo, now twenty-nine, still working as a waiter in one of the town's three good restaurants, a place where Milly and Stephen's friends often dine, always overlooking the fact that Leo, who should have moved on by now, as their own children have, is still waiting tables?

156

"How's Desiree?" Stephen asks, the absurdly seductive name all too fitting for the slight flaxen-blonde with sharp green eyes who rarely buttons the top three buttons of her blouse.

"Good," Leo says.

"And the baby?" Stephen asks, tenderness creeping into his voice.

"Actually," Leo shifts his weight from one foot to the other, "that's one of the reasons I'm here."

"Can't you come to the house later?" Stephen says, sitting down opposite him in the leather desk chair, on the walls the framed photographs from travels to Peru, Italy, and Switzerland that Milly chose with such care. "I have half a dozen clients waiting to see me before lunch."

Leo shakes his head. "I'm due in at the restaurant at 4:30, remember?"

"Very well," Stephen says, noticing the way Leo's jaw twitches a little, a habit he's had since he was a boy, a sign of discomfort, stress. "What's going on?"

"It's Desiree. She wants to go back to school. Now that we have Gretchen, she thinks it's important to finish her degree."

Stephen's first reaction is relief. Milly would be happy about this. "Great," he says.

"Yeah." Leo grins. "Desiree wants to go to Oceans, the massage therapy school downtown."

"Is there enough of a market for that here?" Stephen asks, though what he is really thinking: Could Desiree, who weighs at most one hundred pounds, have the physical strength, much less the stamina for such work? She can barely handle taking care of the baby.

"She only wants to work part-time, Stephen. She wants to be with Gretchen the rest of the week. The good thing is," he continues, more flexing of the biceps, "she could start seeing patients, under supervision, as early as March."

"Sounds promising," Stephen says, wishing Leo and Desiree would get married, though as Milly reminded him, more times than he could count, Desiree doesn't exactly seem like long-term wife material. If Milly hadn't been dying, Stephen would have said, "And you think Leo's going to be a responsible husband? Until last year he lived with us, left his room a mess, and even now he comes to us for money."

157

The baby, as green-eyed as her mother but with Milly's dimple—amazing how that worked out—was born on November 1st, just two weeks after the devastating return from the cancer center.

"So what can I do for you?" Stephen says.

"There's Desiree's tuition, and then we're going to need some childcare for Gretchen."

"Money," Stephen realizes. *Of course. He came here to ask me for money.*

It's nearly midnight before Stephen gives up on trying to fall asleep and pads across the mohair rug that he and Milly found in Istanbul to the bathroom, its pristine whiteness antiseptic and a little forbidding at this hour. Before Milly's diagnosis, Stephen had never even taken a sleeping pill, always managing to deal with the occasional insomnia by plodding through the following day. Now, he has nothing in reserve.

In the too bright light, he faces himself in the mirror. These last weeks, he has grown a salt and pepper beard to hide the sunken quality of his cheeks, though the effect, as he's keenly aware, is unfortunate. The beard dwarfs his thin face, and his gray eyes, which Milly had so loved, have gotten lost in the process. He stands there staring at his aged self, and the memory of a much-younger Milly kissing his lips, his cheeks, his forehead, rushes back so intensely that his lungs and belly expand then deflate like balloons. Almost immediately, he begins searching for the scissors, then fervently snips away at the beard it has taken him six weeks to grow. He nicks the skin above his lip, and it bleeds. "Shit," Stephen murmurs. "Shit, shit, shit."

Footsteps pierce the silence, and for a wild, irrational moment he almost expects to find Milly there. "It's about time you shaved off that beard," he can almost hear her say, with that West Texas lilt that endeared her to him the night they met at a symphony gala here in town. Stephen turns around, his heart throbbing, but the shuffling belongs to Toby, the corgi, who gazes up at Stephen with milky eyes. The dog, now fourteen (a preposterous ninety-eight in human years), has cataracts. "Are you waiting for her to come back, too?" Stephen asks, bending to stroke the dog's thick coat. Toby buries his head in Stephen's chest, and he wraps his arms around the dog, breathes in his fur, which smells of grass, drying leaves, and winter.

At 10:30 the following Saturday, Leo shows up at the house with Gretchen. Leo has a key, but he rings the bell, which feels significant to Stephen, as if without Milly around Leo understands he no longer has instant access to his stepfather's house, his life.

"Well, doesn't she look beautiful," Stephen says, taking the twelve-week-old baby in his arms. Though the forecast said the temperature would reach fifty by mid-afternoon, it's still cold. For the drive over, Leo—or Desiree—has dressed Gretchen in a fleecy snowsuit with lamb's ears. Underneath, the baby wears a long-sleeved lavender onesie with rosebuds at the neck, feet, and wrists.

"How is she sleeping?" Stephen asks, once they sit down on the dusky rose sofa in the living room, the curtains on the windows overlooking the garden still partly drawn at this hour.

"She wakes up every two hours or so," Leo says, but happily. "I'm sleeping on the nursery floor. Best sleep I've had in a long time."

"And Desiree?" Stephen asks, as Gretchen relaxes into his arms, and he feels the dreamy weight of her small being—*For me,* her body says, *everything lies ahead.*

"She's fine," Leo says as he stands to open the curtains.

"I mean," Stephen says, squinting in the bright light, "does she wake at night to feed the baby?"

"Not usually. You know we're using formula. I take the night shift."

The baby food companies send formula samples to the medical center, but Stephen can't bring himself to distribute the stuff to his patients. He tightens his hold on Gretchen, and she wriggles in his arms. "So what brings you here on a Saturday morning? And where is Desiree? I thought she would have come, too, especially since you brought the little one."

"Little One" was the phrase that Milly had used when the three other grandchildren were babies, and its resurrection lands like a punch to the stomach.

"At school," Leo says, staring out at the wintering garden, the pool covered by the blue tarp, the urns and terra cotta pots empty. "*Des* has anatomy on Saturday mornings, then a two-hour practicum in the afternoon."

"So she's gone most of Saturday?" Stephen hears the disapproval in his voice. "And don't you have to be at the restaurant at noon?"

Leo's face turns sheepish, a look Stephen remembers from his stepson's boyhood. When Leo was caught doing something he shouldn't or wanted to get out of, his face assumed that same secretive, avoidant expression. "11:30 actually."

"Oh no," Stephen says, getting to his feet so suddenly that Gretchen moans in protest. "You didn't bring Gretchen over for me to——."

"I have no choice. Her babysitter's sick. She called up at nine. Desiree had already left. Besides," he adds, "it wouldn't be right for her to miss class. It's the second one of the semester."

Stephen restrains himself from saying that maybe they should have worked out the childcare situation more effectively before Desiree plunged into school. To the best of Stephen's memory, Desiree, who is twenty-five, left school at nineteen. What difference would another six months have made? In the autumn, Stephen would like to remind them, Gretchen would be nearly a year old, and her routine more reliable.

"I'm sorry." Leo shifts his weight from one foot to the other. "I'm in a bind. We're going to have a wedding reception in the back room. There's no way I can call in sick today."

"Why didn't you phone first?" Stephen says, wetness seeping through Gretchen's clothes, and the unmistakable stink of poop.

Leo just stares back at him, his expression unyielding, and Stephen remembers the string of messages on the answering machine, the "filled-to-capacity" signal on his cell phone. "Very well. This once. You brought diapers? Bottles? Plenty of clothes?"

Leo nods, smiling now. "Thanks, man," he says. "I mean, Stephen."

Well after one o'clock, once Stephen has changed Gretchen's diaper for the second time—poop both times—he stands before the family room's unlit fireplace and studies the photographs on the mantel, realizing he forgot to ask when Leo or Desiree would come to pick Gretchen up. Not that Stephen has

160

any plans. The McNultys invited him over for an early dinner, one he didn't know exactly how he was going to get out of, for they have been so persistent. Edie McNulty was one of Milly's oldest friends, the relationship going all the way back to high school. Now, at least, he can provide an honest reason for not coming, "I have to watch Gretchen." He has not yet called her "my granddaughter," and he registers this.

Once she has been changed and dressed in a clean onesie, this one decorated with grinning yellow ducks, Stephen holds her face to his cheek. Her tiny fingers explore his nose, eyes, chin, and he's glad he shaved off his beard, the consequence of his midnight panic. The oldest grandchild, Annabelle, Thomas's daughter, has refused to kiss Stephen since the beard. "Too scratchy," she said, even when her mother tried to coax her forward in those bleak days after Milly's death. "It's like bristles, like the rough brushes we use on Tippy." Her pony.

At four o'clock, Stephen leaves a message for Leo on his cell phone, though he senses his stepson will not pick it up, not anytime soon anyway. He's probably harried if he's working the wedding. But what about Desiree? He certainly expected to hear from her by now.

The sun has come out, and Toby has been shadowing Stephen all afternoon, determined to work in a walk. Soon he brings over his leash and lays it at Stephen's feet. "I know, old friend," Stephen says. "It's time." He stands to examine the Baby Björn that Leo left on the couch beside the diaper bag. "What do you think?" he says, speaking both to the baby and to the dog. "Do you think I can figure this out?"

He straps the carrier onto his chest, amazed at how much he must tighten the straps so that they fit. His fingers skim his ribcage, palpable beneath the sweater Milly gave him last Christmas.

The feel of his own bones, the memory of Millie's wasting at the end, seizes hold, and all at once he's wracked by sobs, guttural grief erupting from the deepest part of himself, demanding to be given presence, space.

Lying on her back on the ivory carpet, Gretchen watches him. Absolutely silent, still. Toby, who was never a children's dog, sits beside her, his sharp, pointed ears pricked at attention.

It's not until close to 8 p.m. that Desiree's battered Toyota Corolla pulls into the driveway, and Toby begins barking with unusual fervor. "Looking out for the little one, are we?" Stephen says to the dog, the phrase less foreign now, its syllables almost familiar, a bridge back to Milly.

He opens the door to Desiree, her baby-fine hair loose around her shoulders, her cheeks pink with cold. It's thirty-five at most, but Desiree wears only a purple velour sweatshirt and leggings, and Stephen is shocked to see some expensive flip-flops on her feet. "Thanks so much for watching her," Desiree says, stepping onto the tile floor and taking the baby in her arms.

"You're welcome," Stephen says, wondering if she will tell him why she has arrived so late.

"Did she give you any trouble?" Desiree asks as Gretchen tugs at a strand of her mother's hair, coos.

Stephen considers inviting Desiree inside, the two having never actually had a private conversation, but her posture, and her tone, tell him that she's eager to get going. "No," Stephen says. "She was no trouble."

"Leo and I appreciate your help," she says, but she doesn't meet Stephen's eye.

He expects her to say something else—what he does not know. But something. "You're enjoying the anatomy class? If you want help sometime—"

"Thanks," she says. "I'll keep that in mind. Now, I should get her things. It's late."

On Monday, in his office, Stephen sits behind his heavy desk and studies the laboratory results on Lena Sanchez's son. Though there is some uncertainty about the cause, the tests show one thing conclusively: the boy's hemoglobin levels are dangerously low; his body is not absorbing iron. Already there's been some damage to his organs, to his kidneys in particular. This has to be the reason, Stephen suspected at the first appointment, for the boy's shrunken veins. They'd had to try several times before getting the needle into the vein at his throat for a blood draw, and the poor child had screamed and screamed, covered with punctures that would now be bruising. The boy and his mother are due in an hour for their follow-up appointment.

Thankfully, Marjorie, the gentle nurse, has been assigned to work with Stephen today. She is already in the sunflower-yellow examining room with Lena Sanchez and her son when Stephen joins them.

"Anemia," Lena Sanchez says. "I don't believe my son has anemia. I eat lots of red meat. I feed it to him several times a week, sometimes every day."

Stephen has to suppress reading into what she is saying, as if the old rules still apply. Thirty years ago, red meat was a luxury; but no longer, not with the endless strips of six-lane roads in this town, the roadsides dominated by McDonald's, Burger King, Taco Bell. And eighty miles beyond Lubbock, the cattle feed lots begin, stretching all the way from Muleshoe into Clovis, New Mexico. "What you don't realize, Ms. Sanchez," Stephen says politely, "is that anemia is not a reflection of your care."

She folds her arms across her chest. Last time, she hadn't worn her Walmart uniform. Today, the effect of the polyester is startling. When Stephen goes into Walmart, which is rarely, for he avoids the place at all costs, he never really sees the checkers in their cheap, stiff uniforms. Not really, and this shames him now.

"Marco's body is not absorbing iron," he says, determined to hold her eye.

"And what will you do to get him to absorb iron, doctor? What can you do?" Her shoulders collapse as she sits down in one of the plastic chairs while Marco lies, remarkably silent given his last traumatic experience here, on the examination table.

"There are two courses of treatment," Stephen says.

"Okay. What are they?"

"We could try a blood transfusion," he says. "I'm reluctant to take that route given how shrunken your son's veins are. Anemia does that to the body."

"What's the other idea?" Her voice is soft, drained.

"We install a catheter that brings blood straight to Marco's heart."

"Surgery?" Fear registers in her eyes.

"This is going to take a few months to correct," Stephen says, "if we can correct it. If we elect to do transfusions, you will need to bring Marco here every week, maybe two times a week. Each time, we will have to search for a vein. You saw how difficult it was the last time, how painful. It will be like that every time until his body starts to repair itself."

"Alright," she says. Her lower lips trembles as tears gather in the corners of her eyes.

At home that night Stephen fixes a whiskey and soda at the bar, a marble-topped counter with a mirrored backdrop for their wine and liquors. He sips his drink, his gaze inevitably drawn to the spot where Milly's hospital bed had been. What to do with the remaining weeks, months, years without Milly?

At his feet, Toby, too dignified to whine, lets out a series of low baritone barks.

Stephen stares at him, and the dog wags his stub of a tail, not affectionately, but with a kind of urgency, as if there is some message that Stephen's not registering. He fed Toby as soon as he came home, but one look at the food bowl, still half-full, shows that dinner is not the issue. "What is it, old boy? You need to go out?"

Toby holds his gaze for a moment longer, then retreats to his dog bed in the corner, leaving Stephen with the feeling that he's failed the animal somehow. "Ridiculous," he says aloud, swallowing the whiskey.

He pours just a finger more, trying to dull the longing for Milly. How many evenings did he come home from the medical center to sit with her over drinks here. As the sun dipped below the horizon, they talked about their respective days, and when he told her about his difficult patients—the painful ones—she always found a way to discover some point of light.

"You must have been lying here all night like this, Mr. Hummel," Melody says, after he opens his eyes to find her staring down at him, her lips pursed with concern.

He sits up, registers the empty glass on the coffee table, the morning sunlight, and realizes that he must have fallen asleep on the sofa. "What time is it?" Stephen asks, already peering at his watch.

"Time for you to get in bed," Melody says. "I wasn't going to say so, but I have no choice now: you need a good, long rest, Mr. Hummel. You've been doing way too much ever since poor Mrs. Hummel got sick, and now—"

"I appreciate your concern, Melody," he interrupts, "but I'm not an invalid."

She frowns, fixes him with her beautiful dark eyes. "You're skinny as an alley cat, pardon the expression."

"Very well," he says, amazed, a little, at how good it feels, her concern. "I will stay in today, on one condition: I don't want you fussing over me."

"You don't need to worry about that," she says. "I've got far too much to do around here without you to look after. Besides," she tilts her head to the side so that he can almost see the pretty young woman she had once been, "you're paying me to clean, not to fuss."

"Yes, of course," Stephen says kindly, remembering the hours that Melody spent sitting beside Milly's bed, reading to her from any one of the nineteenth-century novels that Melody, surprisingly, seemed to like so much. What this no-nonsense black woman from West Texas found in Jane Austen, Stephen couldn't say, not being fond of the author's sitting room chit-chat himself. Yet he could not deny that Milly grew calmer while buoyed by Melody's voice, the pain troubling her less.

In the end, Melody does fuss over Stephen. At least she looks after him.

At noon, she brings him a bowl of minestrone soup along with a glass of orange juice. Stephen knows he didn't have any juice in the refrigerator, but he doesn't ask Melody where it came from. He just drinks it down, along with the tea she carries in later; and with it, a plate of Chessman cookies. These, he remembers seeing in the pantry.

"How's that grandbaby of yours?" Melody asks, as Stephen sits in the roomy, floral armchair by the bedroom window.

"Gretchen is fine," he says, though as soon as the words are out, he knows they aren't true.

Melody seems to understand this, for she says, "Fine?"

"If we're going to talk," he says, "then let's do so properly. Why don't you sit down? But first, go and fix yourself a cup of tea. There are too many cookies on this plate for me anyway."

Melody smiles, nods. "Alright, Mr. Hummel."

"Stephen, please," he says. "You found me on the living room floor."

"No, sir," she says, shoulders back. "I need to keep a degree of formality, especially if we're going to be sitting down in here."

"Very well," Stephen says. "Let's go into the living room. The sun's out."

The room is warm and cozy at this hour, the windows bringing in as much light as any room can hold, and anointing the marble-topped surfaces and their contents—porcelain vases, ancient stones, even a jade eye framed in gold from some ancient Egyptian tomb—with a softness, a sense of harmony and order that Stephen has not felt in a long time.

By the time each of them has drunk a second cup of Earl Grey tea, Stephen has told Melody a good deal about the Saturday he spent with Gretchen, Desiree's return to massage school, the odd distance of her behavior when she came to pick up Gretchen, the fear that his stepson isn't telling him the whole story.

"What do you think Leo's not saying?" Melody asks, while Toby, no lap dog, curls up at her feet, his nose resting atop her shoe.

Stephen looks out into the garden, notes the flash of red, a cardinal moving among the live oaks, and remembers Leo as he had been when they first met, a shy, eight-year-old with asthma. Stephen had tried to teach Leo to ride, thinking horses might create a bond between them, but the boy couldn't breathe around horses, so they had to quit. In the end, it was Thomas, Milly's oldest son, who accompanied Stephen to the stables—Thomas with whom Stephen became close.

"I'm not entirely sure," Stephen says at last. "Leo's never talked to me, not really. It was always Milly he turned to."

"She took such good of care of him, she did," Melody says at last.

Stephen meets her eye, wondering what else she has noticed and concluded over the twelve, maybe fifteen that she has worked for them.

"I know they say a mother can't do too much for her child, and I'd like to say I agree."

"But you don't?"

"The world isn't an easy place," Melody says. "My mama died when I was sixteen. I was her baby until then. After, I learned

166

the hard way. I had to drop out of school, get a job. You wouldn't know it now, but I planned to be an English teacher."

Stephen nods, reminded again of those hours that Melody spent reading to Milly, his image of her transforming before his eyes. Though if he's honest with himself, how much thought has he actually given her until now?

Late afternoon on Thursday, and Stephen finishes seeing patients at the unusually early hour of 4:30. Seated at his desk, he stares at the photograph of Milly before him, one taken during their last holiday in a village in the Spanish Pyrenees. She sits smiling back at him, a glass of red wine on the café table before her. What had they talked about that afternoon? Stephen wonders, wishing he could recover the circumstances, the reason for the delight in Milly's eyes. He takes the photograph in his hands, raises it to his lips, missing her fiercely. Had life not taken the turn it did, he would go home now and take Milly out to dinner; or they would sit in the living room and watch a movie, something with Bogart or maybe one of the *Thin Man* series.

Outside the sky blooms violet, and Stephen's thoughts return to last Saturday when he stood at the reservoir, Gretchen strapped to his chest, Toby bounding ahead—almost like a young dog—to chase the errant squirrel. He misses Gretchen, hopes that Leo will call him again and ask him to watch her. And what of Desiree, the lateness of the hour when she turned up? Her eagerness to get going? Of Milly's grown children and their partners, it was Desiree, whose father died when she was nine, who seemed the least comfortable in the house once Milly got sick. At the funeral, he wasn't sure he even remembered seeing her though she would have had the excuse of the new baby to stay away.

Marco Sanchez's surgery to install the catheter has been scheduled for today. A specialist, an Iraqi woman whom Stephen met only once at a lunch meeting, performed the operation. Stephen picks up the phone, dials her number.

"The procedure was successful," she tells him. "Mrs. Sanchez and her son are at Covenant through the weekend. I'll go and see them tomorrow afternoon. What we need to watch for is infection. We've introduced antibiotics intravenously."

167

Stephen wants to ask her more, but it's clear, from the fatigue tugging at the edges of her own voice, that she is ready to go home, or at least get back to the work that will bring her closer to getting there.

Not long after that, his own cell phone vibrates on the desk. If it wasn't right in front of him, he wouldn't see it. The caller is Leo.

"Where are you?" Stephen asks, for the connection is bad, full of interference.

"At the apartment," Leo says.

"Alright then," he hesitates, "and Desiree? Where's she?"

"Not here."

"At school?"

"No." Leo's voice comes out hoarse. "She left me. There's a note on the table."

Panic surges through his body. "Where's Gretchen?"

"With me. Here. She's fine," Leo says. "She was here with the babysitter, with Karen, when I came home from the restaurant. Thing is, I need to be back there in an hour. I only came home to—"

Fury overtakes Stephen's fear. "This girlfriend of yours, this mother of your child, takes off, and you call me to say that you have to go back to work?"

"I knew I couldn't count on you," Leo says, though the words lack their usual force.

Stephen slumps against his chair, the anger still there, but accompanied by something else. Why does it feel almost as if Milly is in the room with him? "Very well, Leo, what do you want me to do?"

"I want to come back to the house," Stephen says heavily, "and I want to bring Gretchen. Not for long, just until I get things straightened out."

Stephen stares out the window into the fading light— gloaming, this time of day used to be called. "I'll meet you at the house in an hour."

Saturday is Stephen's seventy-fourth birthday, and Milly's will follow within the week. Ordinarily, he and Milly would have celebrated in some extravagant, private way—a candlelight dinner with a bottle of French Bordeaux, peonies in a Lenox vase, a buttery pastry for dessert.

Instead, once Leo leaves for the restaurant, Steven stands on the threshold to his stepson's old room, Gretchen in his arms and Toby at his feet. The walls are still covered with the pop art posters he collected throughout college, along with several of his vivid, abstract acrylics. The space, Stephen thinks, looks almost as if he'd never left. Thankfully, Leo has developed at least some of the habits of neatness since he last lived here. Yes, there are mismatched socks on the floor, and baby wipes litter many surfaces, but his clothes are hung up in the closet, and the box of books he brought—many of them volumes of Buddhist-influenced poetry, or so Stephen gathers from reading the blurbs—have been unpacked and set on the shelves that once held Leo's dog-eared thrillers.

On the night Leo and Gretchen arrived, the two men set up a nursery in the guest room across the hall, though with the exception of the makeshift changing table on the dresser, Gretchen rarely uses it. Most nights, she sleeps in the bed with her father, and although Stephen initially feared Leo would roll over and crush her, four nights have passed, and all seems to be well, well enough anyway.

"It's just you and me and Toby today," Stephen tells Gretchen as they make their way downstairs, once he has changed yet another soiled diaper.

When Stephen and Milly first got married, she was forty-two. These days, several of his junior colleagues and his friends' professional children have babies in their forties. A neighbor down the street even had twins at forty-seven, thanks to IVF. He and Milly thought about it, yes, but only very briefly. She already had Leo, whose father died when he was six; and her eldest son, Thomas, from a very brief marriage to another graduate student while earning her history degree at Columbia. Having been a single mother for three years until she married Stephen, she didn't really want another child. And Stephen, the doted upon, only child of his Austrian parents, had never felt the visceral need for children. At least not until his mother died. By then, Milly was nearly fifty.

These thoughts linger as he stands in the turquoise kitchen, with its glass-door cupboards, its warm red tile floors, and fixes Gretchen's bottle. What would his mother, a founder of Planned

Parenthood, say about Leo and Desiree? And really, what would it matter?

He tests the formula to make sure it isn't too hot, nudges the bottle into Gretchen's mouth. What a good baby she is. Nights, he hears her wake a few times, but Leo seems to quiet her easily. She naps on and off during the day, and when awake, she proves alert, quiet, not fussy. Her behavior amazes Stephen for Gretchen hasn't seen her mother for four days now, at least as far as Stephen knows.

Karen, the babysitter, was supposed to come at one o'clock; but Stephen told Leo that since he was home for the day, he would watch Gretchen. Leo had looked at him skeptically. "You sure? I thought you had work to do."

"If I had a problem with it, I would say so," Stephen said, careful not to smile, and not in the least bit surprised that Leo did not remember his birthday—or Milly's. Leo wasn't good with dates under the best of circumstances.

His plan is to spend the afternoon going through the stack of medical bills that piled up those last months. Once he gives Gretchen her bottle, he will settle her into the Moses basket in his study, turn on the classical radio station in any one of the countries he can access online, and get down to work.

"I appreciate this," Leo said just before leaving. "Not just today, but everything."

"Good," Stephen said.

For the first hour, Gretchen watches peacefully from the floor as Stephen works at the desk beside her. He has hung a mobile above the basket and just beyond is the light from the window that slants delicately across her face. Toby, who had appointed himself her other caregiver, positions himself near the Moses basket. When Melody saw this, two days earlier, she told Stephen the dog had found a new person to protect—a new "job." Neither one of them has to say that the last person, the only other one, had been Milly.

By the time the grandfather clock in the hall strikes two o'clock, Gretchen is fast asleep, and Stephen looks up from the paperwork to study her features. Desiree has a high forehead, and her daughter has inherited this. Where is Desiree? He senses that Leo could press charges, that there could be custody issues, but he doesn't have the energy to think about any of this now, and he doubts that Leo does either.

Leo had required so much more than his older brother, and over the years Milly spent thousands of hours helping him. All that homework all through high school, college, and then graduate school, so that friends only half-joked that she had earned several other degrees. "Don't you think you should let Leo handle this one on his own?" Stephen asked two years ago when he found Milly up past midnight reading the study guide for her son's education exams.

Milly just fixed Stephen with her eyes, her gaze neither irritated nor defensive. "No, I don't."

"He's twenty-seven, Mill, and I don't think he's ever studied for an exam or written a paper without your help."

Milly just shook her head. "Leo was six when Jacob died. I've told you that he didn't speak for six months after that."

"That was twenty years ago."

"I'm sorry, Stephen," she said, behind her immovable voice the generations of homesteaders who'd come out West. "*This* is one decision that is not up for discussion."

Regardless of what she'd said, over the next few months Stephen continued to fight Milly on this issue, as he'd fought her on other situations in which she seemed to be doing far too much for Leo.

But really, Stephen asks himself now, how could he have been so sure? Despite their intimacy, Milly never did tell him a great deal about her marriage to Leo's father, a defense attorney who had taken his own life after one of his clients—whom he'd gotten off on murder charges—was later convicted for killing a mother and her two small children. Nor had Stephen known much about the aftermath, excepting Leo's silence and the fact that it was only then that she left the East Coast and returned to Lubbock.

How is it possible that despite Milly's unparalleled devotion, Leo was practically absent from the house during the last two months of his mother's life? During those last weeks, Stephen had waited for Milly to say something to him about this, but she never did, though Stephen knew she registered it. Not even the morphine could make her forget her son's staying away.

Stephen isn't sure what time Gretchen wakes screaming,

171

her tiny hands balled into fists, her face the color of a raspberry. "My goodness," he says and stands, his legs cramped from his position at the desk. "What is wrong?" He scoops her up. "What is it?"

On the way upstairs, Stephen's legs continue to cramp, so he holds on to Gretchen with his left hand while using his right hand to keep in contact with the banister. Toby stays a step behind him.

As soon as he lays her down on the changing table and gets her undressed, he sees that she has developed a rash since he changed her—when was it? Eleven? Or just before noon? The clock on the nightstand says 3:45 p.m. How often he's counseled frantic new mothers about diaper rash, teething, colic, and other ailments. And how easily. Now, as he tries to dab the ointment onto Gretchen's bottom, first with his fingertip, then when she continues to scream with a q-tip, he thinks about those new mothers. He can imagine them standing beside him, laughing, or saying, "See, I told you so. It isn't as easy as all that, is it?"

When Stephen was in his thirties, a friend's wife had taken an axe to the piano after her twins were born. After that, her husband agreed to get her some help. What about the women who don't have any help? Resources? An image of Lena Sanchez flashes through his mind.

Back downstairs, Stephen fixes Gretchen a bottle, keeping watch over the milk on the stove as she squirms in his arms. "You're hungry," he says. "Food's coming."

But when he holds the bottle to her lips, Gretchen turns away, puts forth a series of piercing screams.

"What are we going to do about you, Mr. Stephen?" Melody asks, when he opens the door some two hours later, amazed at his relief at seeing her there, a sturdy figure in a pink down coat, the hood edged with fake fur, her lips made up with that same shade of pink.

"Well," he says, ushering her inside and out of the cold, for the wind has picked up, and it is down to thirty. "At least you're not still calling me 'Mr. Hummel.'"

She shrugs off her big coat. "That's not answering my question."

"It's not me I'm worried about," he says, then leads her

172

down the hall to the study where Gretchen lies in her basket, asleep at last after exhausting herself.

"Her mama hasn't come to see her in all this time?" Melody says, scooping the sleeping Gretchen up and into her ample arms so gently that she manages not to wake her.

"Is that a question?" Stephen says.

Melody shoots him a stern look. "Mr. Hummel, *Stephen,* you call me up on a Saturday night when I'm home with my family, and I come straight over. Now that I'm here, I think we should talk straight to each other if you know what I mean."

"Yes," Stephen says. "Thank you. I'm sorry."

"No need to be sorry," she says, expertly tucking a finger into Gretchen's diaper. "I just think it's important that we get the situation straight, know where each one of us stands if we're going to work together."

"Yes, of course." Watching Melody hold Gretchen, Stephen is half-seized with the desire to thrust himself into Melody's arms, knowing that they would smell like butter and sugar and something faintly floral, the scent of the house after she leaves.

After they've closed the study door and find themselves seated side by side on the living room sofa, two mugs of peppermint tea before them—"to soothe the nerves," Melody said—Stephen stares at the place where Milly's hospital bed had been. How is it possible that she's been gone now for four weeks? The time seems both inordinately long since then, and abominably fast.

"You think her mama's going to come back?" Melody says, holding her teacup in her hands.

"Honestly, Melody, I have no idea. Thomas's wife, Betsy, I've known since they met in college. But Desiree. Well, that one's a mystery, to put it mildly—"

Melody purses her lips. "How old is she?"

"Twenty-five," Stephen says.

"I had two babies by the time I was twenty-five," Melody says, "but that Desiree, she's still a girl. It might take her another ten years to grow up."

"Gretchen will be in fifth grade by then," Stephen says, calculating. "I certainly hope it doesn't take her that long."

"All I can say is it's a good thing that Leo's come home to you with his daughter."

173

"You think so?" Stephen meets her eye, warmth suffusing his body.

"I do. It's good for you, too," she says, her gaze softening. "I'd say, she might just be the saving of you, and you of her."

Stephen hasn't cried before anyone since the day Thomas drove off. Now tears sting his eyes. He thinks of all that paperwork on his desk—the itemized bills for the nurses, the hospital bed, the IV—and he's afraid he'll give way.

Then Gretchen begins to cry.

Both Stephen and Melody get to their feet at the same time, though it's Melody, this time, who hangs back once they reach the baby, and Stephen bends down to pick her up, amazed, given the afternoon they've shared, that she quiets as soon as he takes her in his arms.

Marco Sanchez's catheter does become infected. The Iraqi specialist calls Stephen on Tuesday to tell him so. The child should have been released on Monday, but because he continued to lose weight—and they feared further organ failure—they kept him on another day. By Tuesday, the specialist realizes the catheter will need to be removed, the area cleaned, another catheter installed, and of course more antibiotics in higher doses.

Stephen listens to this news then asks, "How's the boy's mother, Ms. Sanchez?"

"Frightened," the specialist says. "She's been sleeping on the sofa in his hospital room for five days, and her mother comes every day to pray over the boy. I wrote up some elaborate documentation for Walmart to ensure she gets leave. Ms. Sanchez wants to stay here with Marco. We'll need to keep him for at least another week, more likely two. I hope she won't lose her job."

"Thank you," Stephen says. "Thank you for telling me."

If Lena Sanchez is religious, too, Catholic, and most likely she is, Stephen thinks, then an abortion was never part of the equation, even if she'd known that the child she was carrying had Down's. Stephen knows that his thinking is out-of-step in a Pro-Life town where at least 25 percent of the population lives below the poverty line.

When Leo told Milly and Stephen that Desiree was pregnant the previous spring, Stephen had recommended an abortion. Without any hesitation, Milly reminded him later in defense of Leo's anger. Leo didn't speak to Stephen for months after that, staying away until late summer when Milly's cancer was diagnosed. Leo made some semblance of peace with his stepfather only in October after the specialists in Houston said that the tumor had grown back, and Milly had at most three months.

Stephen thinks about this now, holding Gretchen in his arms and standing beside the windows overlooking the wintering garden, rocking her back and forth, and singing a German lullaby he remembers from his own childhood. What if Leo had taken Stephen's initial advice, made in anger as much as in so-called common sense? How was Leo to support a baby on a waiter's salary? And what kind of future would she have with a college dropout for a mother who stayed on working at Victoria's Secret through her eighth month of pregnancy? These exact words Stephen did not say.

But Leo had gotten the gist of it. If Leo had taken his advice, Stephen would be absolutely alone now in the big house with its cathedral ceilings, its five bedrooms, its tasteful collection of antiques, art, and the objects that he and Milly brought home from their many travels. Instead, he is here with Gretchen—and with Leo, too. And Toby, of course.

He looks down at Gretchen, who has at last fallen asleep. She is nearing her fifteenth week of life, and since she has come into Stephen's home, she has already changed so much. There is more substance to her now, and her hair, that downy tuft with which she was born, is beginning to fall out. How can Desiree bear to miss any of this? Stephen asks himself, touching his lips to Gretchen's forehead and breathing in her milky, slightly sour scent. How?

Every day he expects Desiree to call and reclaim her. He expects her to make some peace with Leo. And every day that passes without word from her, Stephen, though he says nothing of this, not even to Melody, who comes three times a week now to help with Gretchen, is grateful. A part of him knows this situation will not, cannot last. At some point, Desiree will return. She may not try to claim custody of her daughter, or even partial custody, but he cannot imagine that she will remain totally absent. As for Leo, for how long will he want to stay here in the house with Stephen? Six months? Another year at most?

The front door opens, and Toby, ears pricked, makes for the hallway, but does not bark, intuiting perhaps, that the baby over whom he stands guard at night—for Toby sleeps in Leo's room now instead of with Stephen—must not be woken.

Stephen steps away from the windows, makes out Leo's silhouette in the hallway, and is filled with surprise. He didn't expect Leo until much later that night, not until after 9 o'clock. Leo comes closer. He holds a white box in his hands, a box just the right size for a cake. "Happy birthday, Stephen," Leo says, very close now, so that he brings with him the wintry smells of the outdoors, of gasoline, and smoke. "Happy birthday."

At the sound of her father's voice Gretchen's eyes flutter open. No matter that Leo got it wrong. Stephen finds himself buoyed with gratitude. With joy. Not his birthday, no, but Milly's—he remembers only now—it's today.

HEROIN(E)

"It is a great shame that anyone so good should be so ugly."
—Beauty and the Beast

Lucifer: The archangel cast out of heaven for leading the revolt of the angels. The Roman name for the planet Venus in her appearance as morning star. Bearer of light from the Latin (lux, lucis + ferre).

Ramble: The roses I love do not possess names like Red Masterpiece, Royal Highness, Savoy Hotel, Prince's Trust. No, the roses I love are hardy, often single-flowered blooms with names like Summer Wine, Pinkie, Soaring Flight, Enigma, Remember Me. Refusing to be trellised or tamed, they ramble across landscapes like sea foam, twine around fence posts and up crumbling gables, hiding the cracking paint, the broken shutters, the missing step, while never trying to hide their thorns. Prick a finger, and you bleed. Everyone knows that. Still, the fragrance of roses kindles in me a hunger. To overreach myself. *Luciferin, luciferase.* Surrounded by summer's ever-blooming roses, I begin to believe I will not—cannot be erased.

Myth: The rose may be the oldest garden plant in cultivation. The flower is depicted in Egyptian tomb paintings long before Cleopatra's reign. Yet it is the queen's love of roses—supposedly she rendezvoused with Marc Antony in rooms knee-deep with their fragrant petals—that created a demand for them throughout the world.

In Greek mythology, the rose obtains its red color when Aphrodite rushes to the dying Adonis's side. Panicked, she accidentally treads on the thorns of the white rose, and her blood stains the blossoms red. In sympathy with the doomed lovers, the rose keeps its bloody color.

Unspoken: *The Beast opened his eye and said to Beauty, "You forgot your promise."* Yes, and now six days later than expected, she has returned to his garden—*her* garden, too, for he gave it to her—just as he gave her the high glass room filled with magenta and turquoise birds that spoke her name and the chattering gold-green finches who perched on the tips of her shoulders, then darted high up into the reflecting arc of a bound sky to thread her mouse-brown hair into the nests they tucked into the shadowy eaves. Why, there was even a snow-white owl with the face of a prophet whose amber eyes watched over her on those nights when she could not sleep.

The entire place, but especially the garden, ignited in her the desire to record the stories begun with tales spun from roses, and how could she not given that they possessed names like Yolande d'Aragon, Souvenir de la Malmaison, Eglantyne, Jude the Obscure, Bridge of Sighs? Buoyed by stories he placed in her arms like so much overflowing bounty, this nearsighted, mouse-haired girl who had not done well in school for a long time (for there was her father's drinking, not to mention the walled-in loneliness of the white room where she still heard her absent mother's footsteps) traveled to countries she never dreamed of. There she met people who redefined words she'd gleaned from books: bravery, fidelity, grace, discovery, purpose, compassion.

All this he gave to her on the cool, purple nights among the drifting perfume of roses, the stars whispering other stories—older stories—in the galaxy beyond them, the trees leaning close to listen; ah yes, the dark forest of deep green trees.

"Is it really you?" he asks, stepping into the light of the glass room where this morning's birds are strangely silent. "Have you really come back?"

She knows he wants her to speak the one word he has never spoken, despite the way his stories circled around it; despite the way the profuse hearts of the roses—petals dropping cleanly, clearing the way for further blooms, such a pleasure to behold—dared him to speak it.

Perhaps, she thinks, catching sight of her hair glinting high up in one of the nests where six tufted heads are watching her, it is up to her to speak it. Perhaps this is her part in the story. She calculates the number of days and weeks that she has been gone, astonished to see that every nest is now filled with nestlings. Is it possible so much time has truly passed?

"Is your father alright?" he asks, as the downy winged, amber-eyed owl soars through the air to alight, not on her shoulder—the owl never touched her, always kept its distance—but on his. "Did your visit make him happy?"

"Yes," she says, understanding only now that the owl moved through the air with absolute silence. No wonder the other birds are watchful of him, mistrustful, even in this safe place where they are cared for, cherished. Doesn't nature teach you to fear what you cannot see or hear?

"I'm glad," he replies.

She feels the word on her tongue. If only she could speak it.

Around them now, darkness seems to lift, a heaviness even here in this glass-ceilinged room with its dome of light. House, branch, expanse, leave, solace, love.

The snowy owl's eyes, although amber, point into the shadows.

Does she dare look past that? Will loving him enable her to look past the long shadows, the never-ending gloam that seemed to swallow her whole; but not here, no matter that he is more beast than man, never here in this house and garden of light, birdsong, story?

If words are not spoken at the proper moment—when a white owl soars through the air, when the finch's green-gold chicks blink in the morning light—will the moment disappear? The chance. Will it no longer be possible? Are the gods listening? Is the deep forest of trees?

Her fingertips alight on his scarred arms, where the needles left tracks, a kind of Braille she has never before attempted to read.

"You are braver than I expected," he says, holding her close, this woman with a beating heart, this woman who will grow old, but first there are the chicks in the nests above their heads. There is the future rambling towards the present. Twining round them like a wild, untameable rose.

179

Heroine: A woman noted for courage or daring action. The principal female character in a novel, poem, or dramatic presentation. In novels, the heroine is often an idealistic young woman from a privileged background. This young woman, rarely one with mouse-brown hair but one who has often lost her mother, longs to distinguish herself through good deeds that simultaneously reinforce an idealized image of herself. One in keeping with an understanding of the world gleaned from books. The heroine's text typically follows her self-education in the differences between book learning and real life, selflessness and egotism. Think of Emma Woodhouse and Dorothea Brooke, of Isabel Archer and Helen Schlegel.

Pilgrim: I have been walking Guadalupe for miles, hoping to see the Number One Bus over my shoulder. Grit coats my teeth and grazes my eyelashes. How could I have forgotten my sunglasses? How I long for a shower. Two miles to go, and I finally stop just outside Urban Outfitters. Another person waits there, too. I take this as a sign that the bus will be here soon.

He smiles. In the windblown sunlight, his hair is the color of bottled honey. "Late?"

I nod.

"Me, too."

The cars go by.

Minutes later I know his name is Tobias, and he is twenty-four and has been living in a halfway house since February. "Heroin," he says, "I lost four years of my life. Four years." He snaps his fingers. "Gone."

Lateness no longer matters, though already I can trace the furrows in my husband Will's brow despite his smile; but once, wasn't Will—who had come from a land of rivers and lush green to arid air and an absence of trees—a stranger too?

"When I walked the Way of Saint James," I hear myself say, "the miraculous happened. It was part of the journey." ("But how," Will will ask, "did you and this guy get on the subject of miracles?")

Tobias leans closer, the pupils of his eyes opening like an animal's when it trusts you. "Like what?"

"I met a woman named Erika in Navarre. She was Brazilian. She wore diamonds in her ears, yet she slept beside me on the cool, stone floors. She told me to live only in the present, not in the past or in the future. 'The past and the future are fictions,' she said."

It's clear Tobias isn't sure what to make of this. Still, his eyes—more amber than hazel—hold my own, the pupils open wide.

"A pony stepped onto a path in the Pyrenees," I tell him, shrugging off all I have been told about divulging such petaled secrets to strangers (from the French *éstranger*, which is also *inconnu*. And yet the Spanish word for pilgrim, *peregrino*, is also the word for curious, strange. "The pony brought back a poem I love. A poem I'd been carrying around for nearly a decade. 'If I stepped out of my body, I would break into blossom.'"

"All day," Tobias says, "I've wondered what I did to let the hope in. He names the poets he likes. Sexton figures prominently, but there is also Wilbur, O'Hara—a natural choice, and remarkably, John Donne. "Though I hate Bukowski," he says, "and Kerouac. What show-offs. What goddamned frauds."

Tobias may wear short sleeves, but somehow I don't think to look at his arms, not even when he tells me he got down to a hundred and nineteen pounds. He and I stand eye to eye. That makes him five ten.

"If I had the money," he says, "I'd still be doing it. But I had to do things, really bad things. For the money, that is."

His mouth is wide and his jaw square. *A beautiful kid*, I think, though twenty-four makes him a man. Twenty-four. *What if his life had ended there, this boy-man with honey-brown hair and the eyes of an owl*

181

who wasted himself down to one hundred and nineteen pounds?

"I changed," Tobias says, "to chase the dragon. And it scared me real bad."

"I understand," I say, reminded of the morning I hurled a lamp down the attic stairs. I didn't want to hit Will who stood below, but I did want to make him and the argument burning both our tongues—the shame, the ugliness—go away. Vanish. The way a gust of wind can clear a rose garden, leaving only the thorny stems. Blinking in the exposed attic light, he slammed the door so hard the wood cracked, and the door jammed. I sat down on the stairs and wept. He listened, but after a while—how long? I could not count the minutes—he jimmied the door and let me out.

But what if we'd let the anger escalate? What if it burned and spread like the wildfires raging just north of the drought-infested country where we live?

"If you were still doing it, the heroin," I say, "there would be only one ending to your story."

"I know." His eyes slant closed. The sun is bright.

The bus pulls up, and we board, sit side by side in the narrow seats, knees bumping.

All day I've wondered what I did to let the hope in.

The cars go by. The bus chugs down Guadalupe.

"I'm getting off at the courthouse," Tobias says, then rattles off a day filled with the kind of errands that require one to wait and fill out forms and never use one's head.

"You should go back to school when you get out," I tell him.
He stares hard at me, shrugs, tells me he'd like to. "But how?"

I want to ask him about his family in Baltimore. Doesn't he have any contact with them? Isn't there somebody? He shakes his head no, shrugs. "Give me your address," I say. "I'll send you a parcel."

"Yeah?" He half-grins, writes down the halfway house's address where he'll be living through May.

"Even better, I'll send you poetry, a parcel of poetry. We'll keep in touch." I scribble my email address on a postcard, reminded that there is a risk here I cannot lose sight of; for the desire to help carries with it a responsibility. Do I really want to take that on—do I really want to take him on, a boy-man I just met at a bus stop?

I hesitate; but Tobias is smiling at me, his eyes shining. Quickly, I hand him my address, heroine@gmail.com, telling myself that one letter separates an exemplar from the irretrievable, one letter spans the distance between possibility and addiction. But he's here beside me, so the single vowel must matter infinitely more than its absence.

The card changes hands, and it's then I see the tracks. They remind me of journeys through northern cities in Germany on trains that gray, cold, rainy season I lived in a centuries-old village outside of Nuernberg and missed home so much I spoke English aloud in my room, rolled my loved ones names around on my tongue, and went for endless runs in the maze of forest beyond, never once considering I'd lose my way.

But the tracks also bring back the night I stole into my neighbor's garden and plundered her roses. Because her husband had hurt my dog. He said he'd scared the dog off with a shovel because the dog had been digging in their prized rose beds. The dog limped home and wouldn't allow me to touch his right side, though the neighbor's husband denied hitting him despite that gleaming evidence of steel. It was the height of summer, and the roses were sachets of long-necked blooms of a red so velvet dark they looked black. Bleeding hearts in starlight. I broke the roses off one by one, twisting the stems with my bare hands, the thorns puncturing my palms and the delicate undersides of my wrists. Did I think she'd catch me? Dream that her husband would come after me with a shovel? Bruise my ribs?

And if I was Tobias, the shadow-self chasing the dragon that Freud talks about, a self I have met, more than once, in the mirror's reflected eye? (Consider the shattered lamp below the staircase, shards so sharp they cut my palm.) If I were Tobias, I might have stolen into their house after dark and filled my jacket and jeans pockets and armfuls of black trash bags with the things they'd valued. And I don't mean roses. And what if they caught me? Would the neighbor's husband have broken my ribs? Or maybe I would have carried a gun. Would I have fired? What if the story had ended there? What if the police hauled me away in cuffs, another kind of gleaming steel (so close to steal)?

The bus stops. "Well, that's me," Tobias says, and stands.

"Keep in touch," I say.

"You won't forget?" The honey-gold hair falls across one eye.

"Absolutely not."

He grins, gives me a thumbs-up.

The cars go by. I settle my head against the window, follow his retreating figure into the crowd until the bus propels him out of sight.

Heroin: Meaning heroic from the German *heroisch*. After an injection, the heroin user feels a rush of euphoria accompanied by a flushing of the skin and a sensation of warmth, a rush so powerful it outweighs the fatigue and clouded mental functioning that follow. With regular use, the user must rely on increasing amounts of the drug to achieve the same effect.

The body responds to heroin by reducing and sometimes stopping the production of endorphins, that essential substance regularly released in the brain and nerves to attenuate pain. Within six to eight hours after the last dose, withdrawal sets in. The diminished or vanished endorphin production results in extreme symptoms of pain even when there is no physical trauma.

Myth: Hypnos, the Greek god of sleep, created a poppy drink to ease the goddess Demeter's grief after her daughter Persephone's abduction to the underworld. Because of Demeter's mourning, nothing grew, and famine overtook the earth. After drinking Hypnos's potion, Demeter fell into a deep sleep. When she awoke, she felt comforted, and the earth once more became fertile.

Reality: Heroin comes from the opium poppy, which the Sumerians called *Hut Gil* or flower of joy. It flourishes in dry, hot climates. Today it is mainly grown by farmers in the mountains that extend across South Asia from Turkey through Pakistan. Heroin is obtained from the egg-shaped seed pod left behind once the flower's petals have fallen away. Inside the pod is a milky sap: heroin in its crudest form. To begin the purification process, the sap is mixed with lime in boiling water, and the white substance that collects on the surface—morphine—is collected, reheated with ammonia, filtered and boiled until it becomes a brown paste. This paste is poured into molds and dried in the sun, the resulting substance is smoke-able; or ready for further processing as heroin, a much more complicated process of purification involving a series of chemical distillations.

Tobias: In the *Apocrypha*, Tobias is both good father and good son. After losing his property, his station, even his eyesight, the elder Tobias sends his son and his dog on a journey to the distant city of Rages to recover the money he left in the care of a friend. Before the younger Tobias sets out, a traveling companion joins him. The man calls himself Azarias though he is in reality the angel Raphael in disguise. Azarias promises the father that he will lead Tobias to Rages and bring him home alive. Along the way, Tobias meets Sarah, a kinswoman whose life has been a series of miseries because a devil has strangled each of her seven husbands (on the wedding night) in the hopes of possessing her. Sarah is beautiful and good, and Tobias would like to make her his wife. But he fears the fate of the men who came before him.

To conquer the fear, Azarias shows Tobias how to destroy this devil that has secreted himself inside the sequined body of a giant fish. "Cut out its heart and liver and burn them," Azarias instructs. "It will drive the devil far away, but save the gall. The gall," he says, a flutter of wing beats hovering, "will heal your father's eyes."

In the apocryphal story, events turn out just as Raphael says. Tobias marries Sarah and is not strangled. In the city of Rages, he recovers the money from his father's friend and returns home. With the gall of the fish, which he has carried all this way, Tobias anoints his father's blind eyes. *For be assured,* the angel tells him*, that his eyes shall be presently opened, and thy father shall see the light of heaven, and shall rejoice in the sight of thee.*

Ramble: If words are not spoken at the proper moment—when a white owl cleaves the air, when the finch's green-gold chicks blink in the morning light, when a boy-man with honey-gold hair speaks to you on a windblown afternoon at a bus stop, when an angel reveals himself—will the moment disappear? The chance? Will it be no longer possible? Are the gods listening? Is the deep forest of trees?

Apocrypha: Lucifer as Venus as morning star. Lucifer as bringer of light.

Long after Lucifer fell, Raphael accompanied Tobias on a journey to the distant city of Rages. Before Tobias left, his father said, "See thou never do to another what thou wouldst hate to have done to thee." Yet to destroy the devil, Tobias had to burn his lungs and liver. But, a small voice says—a child's voice perhaps—the gall restored Tobias's father's sight. And so restored his own. But the *Apocrypha,* as we have all been told, is not the official story. So do we dare believe it? The real question is: How do we dare not believe?

Ramble: Prick a finger, and you bleed. Everyone knows that. Still, the fragrance kindles in you a hunger. And perhaps also a desire. To fly. To overreach yourself. *Luciferin, luciferase.*

Once Upon a Time: Imagine the boy-man with honey-blonde

186

hair and the amber eyes of an owl meets a girl at the courthouse. Imagine that she is reading a book with gold-leaf pages that carry the musty smell of a childhood library thousands of miles from this mid-size Texas city where addiction led him. A hundred and nineteen pounds. The city's name? It might just be Rages. Under other circumstances, it might not.

The boy-man wants to know what she is reading.

"Fairy tales." And when he blinks at her—wondering who will slam the door on his sunlight—she adds, "But it's not what you think."

"How do you know what I'm thinking?" he says. "I mean, you've never met me. Until now."

So he introduces himself. And so does she. After all, there must still be a few stories that begin *Once upon a time…*

Even though the cars go by. Even though people slam doors. Kick dogs. Carry scars. Steal.

Once upon a time in a mid-size Texas city on a hot, dusty day, a boy-man with honey-blonde hair and the amber eyes of an owl meets a girl in a courthouse. Her name is not Sarah but Penelope, though she goes by Penny. He asks her why she doesn't carry shiny, copper pennies in her shoes, and instead of telling him to "get lost," she smiles. And so he sits down beside her, and the mindless task he doesn't like—even though it fills the days, and they are so difficult to get through now that he is no longer invincible-euphoric-riding the tail of the dragon—becomes not just bearable, but a pleasure.

All day I've wondered what I did to let the hope in…

Gold Leaf: Birds settle onto branches. At dusk. Two thousand blackbirds chirp, their silhouetted bodies a Japanese ink painting along a cool, stone wall in a clean room on an emerald mountain.

Lovers embrace in a high-ceilinged room of glass surrounded by birds. The birds raise their voices in song.

Rain falls.

A child turns the page, and a girl—call her Beauty—presses her face to the glass. Her father is returning from his journey. In his hands, he holds a single rose, its high-pointed bloom like the hope she kept alive all through his absence.

The amber-eyed boy-man didn't know if he could trust her promise about sending the parcel. So many gaps, so many broken promises. Yet here it is. Wrapped in brown paper. Battered but whole.

One letter separates an exemplar from the irretrievable—but here he sits beside me.

All day I've wondered what I did to let the hope in…

Hope. Admit her.

STRAYS

It began with the marmalade tabby Paul found in a dumpster outside his restaurant. He heard her wincing meow then pulled her from beneath the cardboard boxes and rotting produce. Paul feared some terrible injury, but except for a cut on the cat's left leg and a swollen belly, she seemed okay. Cradling her in his arms, he hurried home through darkening streets lined with row houses, their sun-scorched lawns pocked with massy cactuses, until he reached Twenty-First Street where the houses wore earth-toned palettes, their appearance further softened by canopies of live oak. There was a slight breeze that evening, and it carried with it the spicy, soothing scents of lavender and rosemary, that sun-warmed drift of calm.

Later, curled in a tight ball on a wicker chair on Paul's back porch, the cat's whiskey eyes watched him open a can of tuna. He placed a dish of water beside it, even brought out a favorite afghan. Only after the cat had examined it thoroughly did she nest herself inside its folds. It was then he realized that the name Alley had risen up, unannounced or more likely beckoned. The terrier mixes, Harpo and Lady, watched from the nearest window, their ridiculously large ears on red alert. But they didn't make a ruckus, and Paul wanted to believe they understood the situation with the cat, as they'd understood what had happened to Richard.

In the morning, Dr. Cainan cleaned out the wound and prescribed a high-nutrient cat food. "She's young," the vet said. "But the swollen belly's not due to malnourishment."

Paul stared at the cat. "What's wrong with her?"

"Pregnant. The kittens should be born within the week."

Instantly, Paul found himself reminded of how Richard would have reacted. *That's why we stick to gardening. With certain plants, roses, for example, you can never have enough blooms. As for mint and Virginia creeper, when they threaten to encroach on the others, you cut them back, or pull them out by the roots.*

Gardening's appeal for Richard likely lay in his ability to exert a certain amount of control, impossible in other aspects of his life. There was the fact that before Richard came out, he'd been married to Leahs. They'd had a daughter: Cynthia. That daughter was now sixteen.

189

Four summers ago, Cynthia had come to Lubbock and stayed in the dotted Swiss-curtained guest room. Over the course of three weeks, Paul and Richard took Cynthia to Prairie Dog Town, the artsy Depot District, and Caprock Canyon. When the gusting winds brought the stink of manure and cottonseed oil, they drove out to see the kaleidoscopic play of windmills at the outdoor museum or wiled away the afternoon in the velvet dark of a restored 1950s movie theater. And most nights, they listened to Buddy Holly and the Flatlanders and ate enchiladas at the canopied table in the yard.

A tearful parting at the airport followed, then a flurry of rainbow-papered letters and phone calls that lasted all through the autumn.

Even so, Cynthia didn't make another visit.

Until she stood beside her mother wearing a gray linen dress and chunky Doc Marten's at Richard's funeral. Somehow, she'd inherited his tendency to run her tongue along her top teeth when she was nervous. Paul noticed this when he asked Cynthia to say something during the service. "I wouldn't know what to say," she replied, tongue swishing across her teeth. "I mean, I hardly knew him."

On the fourth morning, Alley dragged the afghan into the recycling bin. By sundown, there were three wet kittens in the bin with her. Two were pitch black. The other was marmalade.

The boy showed up soon after. His hair was the color of paprika, and he wore an oversized *Are We Having Fun Yet?* t-shirt with chartreuse high tops and ravaged jeans. His eyes were the uncanny whiskey color of the cat's.

"These yours?" the boy asked, when Paul found him sitting Indian-style on the back porch, Bathos, the black kitten that survived, and six-toed Marmalade playing with his shoelaces.

"Yes." Paul tried to make his lanky frame seem menacing. "If you steal one, I'll track you down and shoot you."

The boy's eyes flickered over Paul's face, but he didn't flinch. "You got a gun?" the boy asked.

Paul scooped up the marmalade and told the boy to leave.

The boy just motioned to Paul's flowers and said, "I like your place. The plants and shit." He walked over to the most fragrant of the old hybrid roses, now weighed down with a dozen

190

dusky pink blooms. "What's this called?" he asked, lifting a heavy branch.

"Early Blush," Paul said. While waltzing together in the starry garden, Richard would often pluck a blossom, then bring it very close to Paul's face. "If I could choose the form I'd come back in during my next life, I'd take the form of a rose," Richard liked to say. "*This* rose. Paul's Early Blush…"

"How old are you anyway?" Paul asked, wondering not just how the boy had gotten past the six-foot fence, which he always kept locked, but how the boy had gotten past Mr. Marquez's 120-pound-mastiff on the other side.

"Eleven." The boy worried a gray tooth with his tongue.

"What's your name?"

"Matthew," he said, shifting his weight from one leg to the other.

"Well Matthew, if I find you on my back porch again, I'm going to call the cops."

"Gotcha," Matthew said. Then he used the branch of the stately Dutch Elm to give himself the necessary leverage to hoist his body up and over the fence.

"But the dog?" Already Paul anticipated the mastiff's fierce growl.

The boy's gaze met Paul's, and he grinned. "A *Sominex*-packed hot dog tends to do the trick."

The next day, Paul came home to find the boy sitting on the front stoop. He had the kittens in his lap, and the dogs were barking at the living room window, stout paws pressed against the glass. "What the hell? I thought I told you—"

"You told me to keep off the back porch, and I did," the boy said.

"But the kittens. They could run into the street and get hit by a car. A stray dog could come around—"

The boy's smile was lazy, his posture relaxed. "Can't you see I'm taking care of them?"

Paul noticed an open milk carton nearby. "They're still nursing."

"Wake up. I brought the milk for the mother. She's awfully skinny, or haven't you noticed?" Matthew's whiskey eyes and Alley's seemed suddenly accusatory. "You feeding her enough?"

191

Paul grinned, and the pupils of the boy's eyes widened. His friend Susan's daughter once said that horses' eyes dilate when they're glad to see you. Did the same hold true for human beings?

"You owe it to yourself to find out what this kid's situation really is," Susan said a few days later as they drank tart margaritas in the evening cool of the garden, the dogs podded around them. "He could say you touched him, and they'd have the cops on you."

"I just don't believe Matthew capable of that sort of thing," Paul said, then went on to tell Susan about the way he always arrived with some sort of present for the animals. "At first he only brought something for the cats: a new toy fashioned out of string or bits of old fabric. But pretty soon he began bringing *Denta Bones* for Harpo and Lady, telling me that they were developing tartar buildup. A kid who worries about my dogs' teeth is not going to accuse me of molestation."

"You can't be so sure," said Susan. "One word out of this kid, and it could ruin your business, not to mention your life."

Paul refrained from reminding Susan that his life had already been ruined. Susan had been there the morning Richard woke up no longer able to control his bowels. She and Paul had been making scrambled eggs in the kitchen when they heard Richard's almost animal moan.

"Does it take you long to walk home from here?" Paul asked Matthew the next Sunday as they worked together in the garden. It surprised Paul that an eleven-year-old boy would find value in the fact that you couldn't water a zinnia's leaves or it would yellow and die, whereas cosmos and evening primrose loved to be soaked from blossom to root.

"Not too long," Matthew said, carefully transplanting the nasturtium seedlings from a tray into a patch of newly-watered earth.

"And your school? Is it nearby?"

"Sort of."

Paul patted the soil down around the seedlings. "You need to give me a little more than that."

"Why?" Matthew met Paul's eye. "You don't see me poking into your life, do you?"

Paul suppressed a grin. "Oh no? You did just install yourself on my property."

"But I didn't gun you down with questions."

"No, you didn't. Still, I don't really know anything about you."

"You know I'm good with the cats and dogs," Matthew said. "You know I learn fast when it comes to the garden."

It didn't matter that Paul had repainted the bedroom a tranquil shade of blue that Susan said would help him sleep. Most nights Paul woke from dreams of Richard. About a month after the boy first showed up, he found himself dreaming about the week he and Richard spent in Paris, their last big trip. The last time Richard had been completely well. In the dream, he and Richard walked hand-in-hand along the Seine, watching the barges, admiring the decks of houseboats filled with red and pink geraniums, seagulls soaring overhead.

Until his sleeping self registered that something was wrong, then struggled to figure out what it was. When Paul turned to face Richard, he realized that Richard had no eyes. Soon, Richard's mouth disappeared also. Paul awoke tangled in the sheets and sweating.

That's when he heard the pounding on the front door.

Paul opened the door to Matthew's tear-streaked face, his first look both a challenge and a plea to Paul not to mention that he'd been crying.

Minutes later, Paul stood at the old gas stove stirring cocoa and sugar into a saucepan of milk. "Be honest," Paul said. "Does your family have any idea where you are?"

Matthew's eyes were wide and perhaps a little afraid. "You don't know shit about me, do you?"

"And whose fault is that?" Paul stared. "I don't even know your last name."

"I'll tell you," Matthew fixed his attention on the stained-glass chandelier, "but only if I can stay overnight."

Paul hesitated, Susan's words running through his head, but the boy's tear-streaked face and rumpled clothes, and especially the flinty fear in his voice, ultimately won out. "Alright."

"My last name is Orr." Matthew traced the lip of his mug with his finger. "My mom's name is Celia. My dad's Bruce, but he's not around."

"Your parents are divorced?"

Matthew wiped his face with his shirt, laughed. "You live in a romance novel or something? They were never married."

"Do I know your parents?"

"Not Bruce. He's in some oil field. I don't know where." Matthew frowned. "But Celia comes into your restaurant sometimes. She likes seaweed, tofu, shit like that."

"Is she a redhead like you?" Paul recalled just one redhead from the restaurant. She wore her shiny hair in a pageboy and always showed up in twin sets and pearls. No matter how hard he tried, Paul couldn't possibly picture her with this paprika-haired kid with his ratty t-shirts and chartreuse high tops, the laces so frayed Matthew only managed the first three rows.

"Nah, Celia's hair is black. She dyes it. She does hair for a living."

The black hair didn't ring a bell with Paul in a town where too many teenagers and more than a few adults favored inky hair and dog collar jewelry, their torsos, arms, and legs laced with tattoos. Was Matthew's mother one of those?

They padded down the long, oriental-carpeted hallway. There was a spider's web high up on the top shelf, a sign that he hadn't used these sheets in ages. Their friends hadn't visited since Richard's death. Excepting, Paul realized now, the boy. "Does she know you're here?" Paul said. "Celia, that is?"

"Nah," Matthew's voice wavered. "See, she hasn't come home the last two nights. But you can't tell anybody, okay?"

"Where is she?" Paul couldn't resist asking, certain now that child services was involved.

"Probably at some guy's."

Outside the Swiss-curtained guest room, Matthew paused, but Paul shook his head and pointed to the living room, relieved that the boy didn't ask why he couldn't sleep in the bed that Paul had made up after Richard's death and never looked at afterward.

In the morning, sunlight poured through the lace curtains to create fleur-de-lis patterns on the boy's body outlined beneath the white sheets, Harpo and Lady curled up on either side of him.

It had been so long since Paul had seen anyone asleep other than Richard who, towards the end, had always looked so unlike himself with his shrunken cheeks collapsed against a pillow, his bony arms and legs tucked close to his body.

Staring at the boy and the dogs, Paul suddenly understood.

Susan would have told him to contact the authorities; but what made sense to Paul was going to the source: Matthew's mother. At the restaurant, in between mixing up a vat of ratatouille and readying the dough for the next day's bread, he set about telephoning hair salons in town, finally tracking Celia down at Déjà Vu, a trendy place on Buddy Holly Avenue. When the receptionist said, "Hair cut and style?" he made an appointment for five o'clock and asked Diane to close up.

Celia wasn't anything like the person Paul expected. The real Celia was in her mid-thirties, and her clothes—distressed black leather mini-skirt and demure ivory silk blouse—a cross between knock-off Chanel and thrift store chic. Sure, her hair was obviously dyed, but the glossy blue-black color suited her pale skin. And her eyes were a startling shade of violet, the brows tweezed to finely arched lines.

After neatening Paul's sideburns, his already close-cut hair barely needing a trim, Celia swiveled the chair around and handed him a small mirror. "Does it work for you?"

"Sure," Paul said.

Celia placed a hand on the back of his chair, and her eyes met Paul's in the wall mirror. "Come on, why are you here?"

Paul felt the heat rise to his cheeks. "Sorry?"

"I've been doing hair for too long not to know that your last cut was maybe two weeks ago." Celia's voice was sharp. "I get the sense you've been watching me. On a first take, I wouldn't say you were into women, but I've been wrong before."

"It's your son Matthew," Paul blurted out.

"So *you're* his Paul." Celia shook out her inky hair as another stylist turned to stare. "It used to be basketball, especially since Bobby Knight came to Tech, but now all I get is Paul with his garden and those dogs and cats. Listen," an unexpected spaciousness came into her voice, and she leaned close, "my next client's not coming for half an hour. How about going across the street for a drink?"

195

In the brick-lined courtyard of a deserted wine bar, Paul sipped iced cappuccino and watched Celia gobble the half dozen overripe strawberries the waiter had added to her daiquiri without her even having to ask. After ten minutes, Paul knew she was smart, self-absorbed, and likely capable of negligence on an eleven-year-old-boy-sized scale.

"Matthew spends a lot of time at my house," Paul said carefully. "Mostly, he turns up late in the day to play with the animals. But when he showed up at midnight, he'd been crying."

Celia shrugged, and for the first time Paul saw the son in the mother's casual gesture. "Matthew's been staying on his own since he was seven. He never pulled any crying stunt before."

Shocked by the idea of a seven-year-old staying alone, Paul didn't respond. He just thought of how small Matthew had looked standing in that darkened doorway.

Celia folded her napkin into a diminishing series of sharp little squares. "At nine, Matthew conned a sales clerk into believing he'd bought the toy he'd stolen. And last May I found him at home during a school day. He'd been calling himself in for a week. Knowing my son," Celia's violet eyes glinted, "I'd say he's playing you."

Four days went by, and Matthew didn't show. Then Bathos, the black kitten, disappeared. All that week, Paul drove over to the animal shelter, but he found no black kittens among the strays. And every morning and evening, he traversed the hollyhock-lined alleys calling out the creature's name.

Only in the weeks that followed Richard's death had Paul felt such fierce desolation. How many nights after closing up the restaurant had he walked for miles? Revisiting his history with Richard, he went all the way back to the morning Richard first stepped into his diner in San Antonio. That day, Richard had worn a crisp, white shirt and neatly-pressed khakis. And he strode right up to the counter and ordered Ceylon tea, two eggs over easy, and cactus salad with buttered toast. "But you haven't even looked at the menu yet?" Paul said.

"No need," Richard said. "I always know what I want."

Two weeks later Bathos was still gone, Matthew still hadn't

196

turned up, and Paul was running a fever. When the fever hit one hundred and two, Susan came over with chicken soup and Sprite. "I don't drink soda," Paul said, sweating, even though the air conditioner was set on sixty-five.

"It'll settle your stomach," Susan told him. "Besides, you need to stay hydrated, and the sugar will help your system fight back."

Paul was about to protest, but again he remembered how much Susan had done when he'd needed help with Richard. Not even when Paul asked her to go and buy the diapers did she try to offer sympathy, or worse suggest that Paul get Richard into hospice. And after the funeral, once the friends had gone, and the colleagues, it was again Susan who checked in on Paul, sometimes just sitting with him in the garden or on the back porch. He drank the Sprite right down.

On the third day of the fever, Paul woke to mid-afternoon sun pouring through the curtains, the pale blue of the bedroom walls, and Matthew's grin. The gray tooth was gone, leaving a gaping hole and red gums. "You look like shit, man," Matthew said, his paprika hair a disheveled halo.

Paul felt a lop-eared joy rising within. "Where've you been?"

Matthew skirted his gaze, shrugged.

"So, are you going to tell me why haven't you come over?"

"You met with Celia behind my back," Matthew said, worrying the space where the tooth used to be. "That wasn't cool."

"I wanted to know more about you," Paul said, too weak to think through a more calculated response.

"Oh," the boy said.

When Paul asked if he'd seen Bathos, Matthew said, "Downstairs. Celia wanted to keep her, but I knew you'd need her back."

"Your mother wanted a cat?" More than anger, Paul felt stuck in that image of himself casing the alleys while all along the missing kitten had been with the missing boy *and* his mother.

"Yeah, see, we had a kitten once, a little tabby with red streaks in her fur. 'A firecracker,' Celia called her. She followed me everywhere, even slept on my pillow."

"Where is she now?" Paul said, regretting the words as soon as they were out.

"She got hit by a car. Smashed her spine." Matthew's voice wobbled. "We tried to fix her, but the vet said her insides were all shot."

Reminded of those last weeks with Richard—the diapers, the foul smell, the overwhelming grief—Paul said, "Go downstairs or go outside or something, but leave me alone for now."

Matthew ran his fingertips along the edge of the blanket. "You want me to make you mac and cheese or something?" His voice came out almost pleading. "I make really good mac and cheese."

"Not now," Paul said, and turned his face towards the soothing blue of wall.

Morning, and Paul woke to a headache, but at least the fever was gone. He took the stairs slowly, reminded of his conversation with Matthew. But really, what else could the boy have expected? He'd taken Bathos, and then there'd been that terrible story about the tabby. *Her insides were all shot.*

In the bathroom, Paul showered, and although still dizzy, he didn't slip on the slick black tile that Richard had begged him to replace. "A last request," Richard had said. As if slippery tile mattered in the face of Richard's dying. "But it does matter," Richard insisted. "If you slipped and I wasn't here, who would find you?"

Paul managed orange juice and toast, then dressed in one of Richard's old shirts, a white one threaded with traces of blue that still held onto his lemongrass scent. Then Paul drove over to the restaurant, not sure if it was only relief he felt when he learned that Diane and the part-time cook had managed to run the place smoothly enough without him.

After the lunch rush, Paul stood outside and stared at the asphalt lot, reminded of how much Richard had longed for no more than this—a return to health. How many possible remedies had they tried, from acupuncture to herbs to therapeutic massage. Each time they wanted to believe that this last remedy would be the one, but Richard had only gotten worse until his immune system was unable to stave off even a common cold.

198

Towards sunset, Paul drove out to the canyon, the place he and Richard had so loved, especially during those last months when the gnarled mesquite and hunched cactus seemed to reflect back their own tenuous circumstances.

Along the low path that led to a sheltered place among the circle of cotton-woods, a sweet-smelling place where you could actually find small pools of water after it rained, Paul thought back to the evening some nine months ago when he scattered Richard's ashes here. Then there had been a light dusting of snow and a quiet air of solemnity.

Now desert sage put forth its pink flowers, and even the yucca was in bloom.

A breeze picked up, and Paul lay down and breathed in the scent of dusk's prairie grasses. A pair of kites circled far above the earth. A hummingbird moth almost alighted on his shoe.

On the first day of December, it would be a year since Richard's death. Wind-swept West Texas wasn't really home, not in the way of San Antonio with its rolling hills and lush greenery, not to mention its greater tolerance for what they fashionably called "diversity." Still, Paul had managed to build a life here. It wasn't exactly a joyful life, but there was the joy of the garden and the animals. And the restaurant was so much easier to run in a town where good food served in a vibrant atmosphere was a rarity. And then there was Susan, a true friend if ever there was one, whose office had been next to Richard's in the university art department. And now, there was the boy.

Again, Paul thought about what Matthew had said about the little tabby cat he'd loved. It was the one time he'd tried to tell Paul something really important. And Paul had told him to go.

The days passed, and Paul found himself on the constant lookout for a paprika-haired kid in chartreuse high tops. At home, the slightest noise startled him. That third afternoon, he worked himself into such a state he went so far as to phone the salon just to make sure that Celia hadn't left town, taking Matthew with her.

That evening Paul found Matthew lying on his belly in the backyard. He had his nose in a book, and he'd kicked his high tops off to the side. The kittens were playing with his shoelaces, the dogs sprawled out nearby, amused perhaps by the performance, given their tented ears.

"Had a lot going on this past week?" Paul asked.

"Why?" Matthew avoided his gaze. "You miss me?"

"Yes, and I worried about you. What gives?"

Matthew shrugged. "I was thinking."

Paul waited for him to say more, but Matthew just rolled over and looked up at the sky.

"About what?" Paul finally asked.

"You and Celia."

Unsettled, Paul nearly lost his balance. "I don't understand."

"When I found out you went to see her, I thought you two might get together." Paul tried to interrupt, but Matthew said, "It's happened before, and for a little while I've got someone. But the guy always takes off."

Reminded of the way Celia sipped the daiquiri laden with all that overripe fruit in the wine bar courtyard, Paul wondered how often she met men there. Perhaps the bartender was even a lover. And then there were those trips to Las Vegas she mentioned. Surely, she didn't go alone.

"But you won't ever get together with her, right?" Matthew's whole body seemed to arc towards Paul, and his lower lip trembled.

"That's out of the question," Paul said, amazed that Matthew hadn't figured out by now that he didn't exactly favor women. The signs were all around them, most evident in the photographs and more subtly present in the closet that still held Richard's clothes. "My late partner was a man, you know that," Paul said.

"Yeah, but I had to make sure." The boy's tenuous expression showed the beginnings of a smile. "So you're saying we're safe?"

The word propelled Paul back to that first night beside the dumpster. Again, he heard that cry. And within Alley's cry, he heard his own cry the morning he stepped into the guest room bearing Richard's honey-sweetened green tea. Even before Paul had said a word, he'd known that Richard was gone. What did safe mean when the person you most loved could suddenly be gone, leaving behind a lemongrass scent that lingered on clothes and bedding and drifted in through the dotted Swiss curtains you once swore you'd pull down…

Paul could tell Matthew that they would continue to meet in this garden that he had begun with Richard; a garden the two men believed would thrive and reflect back a mature beauty they would need as they aged. He could tell him that they would continue to care for the animals and for each other.

But it couldn't last forever. So, what did safe mean in that context? What could it offer? A kind of refuge for the present? Protection? Reliability—yes, sure, but that's not what the boy meant.

A wind picked up and ruffled the pages of Matthew's book. When the kittens pounced on it, Paul thought the boy might laugh.

But Matthew kept his eyes on Paul. "Well?"

"Let's say we keep showing up, keep holding fast," Paul managed at last.

"What's that mean?" Matthew said.

"'Holding fast' is something like the determination it took to get over that fence," Paul explained.

Matthew sat silent, trying to take this in, and Paul wished he could offer more, but anything else would be a lie, or at least something he could not let the boy be assured of.

"Come on," Paul said, offering his hand. "Let's go in and make something to eat. I brought cornbread home, and I've got chicken in the fridge. "Or better yet," Paul said, and smiled, "maybe it's time you teach me how to make that mac and cheese you say you do so well."

"Alright." Matthew took his time getting to his feet. But when he did, he took hold of Paul's hand and held it fast between both of his own.

EXIT, PURSUED BY A BEAR

In the coming years, walking his daughter to daycare, or holding her hand as they cross the street, Peter Fricke will find himself asking if it was serendipity or fate that brought Agnes Kurowsky into his Shakespeare seminar that year. They've just broken into May, and the bougainvillea in the courtyard are a riot of scarlet and coral. The once burly Peter, who played college football at Notre Dame, has lost more than forty pounds in the wake of Helen's death. Unimaginable still, that his Helen, seven months pregnant at the time, was shot at Albertson's at 8:22 p.m. on March 13th. These days, instead of her pasta salads and curries, he relies on tea and peanut butter sandwiches to see him through the long afternoons at the college.

This afternoon he sits rereading *The Winter's Tale*, his favorite of the late romances. He is teaching the play, and the stage directions—*Exit, pursued by a bear*—replay in his mind; not quite tragic given the play's joyful ending; but given how much Helen loved *The Winter's Tale*, more than a little sad.

Fourteen months have passed since she died, and Peter continues to linger in his office long after his colleagues have gone home. Sometimes, hunkered down in his armchair by the single lead glass window, Peter almost believes he will look up to find Helen standing in the doorway. "Peter Pan," he can almost hear her say. "You didn't think I'd really leave you? How could I?"

Now footsteps in the department hallway crack the silence, and Peter looks up. The late sun blooms through the window obscuring Agnes's features so that it's her very pregnant silhouette and frizzy, golden hair that Peter sees first. "Oh hello," he says. "You caught me just in time. Come in."

Not only is Agnes Kurowsky beautiful in a timeless way, as if she'd stepped out of a Thomas Hardy novel—*Tess of the D'Urbevilles* or *The Woodlanders*—more than this, Agnes's ebullient hair and the heart shape of her face remind Peter of Helen; and though he's more than a little embarrassed about doing so, at times Peter's caught himself staring at Agnes during class.

She smiles, revealing the gap between her front teeth. "My grandmother used to grow these," she says, gesturing at the Christmas cactus on the windowsill which has unexpectedly flowered. "Are you good with plants?"

"Not really, but this one manages to thrive anyway." He motions to the chair in front of his desk. "What can I do for you?"

"I saw my doctor today," Agnes says, easing into the chair. "I'm not due until May twenty-first, but based on the examination, she thinks I'll go into labor before then."

"And you're afraid this will coincide with the exam?" Peter says.

Agnes nods. "I've read everything at least twice, so I'm already prepared. Could I take the exam early? I could even be ready tomorrow."

Peter has not yet written the exam. "Let's say Monday, one o'clock."

That evening, Peter stands in his small kitchen and fixes dinner, his terrier mixes, Lorelei and Milly, and Taco, the overweight Chihuahua, watching his every move. When Helen was alive, the two of them used to linger over dinners on the patio they'd built together after buying the house in Silver Lake, a small 1930s ranch they gradually refurbished. Though they hadn't met until their late thirties, marrying within the year, it had seemed then as if they'd all the time in the world. Over long dinners, they'd talk about the years ahead as they ate salad from the garden, poured more wine, and tried to remember not to overcook the fish or burn the rice.

Is it possible, Peter asks himself, looking out at the leaves gathering on the patio, *that man was me?* Weeds have sprung up between the paving stones, and the flower and vegetable beds are hopelessly overgrown. Only the bird bath Peter still tends with some care, for Helen had loved watching the grosbeaks and warblers and an occasional Western Tanager bathe there.

After fixing scrambled eggs and a salad with a heel of sourdough bread, Peter sits at the Formica table, the collected plays of Shakespeare beside him. There are twenty-three students in the class, and of that number Agnes Kurowsky has not especially distinguished herself. Her essays are clear and at times insightful, but she isn't quite up to the level of analysis he expects from a senior seminar. Yet Agnes will make the occasional remark that abides within Peter long after class.

There was what she'd said about Hermione, the dead queen who returns to the living at the end of *The Winter's Tale*,

203

thanks to the healing magic of her most trusted friend: "There is an art that doth mend nature, change it rather, and yet the art itself is nature." Peter had asked the students to interpret these lines which he'd committed to heart during his first Shakespeare course at Northwestern more than twenty-five years ago. After Helen died, he'd sit in his dark office repeating the words over and over again, as if they were a mantra, though he'd known, even then, that Helen, unlike the queen in the play, could never be brought back.

"Love is the art that Shakespeare's talking about," Agnes said when the others stayed silent. "Love is an art, but it's also natural, a part of us; the most important part."

Pierced by the dead-on-rightness of these words, especially coming from someone who sparked memories of Helen, it was pain that Peter felt then. Standing at the front of the class, he found himself catapulted back to those first weeks after Helen's death, the paralysis that struck him every time he neared the nursery door. How he'd almost wished then that he could shut off—the way a nerve could be severed—that loving part of himself.

More than a year later, Peter catches himself thinking about what his daughter would be doing now, if she'd been born. Sometimes he dreams about a newborn in a cradle. In the dreams, she sleeps, fingers unfurled like petals.

"It's not my baby," Agnes tells Peter when she shows up on Monday to take the exam.

Peter rubs his beard, squints in the bright sunlight. "I'm sorry," he says. "I don't follow?"

"I'm a surrogate." She shifts her weight, self-conscious now, for she hadn't anticipated his furrowed brow, the confusion in his expression. Not that she'd planned to tell him this. It was the way he looked at her when she came in. She couldn't explain it; but just then she'd felt some likeness between them, some "affinity," a word she'd learned from him.

"I'm sorry," he says again. "I'm not quite sure why you're telling me this."

She looks down at the exam, and all at once the reason is there. "The art that doth mend nature," she says, pointing to one of the questions. "The couple whose baby I'm carrying, well, the woman hasn't been able to carry a pregnancy to term. I feel as if those words speak to what I'm going through now, you see?"

He doesn't answer, and she takes in the perspiration prickling his brow, reminded of the newspaper article, the way he lost his wife. "Dr. Fricke?"

"Take two hours. Then bring the essay back to me. And yes," he adds, "you can use your laptop if you like and print out a copy in the library, okay?"

"Thank you, I will."

She stands in the hallway, just outside his office door for a while after that, wishing there was some way she could make him understand. *I'm his student*, she reminds herself. *He probably thinks I'm crazy to have confided in him like that.* Another professor walks by, and the woman's eyes linger on Agnes. She must wear all she is feeling on her face. Hurriedly, she turns and makes her way towards the stairwell.

"You aren't serious," Helen's older sister, Marianne, says when Peter meets her for dinner at the Japanese restaurant down the street from her apartment the following Saturday.

"Perfectly." Peter wishes that Marianne, who was hard-nosed even before her divorce, could muster some enthusiasm just this once. These weekly dinners aren't the same without Helen. Always, she was the glue that held Marianne and Peter together. "Not that Marianne and I have a whole lot in common," Helen used to say.

"Except for the fact that you were raised by two parents who adored you," Peter always replied.

"True," Helen said, hugging him close.

"But Peter, this is crazy," Marianne says, once the waiter has brought their sushi.

"Is it?"

She tucks her silvery hair, recently cropped to chin-length, behind her ears. "You're still grieving."

"It's been more than a year," Peter says, poking at an eel roll. "You're the one who's always telling me to get on with my life."

She lays down her chopsticks, fixes him with her blue-gray eyes. "I've encouraged you to date, to travel—you've talked for ages about going back to England; but I never said you should have a baby. What are you thinking anyway? That you can somehow replace Helen? Clone her?" Her laugh sounds bitter. "A sort of mini-me like in that absurd movie you dragged me to see?"

The couple at the next table, both of them dressed all in black, look their way.

"Don't be ridiculous," Peter says quietly. "And that movie was funny. You laughed as hard as I did. You just won't admit it."

"You're changing the subject," Marianne says, the lawyer in her coming through despite her recent move into real estate.

"That baby would be a part of Helen," Peter says, his voice firmer now. "It would be her child, the child we should have had."

"Yes, if Helen were still alive." She sighs, swishes the wine around in her glass, drinks. "I'm sorry, but the whole idea's just too much. It's crazy, totally crazy."

Peter holds her gaze. "Stop saying that."

"Seriously." Marianne props her elbows on the table. "Think about it. A pregnant student comes into your office and tells you that she's a surrogate for a childless couple, and now you want to find one of your own."

"We have the embryos, Marianne, don't forget that. It's not like this wasn't our idea in the first place."

"But Helen was going to carry the child, her child. She was the mother—" Only now does Marianne's voice waver.

"And she did carry that child, our daughter. If that fucked up kid hadn't—" If Helen hadn't been in the supermarket at night, buying butter, apples, and a tin of tuna, she would still be here, and they would have their daughter, Louisa Marie. Peter, despite every reason not to, still keeps the picture from the last ultrasound in the nightstand drawer.

More staring from the couple in black.

Marianne sinks back into the red leather booth, closes her eyes. "Oh Peter."

"Don't talk to me about moving on," Peter says, a razor sharpness coming into his voice. "Every single day I wake up, and I can't believe she isn't here. I reread the books she loved, trying to find her in the marginalia. People say it's going to get easier, but frankly, that's bullshit. It doesn't."

"God, Peter, I miss her, too, terribly. But raising a child on your own? Really, you need to give this more time." Marianne reaches out, covers his hand with her own.

"That's another phrase I've had enough of." Peter pulls his hand away, reminded of that awful night, some three weeks after Helen's death, when either he or Marianne reached for the other, and for a few moments they were in each other's arms. Thank god, one or the other of them had the presence of mind to stop things from going any further, for what a disaster that would have been.

Marianne's elbows are back on the table, and she is scrutinizing him closely, her eyes as blue as Helen's, though Helen alone had those dazzling gold flecks. "Tell me this: how are you going to pay for a surrogate? It's going to be phenomenally expensive."

"I've already considered that," he says, though in reality his calculations have been pretty minimal. "I'll forego my sabbatical next year and take on summer teaching. The Subaru's old, but it's in good shape. I could even take in a renter," he adds hurriedly, though this he has, in fact, not considered.

"You can't possibly do that," Marianne says.

Peter frowns. "Why not?"

"You love your privacy way too much."

"I want a child, Helen's child, more."

They stare at each other for a while, and Peter senses that Marianne is waiting for him to look away first. Another lawyer's tactic.

"I didn't give away the cradle," Peter says at last, his gaze still riveted on Marianne. "It's in the walk-in-closet in Helen's study, along with the other things I couldn't bear to give away.

Marianne looks down at her hands and then back at Peter again. She was with them when they bought that cradle, having found it in an antiques store in some small town outside the city. And Marianne, with her elephant's memory, must remember the care with which both Peter and Helen refinished the cradle, even stenciling in a moon and stars along the headboard.

Agnes Kurowsky isn't given to gossip, and she doesn't hang out with anyone in the class. But she did read about the shooting at the grocery store, the one in which Peter Fricke's wife, seven months pregnant and out for a few items, had been killed. There are days when his eyes flicker over her face and body, not with desire, though there is hunger there, and sorrow so deep Agnes believes that if she looked too long, she could get lost in it.

Agnes herself has known sorrow; it lingers in her sister Beth's house, and at times it seems to cut through Beth's fury to reveal something purple and bruised with longing.

Even though Agnes isn't majoring in English, she signed up for the seminar because she's determined to read the great writers while pursuing her nursing degree. It's the one thing her self-educated grandmother believed every person should do. And because Agnes loved her grandmother, who looked after her and Beth while their mother had to work, the advice stayed with Agnes, became her own.

What Agnes never expected was the effect Shakespeare's plays would have on her. "So young, my lord, and true," Cordelia tells Lear when he is disappointed, then enraged by her inability to flatter, her inability to "heave my heart into my mouth." Agnes doesn't entirely understand everything in these plays, yet lines like this one burrow deep beneath her skin to become part of her. She thinks of her own father, who left when she was seven, the way she knew, even as a very small child, this wiry, broad-shouldered man who took off on his motorcycle on Saturday mornings, would not stay. Like the loyal daughter in *King Lear,* she'd tried to hold her father, to keep him, with her love. And she failed, just as her mother had. "I am a feather for each wind that blows."

Two weeks later, on a rainy morning just after the semester's final exams are over, Peter sits in the office of Dr. Rayan Murr. The last time he saw Murr was at Helen's funeral. Peter had looked around at some point, a little amazed the man had come though, of course, Murr had heard about the shooting. His office had sent flowers: a dozen white roses and a card that Peter can't remember having read.

"You look different somehow," Peter says, startled when the doctor steps into the office, and Peter stands to shake his hand.

"It's the hair," Murr says, shaking Peter's hand. "I had a transplant."

"Ah, well." A smile creeps over Peter's features, remembering what Helen used to say about their endocrinologist, how certain she'd been that he was "more high maintenance than the vainest woman." And yet there was no denying that Helen had liked him, just as Peter had. After all, he'd made it possible for

Helen and Peter to have a child, and they would have—Peter slams closed this door to his thoughts.

"How are you?" the doctor says, once he opens the folder on the Frickes, a folder dating back to their first appointment nearly three and a half years ago.

"Surviving," Peter says, then realizes this is probably not the best way to proceed given the reason he's here. "I'm tenured now at the college. I published my book on Shakespeare's romances."

Murr congratulates him, the vague look in his eyes suggesting he has no real idea of what Peter's book is about and will, therefore, not press him further. For this, Peter feels only relief.

"So," Murr leans back in his chair, his fine hands folded in his lap. "What can I do for you?"

"I've come to talk to you about finding a surrogate."

"That's a considerable undertaking," Murr says carefully.

"I know." Peter looks the doctor directly in the eye. "If Helen hadn't died, we'd have a baby girl right now."

"She would be a year old," the doctor says, not even looking at the folder.

"Yes," Peter says, swallows. "I'm here because I want to have a child, Helen's child."

Murr, who has aged in the interim despite the gorgeous head of hair, the lines around his mouth and eyes now more deeply ingrained, remains silent for a good while.

And Peter, who's been so keyed up about this meeting since he arrived at the decision, takes some comfort in the space between them, for it lets him breathe.

A few minutes later, Dr. Murr quotes the cost of using a surrogate, explaining that the legal documents will be more elaborate and therefore significantly more expensive. "Each prospective surrogate is subject to significant psychological screening. We need to ensure that there is no way a surrogate could try to keep the child after giving birth. There have been incidents, though very few, elsewhere of course. You see the reason for the safeguards."

Peter nods, rests his large hands on his knees, Agnes's lovely face swimming up into his memory. It's been nearly two weeks. More than likely, she will have had the baby by now. "And the procedure?"

"It will be like the last time. The surrogate will take the hormones, just as Helen did. The main difference will be that this time we will be using thawed embryos and not fresh ones. The chances of pregnancy are significantly lower, so I would recommend implanting four, perhaps even five, depending upon the quality. Your file says there are six in storage. We won't know their viability until we thaw them all on the day before the implantation.

"But," Murr says, his cheeks suddenly flushed, "we're getting ahead of ourselves. First, we must find a woman to carry this pregnancy."

Agnes's obstetrician expected her to go into labor early given the extent of her dilation at thirty-eight weeks, but it doesn't actually begin until two days after her due date. She is standing in her white nightgown in her sister's kitchen fixing breakfast for her niece and nephew when she feels a warm whoosh of fluid down her legs. "Oh, oh," six-year-old Tulia says. "Aunt Aggie had an accident."

Staring down at her soaked gown, at the puddle on the floor, it takes a moment for Agnes to register what's happening. "No, Tuli dear," Agnes says, "my water broke. The baby's coming."

Tulia stands there blinking in the bright light, and then she says, "Should I get Mommy? Maybe you need Brown Bear to help. Are we going to go to the hospital now? I can get your pink suitcase."

Agnes smiles, relieved it's happening at last, despite the fear that courses through her. "Yes, we are," she says. "Wake up your mom, and yes, please get my suitcase."

Within the hour, Agnes is admitted to her hospital room which looks more like a hotel suite with its pull-out sofa, gilt-framed pictures, not to mention the television opposite the hospital bed, as if she could even think about television right now. Leo and Rochelle Goldman, whom she phoned before leaving the house, are already waiting for her.

"At last, the baby's coming," Leo says to Agnes, who nods, smiles, allows him to take her hand. His own is warm, sweaty. Rochelle, a wispy blonde with pale skin and equally pale, green eyes, takes Agnes's other hand. And soon the doctor is there, and the nurses, and within the hour she is squatting on the floor in the throes of an experience she will never be able to describe afterwards. Eight hours in, Rochelle produces popsicles for Agnes to suck on, the too-sweet grape and strawberry reminding Agnes of running through the backyard sprinklers all through the heat of summer when she and Beth were small.

These images are pierced by wave after wave of contractions that cut deep into her, so that she screams with a primal force. Fourteen hours later, she doesn't think she can hang on any longer, but Rochelle squeezes her hand, and speaks in the most soothing tones, "You're almost there. Just keep breathing."

For a time, it seems as if the two women are breathing together, and all the while Rochelle, her fine flaxen hair grazing Agnes's cheeks, keeps sponging Agnes's forehead with a cool cloth that smells of lavender. And then it gets agonizingly hard again, and the nurse and Rochelle help Agnes into an almost upright position, and the nurse tells her "to push with all you've got." Agnes doesn't remember much after that, until Joshua Leo Goldman, who weighs eight pounds and two ounces, comes crying into this life just before dawn on May the 24th.

How much time passes before Agnes is gazing at the wrinkled, purplish face of this tiny human being who grew inside her for nine months, she doesn't know. All she knows—all she remembers later—is the love that fills her when she nurses him that first and only time, a love so complete she almost forgets that she must surrender to this couple this brand new person whose kicks and turns she felt for so long they became a part of her.

Three days later, Agnes is back in her garage apartment at Beth's house on an un-gentrified street on the fringes of Westlake. Friday evening, Agnes stands at the stove making French toast for eight-year-old Zach and little Tulia, who loves Aunt Aggie's comfort food far more than her harried mother's crock-pot chili and crunchy salads.

"But where is the baby?" Tulia asks again, once Agnes sits down beside them at the picnic table in the postage stamp-sized garden.

"She's already told you ten times, Tulip-head," Zach says, stabbing at his French toast.

"Mom said not to call me that," Tulia says.

"Please, Zach," Agnes says, more tired now than she was at the end of the pregnancy. "I could use a little help here."

Zach rolls his eyes. "Fine."

"Thank you," Agnes says, and returns to her meal, aware that Tulia's big blue eyes are still fixed on her. "Like I said, Tul, the baby is with his mommy and daddy."

"But he grew in your tummy," Tulia insists. "You let me feel his kicks, his little 'hellos.'"

"Oh Bumblebee, I told you that he was going to live with his parents."

"The real parents needed Aunt Aggie's body, Tul," Zach explains. "She isn't the real mommy."

"Zach's right," Agnes says. "I just gave the baby a place to grow because his real mommy couldn't."

Tulia crinkles her brow, bites her lower lip. "Mommies give birth to babies. I waited and waited to meet him. I set up a tea party in my room. Ella Funt and Brown Bear are still waiting."

Agnes smiles, trusting it will all sort itself out, though it's a little astonishing that Tulia, who knows all about her father's new family, just can't wrap her head around the idea of baby Joshua, as Agnes calls him, going to live with someone else. "It's a little like Mary-Katherine," Agnes finally says, thinking of the eight-year-old tomboy who lives next door, as she gathers Tulia up into her lap. "Mary-Katherine's parents brought her home from the hospital, but someone else gave birth to her."

"That's because her first mommy didn't want her," Tulia says.

"Mary-Katherine didn't say that, did she?" Agnes asks.

Tulia doesn't answer, just fiddles with Agnes's napkin.

"Mary-Katherine's parents love her a lot," Agnes says, wrapping her arms around her niece, "just like your mommy loves you."

Agnes meets Tulia's earnest gaze, feels the tug at her breasts, once again remembering what she felt after Joshua latched on and sucked and sucked, the tiny eyes with their butterfly lashes closing and opening just long enough to gaze into hers. The dreamiest peace washed over her, a cocooned calm radically unlike anything she's ever known. Now there are two damp spots on her t-shirt, a sign she will have to shower and then press out the milk destined for a child that was never hers to begin with.

"Listen, Tul, I brought him into this world," Agnes says eventually, "but the people who waited for him, the Goldmans, they're his parents."

To her surprise, Tulia nods and goes back to her chair. Soon she is asking Agnes to play *Candyland* with her after dinner, and can she have marshmallows in her hot chocolate, her worries about the baby and Mary-Katherine forgotten, for now anyway.

Agnes clears the dishes and thinks about her tired, unhappy sister who, at thirty-six, seems more disillusioned than almost anyone she knows, her own husband having left nearly two years ago now. And oddly enough, she thinks about another pair of lines from *The Winter's Tale*, which she reread after coming home from the hospital. "What's gone and what's past help should be past grief."

"I married an asshole, Aggie," Beth told her when the child support was late again. "Remember that when you start looking around. Or better yet, get your nursing degree, focus. You'll graduate at thirty-three as long as you don't get distracted. Just don't be like me—or Mom. God, what a fucked up mess I made of my life."

"But you have Zach and Tulia," Agnes replied.

And for a moment Beth's face, her tense body, softened at the words, the truth of them.

Agnes received $25,000 for carrying Joshua Leo Goldman to term. Initially, she planned to use that money to pay for her final year of nursing school, to buy a car that would be reliable enough to drive more than twenty miles, and maybe even to take a trip this summer. Always she has wanted to see her ancestral Poland; at this point, she hasn't been anywhere other than the West Coast.

But she decided to put some of it aside for Tulia and Zach. An educational IRA, she told Beth.

"How do you even know about that stuff?" Beth asked.

"The Goldmans told me," Agnes said, reminded of the hours she spent with the couple who counseled her on her future and invited her to come to their house later this summer, though she isn't sure yet if she will.

"Sometimes," Beth said, "it's really hard to believe that you and I have the same parents."

"You're right," Agnes replied. "Sometimes it is."

The last day of May draws near, and the campus empties out. Peter plans to come into his office only once more before the summer break begins. The previous evening, he emailed his students in the Shakespeare seminar to say they could pick up their exams on May 29th. "After that, I won't be around much before late August." Though he doesn't expect most of them to stop by, given that he will post their grades online, he does expect Agnes to come. Not that her essay is exceptional, only thorough with the occasional glimmer of real insight. She took his earlier advice and steered clear of too many personal asides or "digressions," as he called them, and wrote a perceptive analysis of the role of key lines in *The Winter's Tale*, all the while referring to others, thereby demonstrating her conversance with the play:

The queen returns to life because the king has finally recognized his wrongdoing. The spider in the cup that he talks about in the first act, the spider he believes to be his wife's unfaithfulness, is his "fatal error" or "tragic flaw," and he sees this. And that action saves him—all of them. The queen was loving, and true, and their child is miraculously restored to them. (And here I find the fact that Shakespeare kept her alive to be really sweet but not entirely believable. I mean, a shepherdess who is really a princess? Was Shakespeare reading fairy tales? Were there fairy tales in the sixteenth century?—"A sad tale's best for winter," the king's son says. Not that I don't love that ending. Who wouldn't?)

Peter laughed when he read Agnes's parenthetical statement. Even though he'd gone over all this in class, the fact that the late romances are so very different from the tragedies because in the romances everything that should have ended disastrously—in this case the king's order that the queen be put to death—turns out to have a miraculous ending. "There is an art that doth mend nature, change it rather, and yet the art itself is nature." The art that Shakespeare is secretly referring to, Peter told the class, is Art with a capital A.

I understand that a romance is the total opposite of a tragedy. What I find impossible or at least amazing is that Shakespeare didn't end with the tragedies. He was an old man when he wrote The Winter's Tale. *Why didn't he end on a play like* King Lear's *"Is man no more than this?" That's what I can't figure out. Most people I know are unhappy or at least resigned—that's the word, right?—by the time they're fifty. If I can look at the world like that when I'm old, at this world with all its violence, well then…*

And here, Peter realizes, Agnes strays from the topic significantly. At the same time, she is pointing to the marvelous, unanswerable question that no one can answer, though many, Peter included, have tried. What made Shakespeare's late vision possible?

Peter's own father was nearing forty when Peter, his only surviving child, was born. By the time Peter was thirteen, his mother had died of cancer, and his father, whose red hair grayed early, had arthritis in his knees and hands, and had moved as far up in the railroad hierarchy as he was ever going to. Now that the old man's in the nursing home, he dwells on What Should Have Been.

"What's gone and what's past help should be past grief." Peter actually said these words to his father once; the context, though, he's forgotten. "What in the hell are you quoting that mumbo jumbo to me for?" his father had said. And Peter had wanted to say: "Because truth can be found there, maybe even solace."

"Exit, pursued by a bear." That's how he often feels leaving his father at the nursing home; he'd told Helen this, long after she, too, knew *The Winter's Tale* almost as well as he did.

Helen had cried over these lines when he first read them to her in the weeks after they bumped into each other, literally, while buying apples at the farmer's market. "Those lines mark the change from tragedy to comedy," Peter had said. "The baby doesn't die. She's found by a shepherd and kept safe and ultimately restored to the king, her father, and to her mother, the queen."

"That's why Shakespeare called it a romance then?" Helen said, twining her slender, freckled arms around his neck. "Because of the happy ending?"

"Precisely why," Peter replied, sliding the blouse from Helen's shoulder to kiss her neck.

By the time Peter finishes rereading Agnes's essay, it's nearly five o'clock. He has a dinner date with Marianne at 6:30. He plans to discuss with her the two prospective surrogates who've risen to the top of the list among the nearly fifty profiles he's read. Not that Marianne fully backs him up on this idea now. She remains wary, but Peter trusts, no he believes, Marianne will come around. She's already agreed to help out during the first few months, and she's begun to inquire about nannies. "My financial contribution," she told Peter when she brought the nanny up, "should you decide to go through with this, and should it actually work."

"Marianne moves much slower than I do," Helen used to say. "She always has."

At 5:30, Peter checks his email, just in case. But there is nothing except a memo from the department chair reminding faculty to turn in grades by June 1st. Peter leans back in his chair, plucks a dead blossom from the Christmas cactus, which continues to put forth more blooms. He arranges the exams in a neat pile and then stores them in a folder in his cabinet with Agnes's B+ close to the top. Outside his window, the bougainvillea in the courtyard bloom as brilliantly as ever. He switches out the light on his desk, takes one more backward glance, and closes the door.

ACKNOWLEDGMENTS

Exit, Pursued by a Bear would not be the collection it is without the support and faith of many people, and I would like to express gratitude for those people here.

For the readers, friends, and writers who helped, via inspiration—and faith!—as well as offering feedback and other forms of support, thank you. These people include Milica Trindade, Eileen Bonds, Kanika Batra, Anne Sanow, Liza Wieland, Matthew Lansburgh, Kirsten Sundberg Lunstrum, as well as the late Wendy Barker and Margaret Lutherer. I am also endebted to the writers in Christopher Merkner's wonderful lighthouse class: Cat Fagelson, Ceara Hennessey, and Joe Lyons.

I especially thank Bill and our daughter, Sophie, whose coming inspired "Solstice in the Jardin du Luxembourg," and whose growth over the years nurtured these stories. From the very beginning and for always, I am indebted to my own St. Petersburg-born grandmother and to my father for kindling in me such a passion for story.

Immense thanks to Prize Americana for selecting the collection and to Dr. Leslie Kreiner Wilson for editing it.

I would also like to express my gratitude to the following journals in which several of the stories originally appeared: "The Raven" in *Cimarron Review*, "Boundaries, Bodies, Breath" in *Permafrost*, "Little One" in *The Saranac Review*, "Elegy for a Fairy Tale" in *Copper Nickel*, "Seeing Red" in *The Upper New Review*, "Solstice in the Jardin du Luxembourg" in *Western Humanities Review*, "Heroin(e)" in *Zeus Seduces the Wicked Stepmother in the Gingerbread House: Myths, Fairy Tales and Legends for the 21st Century* Ed. Susan Richardson, and "Exit, Pursued by a Bear" in *The Woven Tale Press*.

Lastly, special thanks to Texas Tech University for funding the magical cover art by Paul Bond.

ABOUT THE AUTHOR

Born in Chicago, Jacqueline Kolosov spent the first thirty years of life in and around big northern cities, only to find herself in arid, windswept West Texas at the start of the twenty-first century. Thanks to her daughter, she soon fell in love with horses and the open expanse of a country defined by sky. A member of the creative writing faculty at Texas Tech University, she has published three collections of poetry including the ekphrastically-driven *Modigliani's Muse*. A fourth, *Talons, Wings*, is forthcoming from Salmon in 2025. Also an essayist and a practitioner of hybrid forms, her collection of lyric essays *Motherhood, and the Places Between* was selected by W. Ralph Eubanks for Stillhouse Press's annual prize. She has published several YA/crossover novels including two set in Elizabethan England: *The Red Queen's Daughter* and *A Sweet Disorder* (Hyperion/Disney). Jacqueline co-edited three anthologies of contemporary writing including *Family Resemblance: An Anthology and Investigation of Eight Hybrid Literary Genres*, 2015 Winner of Foreword's IndieFab Award for Nonfiction. She has been awarded a Literary Fellowship from the National Endowment of the Arts along with residencies at the Banff Centre and an artist's house in Amagansett. Active in the field of Art in Community Health, she is an ad hoc cook, lifelong yogi, and passionate horsewoman. She can usually be found out in the elements with horses and her dog.